1

OPENING MOVES

D r Adam Bascom was in a bad mood. The weather was awful and the roads nearly impassable with mud. Worse still, his patients were far too eager to call him out for minor ailments which would clear up in a few days without treatment. It was enough to make any physician wonder why he had not chosen a career in the law. At least then he could have enjoyed seeing his clients facing imminent ruin.

He could even have become an apothecary and spent his days concocting vile-tasting remedies in a warm, dry compounding room. That was what his friend Peter Lassimer was doing before him at that moment. His mind wandered into fantasies. Could you make the taste of a medicine fit the character of the patient? Say something acid and astringent for elderly females with the vapours. A throat-burning and peppery brew for red-faced squires. A seductively mild syrup with a foul aftertaste for bilious wives. Bland mixtures for arrogant sons, each certain to produce a violent flux after a few minutes?

For several more minutes, Adam concocted ever more venomous tastes to suit odious patients. In time, the warmth and quiet of Peter's room began lulling him to sleep. When Peter spoke, Adam jumped in surprise.

"What in Heaven's name is the matter with you, Bascom?" Peter said. "You sit there looking as if you bear the whole weight of the world on your shoulders. What is amiss, man?"

"What is amiss? You see before you a physician who serves an area packed with hypochondriacs too tight-fisted to settle their accounts for months. What could possibly be amiss?"

"Is that all?"

"That is all."

"Poppycock! Out with it, man."

"By the devil himself, Lassimer, we cannot all be as cheerful as you are. Some of us feel the buffeting of the world's storms more deeply."

"You are a poor liar, Bascom. Something more than the distressing habits of your patients is biting you. It is the Black Dog. I have seen many men in that creature's clutches and they all bear the face of doom, as you do."

"What Black Dog are you talking about? Not Black Shuck, the hell-hound the country people fear to meet on a dark night in the empty heathland? That is but a fairytale."

"The Black Dog I mean is no fairytale," Lassimer said. "It is what many call that state of gloom and melancholy which falls upon them at certain times of the year. They say they have the black dog on their backs ... as I see it is on yours."

"And what, my good apothecary," Adam said, his voice heavy with sarcasm, "would you prescribe to deal with this creature?"

"My professional opinion," Peter said, "is spoken as an almost-admitted Master Apothecary. Your poor spirits are due to an insufficient – nay, absent – exercising of your masculine functions. Find yourself a pretty mistress, my friend, and you will soon see your spirits – and that other part of you too – rise up."

This remark at last produced the briefest of smiles. "As I have told you many times before, Lassimer," Adam said, "all your quack diagnoses focus on but one organ of the body. To hear you speak, sexual congress must cure every illness known to man."

THE CODE FOR KILLING

WILLIAM SAVAGE

RIDGE & BOURNE

For Jenn

This is a work of fiction. All characters and events,
other than those clearly in the public domain,
are products of the author's imagination.
Any resemblance to actual persons, living or dead,
is unintended and entirely co-incidental.

"And so it must. At least, if it does not, it will make bearing most afflictions easier."

"That's as maybe," Adam continued. "But I tell you it is not the lack of female company which makes me look glum. It's just ... well, listen. For a start there are too many inconsiderate mothers who cannot wait to bring their children into this world until a sensible time of day. I have been roused three nights in a row to deliver offspring in this town. Three nights! One woman even had the effrontery to produce twins born a good hour apart."

"Would you have the good folk of Aylsham take vows of abstinence, and their children vows of celibacy, just so you can sleep undisturbed?"

"That is an excellent notion, Lassimer. I will propose it at the next Vestry meeting. Most there are too old for any vow of abstinence to upset them. All would approve a motion calculated to reduce the Poor Rate. Much of that goes on providing for women and children deserted by philandering males."

"My, my, Bascom," Peter said. "You are in a foul mood. The true reason is plain to all but you, of course. It is your cursed good fortune that has caused it."

"You talk nonsense. How can good fortune make a man feel sad?"

"In your case, easily."

"Explain then, O Wise One." Adam said in his best mocking tone.

"It is simple," Peter replied." You expected to spend many years labouring to produce an income that would sustain you. Years of tramping country roads, listening to the woes of millers, shopkeepers and tenant farmers. Instead of which," he went on, holding up a hand to prevent Adam from interrupting him, "you find yourself already established. You have a list of wealthy patients and an income more than enough for your needs. And all this was due to the chance finding of the archdeacon's body in a local churchyard."

"Don't put it like that," Adam said."You make me sound the most ungrateful wretch."

"As you are."

"But if my fortune has been so good, why are my spirits so low?"

"That is swiftly explained." Peter said, "Before you raise your eyebrows any further, the explanation has nought to do with your much-neglected male organ. Being involved in that murderous affair last spring and summer awoke skills and abilities in you that you had not recognised. Now it is over and they clamour for further exercise. Let me put it plainly, Dr Bascom. You are bored."

Adam sighed. He knew that his friend was probably correct. He was bored. His patients might be rich, but their ailments were still those common to all men. The single exception was the gout produced by rich living and hard drinking. Few of their ailments challenged his professional skills. It was his patience and tolerance that were pushed to the limit. The poor, and those of the middling classes, were usually grateful for whatever help you might be able to offer. The rich were petulant and demanding. All were convinced that they were doing you the greatest favour by calling you out to deal with a sore toe or a careless fall from a horse.

"And if you are right," Adam conceded, with some reluctance. "What can I do about it?"

"I know that I am right," Peter said. "As for the answer, that too is plain. Leave this little town. Set up your practice in Norwich – or even in London. Write learned tomes, give incomprehensible lectures and teach terrified students. You are quite unsuited to a country practice, Bascom. You thought nothing else would be within your grasp, so you told yourself to be content. Now you know better and your spirits rebel. I, on the other hand ..."

Adam broke in. "You, my good fellow, are well suited to your life here and make a far better living than you will admit. Aye, on the back of selling patent remedies and worthless nostrums to gullible countryfolk." The age–old rivalry between the university–trained physician and the practically–trained apothecary was a constant source of banter between them.

"A physician lightens his patient's purse more than he reduces their illness. An apothecary uses skill and judgement to effect an actual cure," Peter said. "But wait ... I should be taking notice of what a physician would do in this case. I have given you my prescription, sir. That will be two guineas, if you please."

"Two guineas! What you have said to me is not worth two pence."

"How quickly you fall into the role of a patient, Bascom. You have clearly had much experience of the typical response to the physician's diagnosis."

"You charge your patients five shillings for some worthless powder or box of pills. I suppose they pay with the utmost gratitude."

"Of course. They recognise my professional skill."

"The skill of the huckster!"

"I will tell you another thing, Bascom, and charge you nought for doing so. You spend too much time alone. When did you last visit your brother and his family at Trundon?"

"Well ... I'm not sure ... it was a little while ago."

"And your mother in Norwich – to say nothing of the delectable Miss LaSalle?"

"I write to my mother regularly!'

"Writing is not visiting. A dutiful letter, containing what you choose to think suitable for motherly reading, bears no comparison to being there in person. Do you write to your mother's pretty companion, Miss LaSalle?"

"Of course not!'

"Sometimes, Bascom, I despair of you. There you have a lovely young woman – intelligent too, so you tell me – and you neglect her. Does she displease you?"

"Well ... no. She is most pleasant company."

"Which you are most definitely not in your present mood. Get out more. Enjoy yourself. Do something wild and dangerous ..."

"Now you are being foolish again," Adam said.

"Not at all. You are not yet thirty years old, yet you act like a man of twice your years and half your intelligence. Go and visit our own, lovely Miss Jempson ..."

Fortunately for Adam, at that moment Annie, Lassimer's maidservant, entered with a letter on a small tray.

"Beg pardon for disturbing you, gentlemen," she said, "but there's a man at the door says he is a messenger. He went first to your house, doctor, and was sent here. He says you have to read this at once so that he may carry your reply. A most handsome man he is too." Annie's eyes shone at the recollection. "All kitted out in the finest worsted cloth, with the king's coat of arms on his saddlecloth and holding the biggest horse I ever did see."

Adam hurried to open the letter and read its contents. "It is from Mr Wicken at the Alien Office in London," he told Peter.

"That much I had guessed for myself," Peter said. "See, once again your mysterious Mr Wicken is on hand to involve you in another mystery. Already your prayers are answered, though you have not even prayed them. "

"What prayers?"

"To be cured of your low spirits."

Adam frowned, but decided to ignore Peter's silliness. "Mr Wicken asks me to meet him in Norwich as soon as I may be able to get there," he said.

"Go! Tell the messenger to say that you are on your way. While you are there, you can also visit your mother ... and Miss LaSalle too, of course."

"But my patients! I cannot ride away and forget about them. What will happen to my practice?"

"Have you any urgent cases at present?" Peter asked.

"No, but ..."

"Then there is no problem. Instruct your servants to explain you have been called away for a few days and will deal with medical business on your return. Any urgent requests for help they can send to me."

"But I cannot impose upon you in this way," Adam said. "You have your own business to deal with ..."

"... which is not yet so onerous that I cannot make time for a patient in urgent need," Peter said. "Set your mind at rest. You do not impose upon me, for I have offered you my help of my own accord."

"You are a true friend, Lassimer," Adam replied. "Only ..."

"Do not dose your patients with any of my vile brews?"

"That was not what I was about to say. This is no matter for levity. I wanted to say be sure you do not neglect your business in favour of mine."

"At times, Bascom, you speak the greatest nonsense. Now sit and compose your reply to the great man who waits upon your arrival."

Adam pulled a face at that, yet sat and did as he was told. His reply promised that he would be in Norwich that evening. He would call on Mr Wicken at eleven the next day.

"Where is Annie?" Adam asked, when he had finished.

"Making sheep's eyes at the handsome messenger with the big horse would be my guess," Peter said. "I believe she is giving up on me, since she can see I have no intention of promising her marriage."

"Would she not make a good wife?"

"Have you no eyes, man? She is pretty, wilful and more than confident of her effect on any man. She is young as well and – unlike you – wishes to enjoy life while she may. Any husband would need to spend more than half his time pleasing her – and the same amount of time watching to see she did not stray. I have no taste for such a Herculean task." Peter paused, as if overcome by a moment of regret. "But we waste time. Annie! Annie!" His call brought her running. "Give the doctor's letter to the man at the door ... and leave off distracting him from his duty, you baggage!"

The girl left at once, though her scowl suggested she did not relish being mocked by her master. Adam too rose and made ready to leave.

"I must thank you again for your offer of help for my patients, Lassimer," he said at the door. "If I were a more dedicated physician ..."

"Hush!", his friend said. "Do not waste your time or mine on pointless reflections and self-pity. Haste now! Your Mr Wicken will not have come from London for the simple pleasure of your company. There is some grave matter afoot. The faster you go, the quicker you may return to tell me about it."

∾

ADAM'S ARRIVAL late that evening threw his mother's household into confusion. Since he was not expected, nothing was ready for him. An empty bedroom was no problem, but having to carry up fresh coals and light a fire to warm and air the room meant considerable extra work for his mother's servants. He was also hungry, for he had left Aylsham in such haste he had not eaten or drunk since breakfast. The cook, who knew the doctor's appetite, would not be best pleased either.

In the end, of course, his mother stopped complaining about thoughtless children and accepted his explanation of why he could not warn her that he was coming. Her servants also coped, as Adam knew they would. Meanwhile, Miss Sophia LaSalle, his mother's lady companion, simply smiled at Adam's sudden appearance. Fortunately for her, she was not expected to deal with such practical matters as airing beds and providing fresh linen.

The next morning therefore, during breakfast, the two ladies fell at once to questioning him, since there had been little time to do so the night before.

"It is good to see you after so long an absence, Adam," his mother said. "Even if the manner of your coming was ... irregular. Is it not good to see my son, Sophia?"

"Indeed so," Miss LaSalle said. "Now, sir, tell all. What mystery are you set upon this time?"

"There is no mystery, Miss LaSalle," Adam said. "I believe I have been called here to consult about a patient."

"Indeed," Miss LaSalle said. "Are there no physicians in Norwich? Surely some local man would have done as well. Many are men of great experience."

"Hush, Sophia!" Mrs Bascom said. "I know you are trying to vex him into confessing what he is doing here but that will only make him more stubborn. Leave him to me. Now, Adam. Enough evasion. Why are you here? You mentioned a new patient. What is his name?"

"I don't know, Mother," Adam said.

"And his condition?"

"I don't know that either."

"So ... you arrive here at dinnertime, cause my cook to send the kitchen-maid almost into an attack of the vapours, turn the house upside down, and calmly tell me you have no idea how long you may be staying. All for a patient of whom you know nothing, neither his name nor what ails him. It is nonsense. Who summoned you to come in such haste on these terms?"

After a significant hesitation, Adam said, "Mr Percival Wicken of the Alien Office. You will recall he was involved in the matter of the murder of the archdeacon last year. I am to meet him at eleven this morning."

"Hah! I guessed it!" Miss LaSalle's cry made the others jump. "He has that expression on his face, does he not Mrs Bascom? I saw it as soon as he came through the door last evening."

"What expression?" Adam asked.

"Like a fox-hound when it catches the scent of a vixen. Once it has the scent of a fox in its nostrils, its tail goes up, it presses its nose to the ground, its eyes shine and the huntsman has to ride hard to follow where it leads.'

"You are quite correct, Sophia dear," Mrs Bascom said. "I expected my son to be morose, like his letters have been of late. Yet I find him alert and eager to be off. It is sad that neither you nor I, Sophia, can cause such a change of mood in him."

"I am not sure I relish being compared to a dog," Adam said.

"But it is so precise," Miss LaSalle said. "One of those dogs that is never happy, save when it is herding sheep, or hunting some wild animal, or doing whatever it is meant to do. Give such dogs hard, demanding work and they will toil unceasingly. Treat them like lap-dogs and they droop and languish."

"And what animal best matches your character, Miss LaSalle?" Adam asked.

"That is simple," his mother said. "An elegant cat. One that thrives on attention and stroking, yet will soon scratch those who mistreat it. Beware, my son. Miss LaSalle may – just – be willing to overlook your refusal to involve her at once in your mystery. Yet she is far from purring yet. Her claws, you may find, can make a nasty wound if you continue on this path."

"But I have done no harm to Miss LaSalle," Adam protested, "and there is no mystery. I have told you both that. Nothing but a sick man in need of my help."

"Fiddlesticks!" Miss LaSalle said. "Mr Wicken travels here from London ... it is London where he lives, is it not? Yes? So ... he travels more than a hundred miles for the pleasure of asking a young, inexperienced physician to speak to him about a patient, giving him no information as to the man's condition or symptoms? It is not credible."

"My son did remind us of the little matter of helping the great man solve the mystery surrounding the death of our archdeacon last year," Mrs Bascom added. "Do not forget that."

"Indeed so ... that might explain Mr Wicken's presence now, I suppose. But perhaps it is not Mr Wicken who instigated this meeting. Perhaps it is your son who scents a chance to revisit the scene of his triumph."

"That could be it, Sophia. Is he feeling the loss of so many fine ladies eager to talk with him? I could ask Lady Grandison or Jane Labelior to tea. The Honourable Miss Labelior seemed most eager for a more ... intimate ... acquaintance with my son, as I recall."

"You are both determined to mock me, I see. Well, I will not stay to be made the butt of your humour." Adam rose with all the dignity he could muster. "I will go to see Mr Wicken instead."

His fine exit was entirely spoiled by the peals of laughter that it produced.

ADAM WALKED the short distance to the address Wicken had given for their meeting. It proved to be the Canon Precentor's house in The Cathedral Close.

Once through the gate from Tombland, Adam stopped a moment to take in the full expanse of the Close before him. The cathedral dominated the view, its spire pointing to a sky which promised yet more wintry weather. To either side, houses, halls and other buildings enclosed a space even larger than Norwich's famous market place. What a jumble of buildings these were. The remnants of the monastery seized by King Henry jostled against construction from all the years since. There were even town-houses of recent date and it was one of these which proved to be the house he sought.

As he arrived before the Precentor's door, Adam paused to admire its graceful proportions and fine brickwork. It stood on the south side of the close, with but a short walk to the great west door of the Cathedral. The Canon Precentor had oversight of the music, the choir and the organists. He must be close at hand to supervise their performance in the many services.

A solemn manservant took Adam's card, nodded and showed him at once into an impressive library. There he found Wicken seated with a small pile of books on the table beside him.

"The Precentor, Dr Hanwell, is an old friend of mine," Wicken explained after the opening pleasantries. "He and his wife are in London at present, but they kindly suggested that I could find suitable accommodation in this house for as long as I needed. That will not be long, for events call me back to London as soon as I can make the journey. Indeed, this is no time for me to be away at all. You will forgive me, Doctor, if my explanation for the intolerable presumption of calling you here is brief ... and inadequate to your curiosity." A smile. "You will appreciate anything I tell you of this situation is in the greatest secrecy. It is not reluctance to trust you that forces me to be scanty with details, only time. On another day, I will give you a fuller account."

"Tell me how I may assist you," Adam said. "I will endeavour to be content with that. Your message made no mention of why you need to talk with me. I am merely a physician, Mr Wicken. I have no experience of the weighty matters of public security and order with which you are concerned."

"It is as a physician that I have asked you to come, Doctor. I have a patient for you. Yet this is no ordinary patient. This young man is engaged on work of the greatest importance for this realm. His loss poses a significant threat to our safety."

"But there are many physicians older and more experienced than I. Why ask for me?"

"Because I trust you with information I would not give to others. Also because this man's sickness is more of the mind than the body. I have personal experience of your skill in that field of medicine. I do not believe that bleeding, cupping and other methods used by more ... ah ... conventional physicians will produce a cure. It is his mind that has failed, and it is a physician with an interest in unusual cases of that nature that I sought. At once your name came to mind; the more so because you are already in the locality."

"The man is here?"

"Right here, Doctor. Upstairs."

"What problem has come upon him? You mentioned some failure of the mind ..."

"A simple layman's guess, Doctor, not a diagnosis. That is for you to make. Now ... to tell you all is beyond my capacity in the time available. A bare summary must suffice. I beg you, do not interrupt me with questions while I speak, however well-founded they may be. I know your boundless curiosity from our last occasion to work together."

All the time Wicken had been speaking, Adam had been observing him with the eye of a physician. He looked grey and exhausted – a long way from the elegant gentleman Adam recalled from their last meeting but a few months ago. It might have been the long journey from London, though Wicken had arrived after similar journeys in the past without such an effect. Wicken caught Adam's eye and seemed amused by what he saw.

"Well," he said, "have you competed your diagnosis, doctor?" He was smiling, but there was little humour in it. It was more the grim smile of a man determined to preserve a brave face in adversity. "It cannot be a difficult matter. You see before you a man almost at the end of his resources. These damned French revolutionaries have caused me many problems since we met last. If I am haggard and drained as a result, I believe no man could do better."

"Is it so hard?"

"It is. When tensions arise between nations, all seek a more accurate understanding of the plans of their opponents. That is why I am here, once more needing your help – if you will give it."

"I have already said that I will, if it is within my power." Adam felt a sudden fear at what Wicken might be leading him into. Before they had met, the previous year, Adam had floated on the surface of existence like a contented swan on a lake. It was Wicken who introduced him to the dangerous yet undeniably exciting currents and depths beneath.

"I thank you for that," Wicken said. It was time for business. "I have come because of a man who is far further along the road to insanity than I am. A man I need to restore to his proper senses as quickly as maybe, for the good of this country as well as his own."

"Who is this man?" Adam asked, without thinking, his curiosity aroused at once.

"Doctor ..."

"My apologies. I promised not to interrupt. Pray continue and I will mind my manners."

"The man's name is Charles Sanford. He has for several years been in the employment of part of His Majesty's Post Office. Officially, what he does is dullness itself. In reality, he is our most skilled cryptographer. His abilities are essential in deciphering messages of great usefulness to the government. Nor is he an elderly man. I believe he is scarce past thirty years of age. Indeed, the skills he possesses are more likely to be found in youth than old age.

"The work he does requires great concentration. For that reason – and for others I must omit for the present – I sent him here." Wicken gave a brief, humourless laugh. "I thought it would be a place where he could find a more congenial atmosphere than an office in London. The number of enciphered documents passing through our hands has increased. So too has the need for the utmost speed in discovering their contents. We were caught out badly by events in France; found unprepared and vulnerable to sudden invasion. Our leaders need to know what our allies and our enemies intend to do. Nay, they demand to know – and to know at once. Then they vent their frustration on me, while I must drive willing workers yet harder in an attempt to meet their demands. Sanford has been working harder than any, for he is a most conscientious fellow.

"At first, all went well. I arranged for one of the King's Messengers to bring documents to him here and collect those he had deciphered. I found quiet lodgings for him in the home of my old friend, the Canon Precentor of this cathedral. None there would ask him questions or interfere with his work.

"I said there were other reasons for getting Sanford away from London. We need his skill, Doctor. Yet you must not think I am so unfeeling as to drive a man beyond the bounds of his strength in some careless fashion. I had noted some months ago Sanford's look of exhaustion, his sluggish manner and the grimness that swept away his former spirits. I did not miss this, but I was in the grip of necessity. At least, such is the excuse I give for myself. Sanford needed time to rest and recuperate, but I had none to offer him. Instead, I did what I could to improve the circumstances around him. I removed him from the foul air and constant bustle of London. He is country-born, doctor. He needs space and good air and the sight of trees and flowers."

"I do not condemn you, Mr Wicken, for I have little grasp of the nature or extent of the pressures you mention. Nor would I ever judge you unfeeling."

"I thank you, Doctor. You have never seen me save when I am pressed for time and overwhelmed with conflicting demands. I am not sure I can recall how it was in better days. But I must return to Charles Sanford." Again he paused, then explained what he had done to assist Sanford through this period of constant work. The man was treated as a house guest by the Precentor's family and their staff. He had his own bedroom, with freedom to use a small study for his work. He might call upon the services of the household servants.

Most of all, he could come and go as he pleased and work at whatever hours best suited him.

"It sounds an admirable arrangement," Adam said. "What went wrong? For something has, or you would not be here." His curiosity had again overcome his promise to remain silent.

"One again you are correct, doctor. Something has gone wrong. I only wish I knew what that something was."

Wicken's explanation of recent events was also brief. A coded document, thought to be of great importance, had come into the hands of the authorities. The original was sent on its way so the sender would not suspect it had been intercepted. A copy was entrusted to the appropriate King's Messenger and despatched to Sanford in Norwich in great haste.

Wicken was certain the document had arrived. He had questioned the Precentor's servants himself on the matter. Given the extreme urgency of the situation, the messenger was told to wait in Norwich until Sanford had finished his work on the paper. Then he was to carry Sanford's reply with all speed back to London. The fellow had arrived on the Thursday of the previous week and was expected to set out for London on Saturday – or Sunday at the latest.

"Today is Wednesday," Adam said. "You expected the finished work before this?"

"We did, but let me finish," Wicken said. He smiled and pressed on, ignoring Adam's blushes. "The messenger whom we sent has disappeared. So has the document he gave to Sanford, along with whatever notes Sanford had written or any decipherment. That would be bad enough. For the rest, all I can tell you is that last Sunday Sanford returned in a frenzy from what seems to have been a late-evening stroll. None amongst the household could make any sense of his ravings. Then, as suddenly as it began, the fit ended."

"It ended, you say," Adam blurted out.

"Ended, yes, but in no good way. The man fell into convulsions. Now he is entirely mute and unresponsive. The Canon's manservant must clean, feed and do all else for him. He says it is as if he is handling a body made of wax, not living flesh. Sanford responds to nothing save the most basic needs. He drinks, eats – so long as food is placed in his mouth – and voids into his bed, as a baby might."

"Catatonia," Adam said. "I have heard of it, but never seen one taken by it." He shook his head in sadness. "Poor Mr Sanford is in a bad way indeed."

"He has a fine lump on the back of his head too, so I am told. Perhaps he fell. Perhaps someone hit him. I do not know. Can you help him, doctor?" Wicken asked. "The work he is engaged upon is crucial to this realm. We cannot afford his loss."

Adam hesitated a moment, but the appeal in Wicken's eyes was too strong to be turned aside with some excuse. "I will do whatever I can," he said. "That is all I can promise you."

Wicken relaxed a little for the first time that morning. "That is enough," he replied. "No honest man could promise more. Now ... what comes next?"

"Something provoked this acute state, Mr Wicken," Adam said. "From what you have told me, Mr Sanford was suffering from a severe melancholia long before. That, I expect, was brought on by overwork or fear of making crucial errors in his activities. Yet the progress of melancholia is slow and it does not produce catatonia, as it seems to have done here."

"Could he have been poisoned?" Wicken asked.

"I know of no poison capable of producing such symptoms," Adam said. "There are items in the pharmacopeia medica which should not be given to a melancholic patient. Yet none I know of have results of this magnitude, nor so swiftly reached."

"Assaulted then? The servants told me his head was bloody when he came in, though they could find only the lump I mentioned and a small break in the skin near to his ear."

"That is more likely. A blow to the head sufficient to cause concussion does not always leave much external sign. If I were to guess, I would say that only the severest concussion could result in such a state as catatonia. But my knowledge is limited. I must study the possibilities further before making a final judgment. I must also examine Sanford myself."

Wicken got up, keen to be on his way, now he had secured his purpose in coming. Adam made to rise also.

"No, my friend, do not rise," Wicken said, resting his hand on Adam's shoulder. It was an action of extraordinary friendship and intimacy from such an important man. Adam was taken aback. "I must return to London as soon as I can, for there is much awaiting my attention there. Yet I return possessed of a far lighter heart than when I came, thanks to you. One of the servants will show you where to find Sanford. I presumed on your kindness so far as to instruct them to accept you coming and leaving at will. I also assured them you have my entire confidence in whatever action you undertake."

"That is too trusting, Mr Wicken!" Adam protested. "Pray, do not leave without at least some idea of the course I propose."

"Very well, Bascom. But be brief, I implore you." Again the note of intimate friendship. Some line had been crossed in Wicken's mind, placing Adam on a different basis with him than before.

"When I studied at Leiden," Adam said, trying hard to be both concise and comprehensive, "one of my teachers had much to say on the topic of melancholia. In his view, the primary need is for total rest and quiet. The mind has contracted, as it were, into a tight ball to ward off whatever is threatening its well-being. This case may be worse due to the effects of concussion. Mr Sanford's mind has seized control of his body, shutting off all it can of communication and further threats. Sanford needs seclusion and rest, Mr Wicken ..."

"Wicken," his visitor murmured.

"... um, Wicken."

"For how long?" Wicken asked.

"I cannot say. It may well take some time. Before you protest that any time is too great for your needs, let me add that any attempt to force matters risks making his condition permanent."

Wicken's mouth had indeed opened to speak. Now he shut it again. His grim expression said all.

"We are in your hands, Bascom. I know from experience you will spare no effort. Spare no expense either, I urge you. Whatever money you need, I will provide. Succeed and you will be a rich man."

"I cannot think of money at this stage," Adam said. "I am sworn to help the sick to the best of my ability, rich or poor. Since this poor man is now my patient, I must do my utmost to cure him, or be forsworn."

"Nevertheless ..." Wicken said, but Adam interrupted him.

"Have you more information on his past, Wicken?" Adam had given his word and was all business again. "How long have you known him? For how long had you been worried about him? Had he shown any serious symptoms of mental disarrangement before this time? Can you describe them?"

Wicken held up his hands. "Stop! Stop, I pray you. Will you drown me in questions? I cannot stay longer to answer any of them ..." He raised a hand to stop Adam speaking, then dropped it to rest once more on his shoulder. "I have a long journey back to London. During that time, I will try to recall all I know of Sanford. When I arrive, I promise you to summon a clerk and dictate a letter that will contain everything. Now, I must ... I truly must ... depart. Farewell, Bascom. Look to hear from me very soon."

And with that, he left the room in haste, not even waiting to summon the maid to see him to the door. All Adam heard were hurried steps and the front door shutting behind him.

2

ADAM'S PATIENT

The room in which Charles Sanford lay was modest, yet well furnished. Aside from the bed, there was a stand with utensils for washing, an easy chair in which to relax, a cabinet beside the bed and a small desk. It also had a fine view over The Close to the great cathedral beyond. Suitable lodgings for a normal guest in a house like this. For the young man in the bed, it might well be the finest bedroom he had ever occupied.

It was to that young man that Adam now turned his attention. His patient lay on his back, propped up on several pillows. To Adam's professional gaze, his colour appeared somewhat pale, but his breathing was steady. There was no sign of fever.

Sanford's arms rested beside him on the sheet. Adam lifted one to test the man's pulse. That too was steady enough, though not as strong as Adam would have liked it to be. Adam leaned forward and moved his patient's head to the left. He wished to examine the area behind the man's right ear. The manservant who had attended to Sanford when he was first brought into the house said he had noticed a small amount of dried blood there.

Adam soon found the wound, and though it was not large it must have bled copiously when first inflicted. Scalp wounds were like that.

That was why they often appeared to the layman to be much worse than they were. Indeed, this wound was superficial; the real damage lay to the skull beneath. There an area of swelling suggested a slight fracture. That would lead to a significant case of concussion, Adam thought.

The rest of the young man's head was undamaged. Adam pulled back the bedclothes and lifted Sanford's nightshirt up to his armpits. He could see no sign of bruising or wounding on the slim body. Gently, now much preoccupied with his thoughts, he restored all to their previous condition.

During all this, Sanford was totally unresponsive. His eyes were open, yet he stared only at the canopy of the bed above him. Nor did he speak or demand to know who it was who took such intimate liberties with his person. Wherever Charles Sanford's mind was, it was not here.

At length, Adam seated himself in the comfortable chair and reviewed the situation. Sanford must have received a single, fierce blow to the side of his head, inflicted by a stone or a thick stick. The blow had fallen just behind his right ear, so he had either turned his head away to avoid the attack or was struck from behind. Either way, it must have left him dazed, perhaps unconscious. It had also resulted in a serious concussion.

All this was consistent with the servants' report of Sanford's state when he returned home. Would it alone account for the present cata-tonic state? Adam did not think so. Concussion from a blow could result in a prolonged period of mental confusion. He had never known it produce this state of total unresponsiveness. That was more likely to be the mind withdrawing into itself as a result of some intol-erable stress.

What that stress might be would prove hard to discover, even if he was able to bring Sanford back to a state in which he could answer questions. His memory might well be affected by the concussion. Besides, many suffering from melancholia were unwilling to talk about what caused it. The only hope would be to place Sanford in as quiet an environment as possible. He needed a feeling of complete security. Then, and only then, might Adam be able to win his trust and ask him to describe what had brought about this collapse of his mental faculties.

That would indeed take time. How much time, Adam had no means of knowing. Days? Weeks? Months? Whatever time it took would be too long for Wicken.

He also needed to discover as much as possible of the events running up to Sanford's entry to his present state. Wicken must have men capable of undertaking that kind of investigation. He had best leave it to them and concentrate on trying to nurse poor Sanford back to health. Wicken wanted the young man to be able to return to the work he had been doing before. As for that, it was impossible to say. Such a severe breakdown might have consequences that would last for years, even for the rest of his life.

All that was for the future. For now, Adam must tell the servants how to deal with Sanford so long as he remained as he was at present.

When he returned to the library, Adam called for a servant and asked if the Precentor's housekeeper might wait upon him. A Mrs Mendham arrived – a handsome, middle-aged woman sure of her status. Adam treated her with enormous politeness. She soon decided the doctor was an appropriate person for her to take into her confidence.

"Though I feel right sorry for the young man," Mrs Mendham said, "I must own he is a burden upon us, especially in the matter of clean linen. He fouls his bed several times a day, so that it must all be changed and set right again."

"That is indeed a burden," Adam agreed, "and I thank you most heartily for the way you have dealt with it. When I was in his room, all smelled as sweet as if he had scarcely lain himself down."

Mrs Mendham smiled. Flattery was the way to her heart.

"If I might suggest something to lessen your problem," Adam continued, trying to sound as tentative as possible. "Might you not lay the man upon a pad of folded cloth as you would a baby? For the situation is much the same. While his mind is entirely lost, he has no control over his bodily functions."

Mrs Mendham accepted his suggestion as something for her to consider.

"I have limited experience of such an extreme case as this, Mrs Mendham. Yet I am hopeful that, with rest and a growing sense of security from your laudable attentiveness, Mr Sanford may regain his normal state. At least to the extent of eating and drinking unaided and voiding himself in the proper place. Peace and quiet is what he needs above all, both for himself and for the sake of you and your staff."

"I will see he has both, Doctor. You may be assured of that. My staff are well-trained and know better than to shirk my instructions." Adam didn't doubt it. Mrs Mendham was of a nature and physique to reduce the most troublesome servant to obedience.

He thanked her then and assured her he would return the next day to check on their patient's progress. In the meantime, if any servant should recall some detail of events, however small, he would be most grateful to have it drawn to his attention. The same went for Mr Sanford's behaviour since he came to the house. At length, having received Mrs Mendham's regal acknowledgment of his request, Adam took his leave.

WHEN ADAM RETURNED to his mother's house, he found that she was out paying a visit to a friend who lived in Costessey. Miss LaSalle, he was told, had remained behind, due to a headache and a dislike of the cold wind that had sprung up. So much from Ellen, his mother's maidservant, who let him in. Miss LaSalle was in the parlour, she added, should he wish to seek her out.

Adam did. It was time to take the excuse of her indisposition and offer his services as a physician. She would not be able to laugh at that.

Sophia LaSalle sat in a chair beside the fire, reading a book.

Given the wintry conditions outside, that was no surprise. For several moments, Adam observed her in silence. He felt surprised at how much pleasure this gave him. He would not describe her as beautiful, he mused. Not quite that. Yet she had undeniably handsome features. Her dark hair was coiled up on her head, revealing neat ears and a long, slim neck. Both looked wonderfully kissable. A sudden picture filled his mind of himself stepping forward and doing just that. He pushed it aside and continued the careful enumeration of her charms. A little above the average height, her figure slim but well-proportioned, limbs straight. Sophia LaSalle was, in a phrase Adam had heard his friend Lassimer use, 'altogether nicely put together'.

If she were aware of him looking at her, Miss LaSalle gave no sign of it. She remained still, with her head bent over her book, as Adam stepped fully into the room. When he greeted her, she looked up to return his greeting, then bent once again to her reading.

"Ellen tells me you are feeling a little indisposed," Adam said. "Is there any way in which my medical skills might be of use to you?"

She put her book down at once. "I thank you, Doctor," she said, "but I find myself quite recovered. To be honest with you, I find Mrs Dennison, whom your mother is visiting, a little tiresome. She has no conversation other than the antics of her two lap-dogs and the latest fashions from London. The headache was a regrettable pretence on my part."

"I will not tell my mother," Adam said.

"Indeed you must not, Doctor. To betray a confidence is reprehensible, is it not? Now, enough of such trifles. Tell me all about your new patient."

"He is a young man suffering from a bad bump on the head."

"Tush! Is that all? I had hoped at least for a Member of Parliament crazed by a habit of eating opium. But is this young man handsome?"

"He seems normal enough. I am hardly competent to judge what a lady might find handsome."

"Oh dear. How solemn you sound. Very well, I will be serious too. Tell me what mystery lies behind his injury."

"A few moments ago," Adam said, trying to look disapproving, "you said that to betray a confidence was a reprehensible act."

"Did I? How silly of me. Well, that might be the case in general terms, but to inform your lieutenant of the nature of the task ahead does not come under such a heading."

"And who, if I may be so bold as to ask, appointed you my lieutenant? I do not recall making such an appointment."

"You are so forgetful of important matters," Miss LaSalle replied, "that I have been forced to make certain appointments myself. Besides, did I not help you unravel your previous mystery? If you forgot to appoint me to help you, you forgot equally to tell me not to do so."

"And if I did so now?"

"It would prove you to be a most unkind and ungrateful wretch, quite undeserving of my thoughts and skills."

"Even so, Miss LaSalle, I must not share certain confidences with anyone. They are not my secrets and I have been given no leave to reveal them to any others."

Miss LaSalle jumped on this remark in an instant. "At last you admit that there are secrets surrounding this affair. Of course, any person of intelligence knew that from the start, despite your feeble protestations to the contrary."

"And you are such a person?"

"Naturally, sir. Your mother and I were agreed, almost from the moment you stepped through the door yesterday, that you must be involved in some secret affair. We women, Doctor, may be a little less strong than men in a physical sense, but our minds are every bit equal to theirs. However, if you will not tell me ... yet ... I must be patient. You will need my help in due time. Of that I am sure." She stopped on a sudden and listened. "Here is your mother returned, Doctor. I am sure you have much to do, so do not let me detain you further."

Her dismissal was so firm that it took Adam aback. It was clear that she was annoyed he would not tell her more than he had. Perhaps his mother had asked her to wheedle the facts from him, relying on Miss LaSalle's fine eyes and tempting lips to lower his defences. He would not put it past her, for she was his equal in curiosity. Well, Miss LaSalle would have to report that she had failed. Dr Adam Bascom was not so susceptible to a pretty face as they had imagined.

Yet later, alone in his room, he couldn't help wondering whether he had been too much the stern moralist. Miss LaSalle's thoughts had indeed been most helpful to him in the past. It would be awkward if they could not deal with one another easily. Adam was certain that treating Mr Sanford would involve many more visits to his mother's home. He might well be grateful at some time for another view on matters. Perhaps he should have been less ready to dismiss her offer of help.

By the time dinner came, Adam was feeling more confused than ever. In contrast, his mother was in high spirits. She talked happily about her visit to Costessy, the fine house her friend lived in, and the kind welcome she received. She even had some kind words for Mrs Dennison's lap-dogs, though she had little taste for such creatures herself.

Miss LaSalle also appeared her normal self again. Though she did not speak much to Adam, save when spoken to, he was aware of the covert looks she gave him from time to time. It was obvious she was waiting for some further move on his part. Unfortunately, he had no idea what that might be.

Mrs Bascom made no remark on Adam's business that day until they had all retired to the drawing room.

"Adam," she said when they were seated and she had served tea. "You promised to tell us all about your new patient. From your silence, I can only suppose he has already died."

"I remember no such promise," Adam said, "and the poor man is certainly alive, if not in a good state."

"But you did promise. Didn't he, Sophia?"

"Indeed, madam. Surely he will not break his word now."

"Very well," Adam said. "My patient is a young man engaged on …

important work ... who has received a bad blow to the head and is currently catatonic." There he stopped.

"What does 'catatonic' mean? Do you know, Sophia, for I do not."

"It means he neither sees, hears nor speaks and has lost the movement of his limbs," Miss LaSalle said.

"He is deaf, dumb, blind and paralysed? Is that so, Adam?"

"Effectively, yes," Adam said, wondering at the depth of Miss LaSalle's knowledge to understand such an obscure word. "Catatonia is a problem of the mind, not the body. He has lost none of his faculties in a physical sense. It is his mind that blocks them all."

"Can you loosen its grip?"

"I hope so ... in time."

"He was engaged on important work, you said?" It was Miss LaSalle now, returning to the assault on his reticence.

"I did. What exactly that was, I neither know nor would be able to speak about if I did."

"We were right," Miss LaSalle said to Mrs Bascom. "It is a mystery, exactly as last year. Mr Wicken has summoned your son to solve it for him."

"Nothing of the sort!" Adam said. "I am present only as a physician."

"I have already pointed out that such a great man has access to a great many physicians," Miss LaSalle said. "Why pick on just the one who helped him before?"

"You have answered you own question," Mrs Bascom said. "Of course, there might be that other explanation I suggested."

"What is that? Pray remind me." Miss LaSalle said.

"Last summer, my son here had fully half the ladies of Norwich in a flutter over him. Perhaps this present situation is as he says: simply a consultation over a patient. The cloak of mystery he throws around it is a story meant to spread his fame abroad again. He misses their attention and hopes to lure them back."

"That could well be it," Miss LaSalle said. "He spurns our homely companionship because he is set on attracting something more exotic."

Adam was exasperated. "You both talk nonsense," he said. "I will tell you no more. Mr Sanford is a sick man. Mr Wicken knows of my interest in illnesses of the mind and also knows me. Thus he consults on this matter with a physician he trusts. That is it, in a nutshell." He turned to Miss LaSalle. "Nor would I ever spurn your help in this matter, Miss LaSalle, any more than I would spurn my mother's."

"But you did, sir, only this afternoon." Adam could only stare in amazement at that remark. "When you found me in the parlour, I offered my assistance. With great coldness, you told me you were not able to betray the confidences given to you. You spurned me, sir."

"Did you, Adam?" his mother said.

"Well ... only in a way ... I was confused ... as I am now."

"It is no matter, Doctor," Miss LaSalle said. "As I said, you will soon be pleading for our help, as you did last time."

"Do stop being such a pompous fool, Adam," his mother said. "If we are interested in what you do, it is from affection as much as curiosity. Now, apologise to Miss LaSalle and let us all be friends."

"Apologise for what?" Adam asked.

"For spurning me, sir."

"I did not spurn you. You make me sound like a man turning his rejected lover out of the house."

"You may do that too, for all I know. No, sir. You cannot deny that that you refused my offer of help and told me that it was presumptuous to make such an offer."

"It will not do, Adam," his mother said. "Apologise at once."

Adam could not withstand a double dose of feminine thinking. He apologised. For what, he was quite unsure, but it lessened the pressure for a while.

"Thank you, Doctor," Miss LaSalle said. "Now, as your lieutenant in this affair, it seems to me that I need to know a great deal more about this young man. How did he come by his injury? Is it serious?"

"It is a serious concussion, though the physical wound is not too bad and should soon mend. As for how he came by it, I do not know in any detail. It seems he went out for a walk one night and was attacked ..."

"Attacked? And why did he go out at night? Would that not be asking for trouble?"

"I cannot answer your questions, I fear, for the simple reason that I do not know. He was definitely attacked and at night. As to why it happened or where or anything else, you are as wise as I am."

"Well, Doctor," Miss LaSalle said. "I suggest you take pains to find out the answers to all such questions. Only then can you judge the likely outcome of his medical situation correctly, as well as solve the mystery surrounding him. Is that not the case, Mrs Bascom?"

Adam shook his head. He knew he was utterly defeated. Better to accept the situation than continue to put up a fruitless struggle. Still, he made one final attempt to reassert his authority.

"And is there anything more you have decided I should endeavour to make clear?" he asked. Sadly, this sarcasm too was wasted. Miss LaSalle simply chose to take his question seriously and offer a full response.

"The man's background and history. What brought him to Norwich. Who he knows in this city. What led up to events on the night the man was attacked. What work he has been engaged upon. Who might wish to prevent him continuing with it. Whether he had been visited or contacted earlier that day by anyone who might have caused him to go out alone later, maybe to a meeting. Things like that. I'm sure you can work the rest out for yourself, now I have set you on the right path."

"I will do my best," Adam said. His surrender was now complete. He could see this was going to prove a most trying case.

3

THE FULL PICTURE

At breakfast the next morning, Miss LaSalle seemed a little less sure of herself. Yet she was just as determined to play as great a part in Adam's activities as he would let her. Adam's mother had chosen to take her breakfast in her room, so there were only the two of them at the table.

"What is your plan for today?" she asked Adam. "Are you visiting this Mr Sanford again? What do you hope to achieve?"

Adam had his mouth full at the time, so it took a few moments of chewing and swallowing before he could reply. He was unused to revealing his plans to anyone else. Indeed, quite often they were a mystery to him until put into action. He was cautious in his reply.

"Yes. I am going to visit him, but purely in a medical capacity. I do not expect that he will yet have recovered sufficiently to tell me anything. He may not have changed at all since yesterday. I shall see."

Miss LaSalle considered this for a moment. Then she said, "Have you questioned the servants at all? They might have useful information."

"Mr Wicken told me he had already spoken to them, Miss LaSalle. What they could tell him – which was little enough – he passed on to me."

"Hmm ... But did he ask the right questions? If he did not, they might still know things without knowing they know them ... if you understand me."

"I think so," Adam said. "You mean they might not realise some apparently trivial piece of information is important."

"That is exactly what I mean, Doctor. See how well we work together. You understand my mind, even when I do not quite understand it myself."

"I would never claim to understand any woman's mind, Miss LaSalle, let alone yours. And if we 'work well together', as you put it, it is mostly because we are not working at all. You are simply asking me questions on matters I have already considered."

"But how will I know you have considered them, Doctor, unless you tell me? You must promise from this point on to tell me all, in perfect frankness. If you do not, I shall not be able to assist you."

"I believe my words of yesterday have slipped your memory. It is not in my power to tell you of some matters without seeking Mr Wicken's permission."

"Then you must seek it!"

"We shall see. You may have appointed yourself my lieutenant and gained the help of my mother to prevent me from challenging this state of affairs, but I have still to be convinced. I need no lieutenant in what is, as yet, an entirely medical case."

"Pish! You do not believe that and neither do I. I will not seek to interfere in medical matters in any way. There you may reign in lonely isolation. But regarding the mystery ..."

"There is no mystery, as I keep telling you."

"So ... why was this man struck down? Who did it and for what reason? May they try to finish what they have started?"

"I do not know the answer to any of those things."

"And yet you claim there is no mystery! Have you at least put a guard over your patient?"

"Why should I?"

"Someone attacked him and most likely tried to kill him, Doctor. Let us assume they felt they had good reasons for doing so. If murder was indeed their purpose, will they not try again once they know he is alive?"

Much to his irritation, Adam had to admit – at least to himself – that he had not thought of this. What if the assailant had followed Sanford back to the Precentor's house? What if he was, even now, plotting some way of making an entry to ensure Sanford was dead? He could hardly tell Wicken that he had failed to set a guard because it hurt his pride to act on a suggestion made by his mother's lady companion.

"I will consider it," he said. "Now, I beg you, allow me to finish my breakfast without more questions, or I will never get to see my patient at all."

It was little surprise to Adam that his patient had shown no change. He had said as much to Miss LaSalle. The young man still lay with his face towards the ceiling. Today his eyes were closed, though he did not seem to be asleep – at least so far as Adam could tell. Otherwise, his pulse was slow and regular and his colour as pale as before. Healing was going to be a long process.

On a whim, Adam sat on a chair beside the man's bed. The room was silent, save for the soft tick of a clock on the mantel. Indeed, there was such a sense of calm that Adam was loathe to leave. His mind had been a jumble of thoughts on his walk from his mother's house. Images of Miss LaSalle's eager concern ran through his mind. She wished to assist him and, reluctant as he was to admit it, the prospect of spending more time with her was far from unpleasant. In Aylsham, he had always talked his ideas through with Lassimer. Here in Norwich, he had no such trusted ally with whom he could try out his theories or ask to verify his conclusions. And while Lassimer was no dunce, Miss LaSalle's brain was frighteningly sharp – probably sharper than his own. Could he swallow his pride enough to trust her?

Take the present situation, for example. Should he now walk

away to wait until Mr Sanford regained consciousness? That was what any conventional physician would do. Yet was there more?

Almost before he knew it, Adam began talking to his patient in a low voice. He explained who he was and that he wished only to help where he could. He assured poor Sanford that he was now safe and could rest as much as he needed. None would trouble him. Adam even explained that the servants had tried as best they could to make him more comfortable. If only he could co-operate by eating, drinking and voiding as other men did, he would make that task far easier for all.

Whether any of this reached into Sanford's brain, Adam had no idea. He didn't even know if Sanford could hear him. Still he pressed on, trying to infuse his voice with all the calmness and steadiness he could. He asked no questions, expressed no judgment of Sanford's state or what had brought him to it. Time enough for that, when the man could converse properly.

Whether it was the peacefulness of the room or the need to express the feelings pent up inside him that led him on he could not tell. Whatever the reason, he began explaining something of his own confusion to the still body in the bed. He admitted how much his patients bored him and how little he enjoyed his humdrum life. How tiresome it was to spend more of his time struggling through foul roads than with the patient he had gone to see. He confessed that Mr Wicken's summons had come as a spark of hope that this new case would be something more challenging to occupy his attention. He even asked the silent man to do his best to regain his wits, so that he could explain who had attacked him and why.

At length, Adam touched Sanford's hand and thanked him for listening; though he had no notion whether he had done so or not. Then, wearied and refreshed at the same time, he rose and took his leave.

As a maidservant showed him to the door, she hesitated, plucking up her courage to speak. "Excuse my forwardness, sir. You did say as how any of us what knowed something or had seen something unusual about that young gentlemen was to tell you about it."

"I did indeed," Adam said. "Let us stand here a moment and you can tell me what you know."

"It ain't much, sir, but it did seem odd. 'Twas the day the young gentleman came home in the evening so distraught." Once she had overcome her nerves, the pleasure in telling her tale to an attentive audience took over. "Well, earlier that day – noon or thereabout – the housekeeper sent me to the Anchor Inn to meet the carter and bring back any letters. Master or mistress gets some most times he comes – that's twice each week, sir – for they're both great letter-writers. I can write a little too, sir, though my reading is better." The girl's pride in this achievement was clear and Adam hastened to praise her for her accomplishment.

"You collected a letter for the young gentleman who is so ill?" He decided to risk prompting her a little.

"That I did, sir," she said. "Carter said it had come a long distance, as he believed."

"You brought it to the young man?"

"Tha's right enough, that is." The girl's Norfolk accent was growing stronger as she became less aware of speaking to one of the gentry. "As soon as I comes back, I leaves the master's and mistresses's letters in the master's study, like I'd been told. Then I took the young gentleman's letter to his room."

"And he opened it at once?"

"No, 'e did not. He looked at the writing and must 'ave recognised it, for he seemed eager for me to leave. 'E 's a most polite gentleman, sir, and always says 'thank you' for anything you does for 'im. But that day 'e just sat and stared at the letter and says, 'That will be enough, Lucy' as if 'e was master or something."

"Thank you indeed, Lucy. I am most grateful you have told me this." Adam turned to continue on his way, but the girl protested.

"But I ain't got to the interesting bit yet, sir."

Adam stopped and waited with all the patience he could muster. He suspected the girl rarely exchanged more than the most formal words with her employers. The experience of having a gentleman listen to her with such attention was intoxicating. She was going to draw it out.

"Very well, Lucy. But I pray you be brief, for I must be upon my way."

"Right, sir, I will. Now ..." She paused to try to arrange her thoughts. Adam was touched and determined to be patient with her. "It must 'ave been that afternoon, round about four of the clock. I'd done all the grates and was on my way to the kitchen to 'elp cook finish the pickling of a salmon. When master and mistress are away, there's less cooking to be done, so cook gets on with stocking up 'er larder." She must have remembered Adam's instruction to be brief, for she blushed and hurried on.

"Well, tha's 'as maybe. I noticed that I must 'ave left one of me brushes somewhere. The grate in the master's bedroom was the last I'd done before then, so I went up there to look for it. You'll never guess ... right. As I passed the young gentleman's room I 'eard 'im crying, sir. Bawling 'is 'eart out, 'e were. I wondered whether as I should go in to see if 'e were alright, but I knows men are funny about anyone seeing 'em cry. So I stood where I was and just called out, 'Is everything well with you, sir?' and he went all quiet, then said, 'Yes'. Just that. Nothing more. So I went downstairs ..."

"Can you recall how long this was before the young man went from the house, Lucy?"

"Not more'n half an hour, sir, I swear. Maybe even less, for cook said ..."

"You're quite sure he was crying?"

"Indeed I am. Like I said, 'e was bawling 'is 'ead off. Great sobs, there was, and wailing and sniffing and ...'

"And is there more to tell me?" Adam said. But Lucy had come to the end of her tale. Try as she might, with much screwing up of her eyes and murmuring to herself, she had to admit as much. Adam took out his purse and gave her a silver shilling.

"There," he said. "That is for your trouble in telling me and your cleverness in realising how important it might be. Thank you, Lucy. What you have told me will be a great help."

The girl beamed with a mixture of pride and pleasure. Adam had no doubt that she would hurry to tell all the other servants what had passed between them and show them her shilling. If anyone else in the household had information, they would be waiting with it when he came again.

Walking back to his mother's house, Adam reflected on Lucy's words. First the letter – in a hand Sanford had recognised – then the distress. What was in that letter? Who might it have been from? Adam had seen no letter in the young man's room. Nor was he at all certain that it would be permissible to read such a letter, even if he could find it. To read another man's papers, whatever the circumstance, would be a serious breach of manners. No matter if their contents might be helpful in bringing Sanford from his current state.

Adam turned all these matters over in his mind, but even when he stood before the door of his mother's house, he could find no satisfactory explanation.

WHEN ELLEN LET Adam into the house, she told him a messenger – a special messenger, come right to the door – had brought him a letter. The sender wished him to read it as soon as might be convenient. She had left it for him in the small parlour. Her mistress and Miss LaSalle were visiting, she added, and would not return until shortly before the time for dinner.

As Adam had suspected , the letter was from Wicken. To have sent it via an official messenger, as before, argued haste and great importance. Yet who knew what such powerful men as Wicken might feel due to their position? Perhaps he sent all his missives that way.

By the time he had read the first sentences, Adam knew that his first thought had been correct. The news Wicken imparted was indeed grave, and not just about Adam's patient.

My Dear Doctor,

I promised to write to you with as much information about Mr Sanford's situation as I could glean. However, you must forgive me if I ask you to wait for that a day or two longer. The news that has reached me just now is of far greater import. It should have come to me while I was still in Norwich. Such was my haste to return to London, I had departed before it arrived. As a result, it was sent after me and has not arrived until scarce fifteen minutes before now.

I believe I told you that a King's Messenger carried 'letters' to Mr Sanford and brought back the results of his labours. I also mentioned that the last such delivery was of special importance. The messenger was told to wait in Norwich until he could bring back the response. That particular messenger, Toms, had disappeared. Now it seems he was murdered. His body was found in a patch of weed in the River Wensum, downstream from the Bishop's Bridge about a mile. He had received several severe blows to his head from some heavy object. After the assault he was, they presume, thrown into the river. That this was done at once – and presumably by the same person – was proved by the report of those who took him from the water. They saw copious amounts of water come from his mouth and noticed a great sound of liquid within in him as he was lifted. To make certain, the apothecary made an incision into the man's breast and felt a lung. He confirmed that it contained liquid. Toms died from drowning, though he would soon have died anyway, it seems, such was the severity of the beating he had received.

I have at once despatched two of my best constables to Norwich to investigate this dreadful deed and find the culprit. While this murder is not a matter to concern you, I recall the servants said Sanford's head was bleeding when he returned to the Precentor's house. I myself saw the lump on his head. He too must have been attacked – and on that same evening.

What this means, I do not yet grasp. It may be the action of criminals or cut-purses. Of course, there may be more to it than that. Norwich has also long been a home to all kinds of dissenters and freethinkers. There are many who are infected by seditious ideas, such as those put about by Paine and his supporters. Perhaps some such group wish to provoke the authorities to action. Too severe a response could then lead to resentment and riots on a wider scale. That would be bad. But if this violence was directed at Sanford and Toms because someone knew the nature of their activities, it is far, far worse.

I pray you take care of your patient. Whoever has done this foul deed might yet seek to finish what he has started. Take care of yourself too, Doctor. I can by no means afford to lose you either.

It is time that I told you more about this case than I have already, but you will understand there are aspects of the situation I cannot set down on paper. It is a great imposition I know, but will you oblige me enough to visit me in London as soon as you can? Perhaps next week? At present, I cannot leave here. If you suffer any pecuniary loss from being away from your practice yet longer, I undertake to make it up at once.

Please inform me at the address on this letter of the day and time of your arrival. I will have a carriage meet you and convey you to a comfortable place to recover from the journey and refresh yourself, then bring you to my office.

I remain, sir, your most humble and grateful servant,
Percival Wicken.

Once he had read the letter, Adam called Ellen and asked her to give a message to Miss LaSalle on her return. Would she spare him a few moments before dinner, if his mother would allow it? Not that he imagined there would be any problem in such an arrangement. Still, it was often wise to seek permission in his opinion rather than assuming it would be given. Perhaps Miss LaSalle would even take the hint!

She certainly made haste to meet his request. It always seemed to him that ladies of any age took an amazing amount of time to prepare themselves for any activity. Yet Miss LaSalle had returned home, changed for dinner, done whatever else ladies did in such matters, and presented herself in the parlour within barely fifteen minutes. It was scarce believable.

"You asked for me, Doctor?" she said as she seated herself. In contrast to yesterday, she appeared worryingly demure.

"I did, Miss LaSalle," Adam began. "During the day, I have reflected on what passed between us yesterday and this morning ..." How pompous he sounded! More like a man of fifty than one still to reach his thirtieth year. Too late to change his words now. "... and I realised that my response to you was churlish. Your kind offer ... "

Miss LaSalle interrupted him. "You realised that it would be helpful to have someone as a sounding board, if for no other reason. You also decided I could be trusted not to spread abroad whatever you said to me. Is that not it?"

He knew she was clever, but this was terrifying.

"Um ... yes, I suppose it was," he mumbled.

"You also discovered some matters during the day that are bothering you. Now you feel a need to clarify them in your own mind by seeking to explain them to another person."

"Yes," Adam said, feeling quite helpless.

"I imagine that you are used to seeking such help from your friend, Mr Lassimer. But he is in Aylsham and you are here. Nor do you know many people in Norwich. You have thus decided to take what is offered – even if it is by a mere woman – rather than seek to go on alone."

"I would never call you a mere woman, Miss LaSalle."

"But that is what I am, Doctor. I believe I told you last year that I have no expectations beyond my present position. I am not marriageable amongst polite society, for I have no dowry nor hope of inheritance. Nor would I make a good wife for a tradesman or merchant. I have few practical skills and little interest in managing a household. I am neither pretty enough nor empty-headed enough to make a suitable plaything for a rich man; nor do I believe I would relish the role of mistress. In all, sir, I am what you see. Most happy to be companion to such an amiable person as your mother, who gives me all the freedom I could desire, yet as bored as you are a good deal of the time."

"Bored?"

"Of course. Your mother's friends spend their time exchanging gossip for the most part. They are rich, yet few are clever beyond the little needed to manipulate their husbands or current lovers. You, Doctor, are bored with the humdrum life of a country doctor. Do not bother to deny it. It must be so, for you are too accomplished and too curious for new experiences to be otherwise. I am often bored with the conversation of respectable ladies, especially those of a similar age to your mother. You will, I am sure, one day escape the limits of your present position. I will not. Is it any wonder that I grasp at the opportunity to involve myself in something that may challenge my mind? Even if I scandalise you by the way I do it."

"I admit I was somewhat taken aback by your boldness," Adam said. "I had not understood."

"I have only mentioned the drawbacks to my current position," Miss LaSalle went on. "It has great advantages as well. Unlike any young woman who seeks a husband, I am able to pay little regard to the conventions of society – save for ensuring that I never embarrass your mother in any way. With men who would be shocked by anything beyond the norm, I can exercise my acting skills and play the little mouse to perfection. Only with such as I trust to see beyond such fripperies ..."

"I am touched by your trust," Adam said, interrupting her as she had done him. "I only hope I can live up to it. Now ... I have much to tell you and there is little time before the dinner gong will be rung. Let us leave everything else until another time and concentrate on matters in hand."

Miss LaSalle agreed at once to that and arranged herself in a suitably attentive attitude. If Adam suspected this to be a mild joke on her part, he did not call her out on it.

As systematically as he could, Adam explained the matter. He began with the letter Sanford had received before going out on the evening he was attacked. Then he told her what Mr Wicken had written and of the need to protect Sanford from further attack. Finally, he sketched an outline of the work Sanford had been doing. Now she knew all.

"As to the murder of the King's Messenger, Toms," he concluded, "we may leave that to Mr Wicken and his constables to unravel."

"Indeed we may not," Sophia said. "To send constables here from London is a foolish action on Mr Wicken's part. Who will tell them anything? Most will assume they are officers of the Revenue. The radicals and revolutionaries will judge them to be spies or government agents. Many such are sent to seek them out and bring them to what may pass for justice in these troubled times. No, Doctor. The constables will find nothing, of that you may be certain. Mr Wicken must either give up or turn to you. Yet I agree we may set that aside for the moment and concentrate on Mr Sanford."

Adam was forced to agree with her reasoning. Norwich might be a great city, but strangers still stood out. If they asked questions amongst those most likely to be involved in some violent crime, they would learn nothing.

"What are your thoughts on the letter Sanford received?" he asked. "I imagine it must have been a summons to meet his attacker."

"That is one likely solution," Sophia conceded. "However, I do not believe you should assume it is the correct one at this stage. It may also have brought some news – bad news, I imagine – that Mr Sanford wished to think about. He would not be the only person who thinks best when moving. A brisk walk is often a sovereign way to stimulate the brain. But then, that letter may have nothing to do with what happened either."

"So we are no further forward," Adam said.

"Not at all. I think we may assume that the attack on Mr Sanford and the one on Toms, the messenger, are linked in some way. That would rule out Mr Sanford being the victim of a thief or ruffian who was frightened off before he could rob his victim. It would also rule out an attack brought about by seeking out some whore ..."

Adam's face must have shown his thoughts all too clearly, because Sophia smiled at his discomfort with her last remark.

"Really, Doctor," she said. "I am not so sheltered from the real world that I do not know that any man using a whore is in grave danger of being attacked and robbed as a result. Mr Sanford is, you tell me, young. He may be a scholar and have an uncommon gift for mathematics, but I imagine he feels the urges other men feel. Even you ..."

This was going too far!

"Let us not be distracted, Miss LaSalle," Adam said hastily. "I agree that both attacks are likely to be linked in some way. To discover the reason for one will probably reveal the reason for the

other. But how we are to do that while Sanford remains in his catatonic state I cannot imagine. Listen! There is the dinner gong. Now,
we must put all these matters aside and proceed to the dining room
in a normal fashion. I would not have my mother more involved in
any of this than is necessary. It is not that I do not trust her to keep a
confidence. Merely that her idea of assistance may not be mine."

"Ah," Sophia said. "The Honourable Miss Jane Labelior, for
example."

"Precisely."

4

THE PRECENTOR'S HOUSE

Rev Dr Hanwell, the Precentor, and his lady had returned home the previous evening. Thus Adam, making his second visit of the week to his patient, was able to meet them and discuss Sanford's progress. They were seated in the parlour and he had just imparted an edited version of Mr Wicken's letter.

"I wonder whether it would not be best to remove Mr Sanford to another place?" he said.

"No, doctor," Mrs Hanwell said at once. She was a tiny woman, barely five feet in height and delicate in appearance, yet she more than made up for this in the forcefulness of her manner. "No ruffian shall ever force me to feel fear in my own home! Let the poor young man remain here. Are we not in the same position as the Good Samaritan? It is our Christian duty to care for the sick and I will allow no one to deflect me from that – least of all some murderer."

"Be at ease, Jane my dear," Dr Hanwell said, smiling at his wife's courageous outburst. "The doctor is only suggesting we might consider such a course of action. It is our decision. We must remember we owe a duty of care to our household and ourselves. Still, I agree the young man should remain where he is. I will speak with the servants and ask them to keep a discrete watch on comings and goings. The groom and the gardener are both strong young men. I will make sure they are always on hand in case anyone should offer violence. We are not to be away again for several weeks, so they will have little enough to do."

"I suppose you are right, Elias," his wife said. "Yet it sticks in my throat to be driven to any unusual action by threats, especially from a cowardly knave who creeps up on people and hits them on the head."

During this exchange, Adam stayed silent. What Dr Hanwell was planning would certainly be a help, but it would never deter a determined man. What was needed was a proper guard. Yet Adam had no knowledge of how or where he might find men he could trust to carry out this task.

"What you suggest is sensible, Dr Hanwell," Adam said. "Yet your men have their own duties about the household. The gardener must care for the lawns and flowerbeds at least some of the time. If you or Mrs Hanwell wish to go out, perhaps visiting, the groom must prepare carriage and horse and sometimes accompany you. To assure the safety of all in this house, more is needed, I fear. At the moment, I do not know how this may be effected, but be assured that I will make it my business to find out."

"That is kind of you, Doctor," Dr Hanwell replied. "I have no experience of such matters. They do not normally fall within the purview of a canon of this cathedral. What terrible times these are, when men may not go about their business without fear for their lives!"

"Pish!" his wife said. "There are parts of this city where no woman may walk without endangering her honour and her life, as you well know."

"I spoke of men, Jane," her husband replied. "Women are ever the weaker sex."

Not in this case at least, Adam thought to himself. I would by no means relish the thought of coming to a serious disagreement with your wife, even though I stand a full head and more taller than her.

Mrs Hanwell sniffed at her husband's words, but said no more.

The look in her eye, however, promised that he had not heard the last of such condescension.

"With your permission, Dr Hanwell," Adam said, "might your household be called together? We could investigate whether any suspicious circumstances have already been noted. Your maid, Lucy ..."

"Flibberty-gibbet," Mrs Hanwell muttered. "Always gossiping."

"... told me but yesterday of an interesting observation she had made." Adam felt obliged to defend the girl after Mrs Hanwell's remark. " I feel sure she will have told the others of my interest in anything unusual which has occurred in the past few days ..."

"With a good deal of elaboration!" Mrs Hanwell added, under her breath.

"... so others may also wish to relate matters of interest. At the same time, you could speak to them in the way you have just suggested."

"A good idea, Doctor. Let us call my housekeeper at once and ask that all the staff be assembled in the servants' hall. No need to bother yourself, Jane. The good doctor and I will take care of this matter. I am sure that you have better things to do."

Mrs Hanwell looked decidedly upset at this comment, but years of good breeding won over. She would not contradict her husband before a visitor, however much she made him pay later.

Later, when the housekeeper had made all ready, the two men made their way to the servants' quarters. Dr Hanwell spoke quietly to Adam. "It is better if my wife is not present. She has the kindest of hearts and I have long seen her as a paragon amongst women. Yet I have to own that her manner afrights even the most confident servant. If she is in the room, few, I fear, will speak freely. Though, as you have seen, Jane is little, she can be fierce when her passions are aroused. She feels such a motherly regard for the young man lying upstairs that I would not give much hope for any who might offer him hurt in her presence. If I did not have a better regard for her sex and stature than she has herself, I would suggest setting her to guard the house alone. No malefactor would pass that barrier without grave injury."

As Adam suspected, the servants were eager to share all they knew, if only to stop Lucy from acting in such a superior way towards them.

Several said they had glimpsed a man near the house on the night Sanford was found on the doorstep. Two claimed to have seen him the next night also. Their descriptions of him varied, not least because most had already determined that he must be a villain. These described less the man they saw and more the kind of person they thought a villain should be. Still, sifting the imaginative from the practical, Adam gained an image of a man of middling height, thickset and around forty years of age. His dress was typical of an artisan, it appeared. That he was not present by chance seemed proved by the fact that he had been seen where he could slip into the shadows of a building or behind a cart.

None knew if he had returned a third time. Dr Hanwell and his wife had a well-disciplined household and a housekeeper who was more than capable of keeping all under her eye. Once the house was locked up, usually quite early in the evening when the family was away, no servant would dare to venture outside. Even the groom and the gardener were expected to retire to their quarters at about that time and stay there until the morning.

Adam was reassured by what he had heard. The most desperate of ruffians would not attempt to enter a house if he knew there would be people alert within. In the cathedral close, the houses stood close together and the great gates were shut every night. Any outcry would bring others running to investigate. Even so, Adam asked them all to remain alert and guard the house as best they could.

After the servants had contributed what they knew of this mysterious loiterer, Dr Hanwell also warned them to be vigilant. Adam was relieved that the precentor said nothing that might cause real alarm. Rather, his words implied a nuisance that could be dealt with by measures based on common sense. It was agreed that the groom and gardener would make sure one of them was on hand at all times. For the rest, life would proceed as normal.

When all was finished, Adam spoke again, mindful of the reward he had given to Lucy.

"With your permission, Dr Hanwell, might I be allowed a measure of thanks towards your household for these extra precautions? Perhaps I could ask your housekeeper to distribute say sixpence to each of those present here. Save Lucy, of course, who has already received her share."

"That is too kind, Doctor. It is no more than their duty." Dr Hanwell replied.

"Even so, we both urged all to stay on watch and report anything of interest to me. The labourer is worthy of his hire, as it says in the New Testament."

"So be it then, Doctor, and my thanks for your kindness in this matter. I am sure everyone will show their gratitude by their diligence in carrying out what we have asked. And ... I had forgot this ... by remaining silent about it. No tittle-tattle outside this house! We must not warn this man – if he is the one who matters. That would make him exercise greater diligence in concealment. Far better allow him to become over-confident. That way we may see any threat before it arrives."

There matters ended. Adam gave the housekeeper the required amount of money and the servants scattered to their duties again – all save for Lucy, who showed Adam out. If she was disappointed not to receive a second reward, she had the good sense not to show it.

Sophia and his mother were out when Adam returned. In a way, he was glad. He was now reconciled to sharing all he discovered with Miss LaSalle, but he was glad of a little time to gather his thoughts on his own. Like her, he assumed there must be a link between the injury to Charles Sanford and the death of Toms, the messenger. It was hard not to see some conspiracy behind both events. Had someone come to understand the nature and importance of Sanford's work and decided to put an end to it?

Of course, as Wicken had written, none of this ought to be Adam's concern. Not even if it suggested the man seen lurking near the Precentor's house might be more than a common thief or footpad. Yet if that were so, the danger to those within would be great.

Adam made up his mind to reply to Wicken's letter at once, saying that he was willing to go to London as Wicken asked, but could not yet specify a date. Then, as briefly as he could, he reported what he had learned from the precentor's servants. He added that he had offered to find somewhere safer and more private for Mr Sanford, but Mrs Hanwell would not hear of it. Sanford would stay where he was.

How much credence to give to the servants' tales of mysterious prowlers, he did not know. Many people passed through The Close. Nervous or excitable servants – Lucy came to his mind at once – might change innocent tradesmen or delivery boys into desperate criminals.

Finally, he reminded Wicken of his promise to supply details of Sanford's background, activities and state of mind. Sanford had been badly upset by a letter received on the day he was attacked. Maybe some clue to its nature lay in his past life. Nor should they forget his previous bouts of melancholia. Taken with the concussion, it was possible these might be the cause of his present symptoms. It was vital to know as much about him as possible.

Adam laid down his pen and flexed his fingers to remove the cramp that seized him whenever he wrote for too long. He would send the letter by the next available post. Meanwhile, he must give his mind to making better sense of what he had learned of Sanford so far. There was also his practice to consider. Whatever Wicken's needs, he could not stay away from his home in Aylsham indefinitely. Peter could be relied upon to deal with any grave demands, but it was unreasonable to expect him to spend many days looking after another man's business as well as his own.

At length, worn out with questions to which he could find no answers, Adam sat in a more comfortable chair and allowed his eyelids to close for a moment.

HE WAS awoken by Ellen knocking on his door and asking whether he would be taking dinner with Mrs Bascom and Miss LaSalle. They were already in the dining room. Cook was concerned lest the meal be spoiled.

At first, Adam was too confused by his sudden awakening – and the realisation that he had slept for nearly two hours – to give a coherent answer. When he did, saying he would be down within five minutes, he regretted it a moment later. He had not changed when he came back from the Precentor's house and was still wearing his outdoor clothing. But if he stayed to change, it would be a good deal more than five minutes before he could join his mother and her companion.

Snatching up his letter to Wicken, he fumbled to apply his seal to the flap. At the foot of the stairs, he called out for Ellen, thrust the letter into her hands and bade her send Roger the groom to take it to the post office with all speed.

Thus it was that Adam hastened in to dine. His hair was uncombed, his face unwashed and he wore a coat more suited to braving a rainstorm than sitting down to dinner. If neither his mother nor Miss LaSalle mentioned this grave breach of manners, Adam still felt the weight of their disapproval throughout the meal. It looked like being a vexing end to what had proved a most disquieting day.

After dinner, the three of them sat again in the drawing room. None had any inclination to play cards, or make music, or do any of the other things commonly chosen to while away the time before bed. Nor was there much conversation. Adam felt too embarrassed by his appearance. His mother seemed distracted. Miss LaSalle's fury at being deprived of the chance to question Adam on what had taken place during the day fizzed and hummed in the background.

Thus they sat, until Mrs Bascom announced that she was tired and would go to bed at once.

"Visiting Lady Grandison is always a draining experience. She is so ... so vibrant and demanding. I feel pale in comparison. You recall her, Adam?"

"No one could forget her, Mother. Yet she was kind to me."

"You have the advantage of being a more than presentable young man. I, on the other hand ... no matter. I shall retire. I am not blind. I can see that dear Sophia will burst if she does not have the opportunity to quiz you and I am too tired to take in any more about your mystery. So ... I will leave you together."

Once she had left, Sophia sprang to the attack. "What did you mean by avoiding me before dinner, sir? I could hardly come to your room to seek you out. I sat waiting for nearly an hour in the parlour, yet you did not come. It is unkind, sir. Most unkind."

Adam was prepared for questions but not this onslaught. He was about to reply in kind when he realised that to do so would be futile. Fuelling Miss LaSalle's anger would only prolong it.

"I fell asleep," he said. "That is all there is to it. Did you not see that I came into dinner most improperly dressed in the clothes I had worn earlier in the day?"

"What of it?" Sophia was in no mood to be distracted by such a paltry excuse. "You are hardly staying with the Royal Family that you should be so concerned about the proprieties. Why did you not consider that I would be waiting to hear your discoveries?"

"I did consider that," Adam replied. "It was not malice that kept me from joining you in the parlour, merely weakness. I came back to this house with a good deal on my mind. Matters which I felt I should share at once with Mr Wicken. I therefore composed a long letter to him. Having done that, I felt weary, so I closed my eyes for what I intended to be but a few moments. Ellen woke me by calling out that you and my mother were already at table and waiting for me. There, that is all."

Sophia stared at him hard for a moment, then relaxed. "I believe you," she said, "and I should not have berated you so. It was my frustration speaking – and my fear that you would go back on your word and exclude me from this mystery as before."

"I will not do that," Adam said. "As you know, I must go to London soon to meet with Mr Wicken. I must also return to Aylsham to see how much damage my long absence has inflicted on my practice. It will ease my mind to know there is someone here whom I can trust to receive messages and know which need urgent action."

"Very well," Sophia said. "Now ... enough of apologies and explanations. Tell me what more you have found out."

Adam related the details of his day with as much clarity as he could. He left nothing out, even adding some brief details of his impressions of Dr Hanwell, the precentor, his wife and the rest of the household. To his surprise, Sophia kept silent and listened intently.

"I should like to meet Mrs Hanwell," she said when he had finished. "I'm sure I could learn much from her."

The notion of Miss LaSalle adding Mrs Hanwell's vigour and belligerence to her own intellectual sharpness caused Adam to wince. Still, he had no choice.

"You will meet her soon," he said. "With her agreement and yours, I intend to ask that you visit her house regularly in my absence to receive information on Mr Sanford's progress. I do not expect any sudden changes, but in matters of the mind little is certain."

"That will do very well," Sophia said. It is clear she thought her acceptance settled the matter. "Now, I have thought about your news enough for it to be clear that we need more help."

"More help?" Adam's voice sounded shrill even to him.

"Of course. Do you not see? My, how slow you can be. If the attack on Mr Sanford and the death of Toms are connected – as we agree they must be – we need to know how Toms passed his time in the city. What did he do between delivering his packages to Mr Sanford and ending up dead in the River Wensum? Enquiries must be made amongst the inns and grog houses for a start. You can hardly undertake such a task. Nor can I."

"But Mr Wicken has sent constables ..."

"Who will discover nothing, as I believe I told you already. What we need are local men who will attract no particular suspicion. Unfortunately, I know of no suitable persons."

"Nor would it be proper for you to have such acquaintances," Adam said.

"Fie on what is proper! You can have no idea how much ideas of what is proper grate on any woman with spirit, sir. I said unfortunately and that is what I meant."

"Well, for what it is worth, I know of no such persons either."

"Then we are blocked ... no, wait a moment. Do you have any acquaintances who might have dealings with the lower classes?"

"I don't think ... yes! I have it. Captain Mimms."

"I believe I met him once. Is he not a retired sea captain?"

"Indeed he is, but that is to do him an injustice. In his time, he has been an officer on both merchant ships and those of the King's Navy. He also built a prosperous shipping business from Yarmouth. His sons now run things on a daily basis, though it is clear they defer to their father in all matters of greater moment. He has spent his life amongst sailors and wherrymen and must know some who might serve our purpose."

"See? You are not as dull as you pretend, given some pushing. Captain Mimms it is."

Adam chose to ignore the jibe. "I will contact him as soon as I may," he said. "Now, you may be full of excitement still, but I have had a long day and need my sleep. Goodnight to you, Miss LaSalle ... and thank you for your assistance."

"Goodnight, Doctor," she replied, looking now the picture of demure respectability. "Maybe once we have become easier with each other, you will cease to look so askance at my lapses from strict propriety ... and I shall learn not to provoke you so much by flaunting them. I hope you sleep well."

5

PREPARATIONS

The next morning was Sunday, so Adam's mother said she would attend the morning service in the cathedral. Miss LaSalle would, of course, go with her. Adam had little taste for religion and less for lengthy sermons, so he felt considerable relief to a have a ready-made excuse for not joining them. He would instead make yet another visit to check on his patient's progress. Then perhaps he might take a turn along Gentleman's Walk and past the fine new buildings in the Chapel Field to take the air. By doing so, he hoped to find an answer to the problems that he had taken upon himself. Besides, it was a fine day and he told himself he should not waste all of it indoors.

His patient was still catatonic, but there was no doubt his position was improving a little. The servants reported that he seemed to be trying to co-operate more when he was fed or given a drink. He had even started making inarticulate noises when he needed to urinate or defecate. The precentor's manservant could then bring an appropriate vessel. Poor Sanford did not always manage to restrain himself quite long enough, but it was cheering that he was trying.

Once again, Adam sat by the bed, talking to Sanford in a low voice and touching his hand from time to time. He told him that he was showing signs of improvement. That he – Adam – was pleased with his progress, and that all was quite calm and safe within the house. This was, perhaps, something of a white lie, but justified in the circumstances.

It was thus well after noon when Adam finally managed to leave Dr Hanwell's home. His path took him past the dark mass of the castle's keep, then along a narrow street to the Market Place and Gentleman's Walk. He had expected it to be crowded with walkers and idlers. Of course, today was Sunday. Most respectable families would likely either still be in church or chapel. The Dissenting ministers especially had a reputation for lengthy sermonising. Others would have returned home to various pastimes suitable for the Sabbath. Only heathens like himself and the inevitable idlers and loafers would be abroad.

Yet Adam had proceeded no more than a dozen steps when he heard someone call out his name and beseech him to wait a moment. An elderly man now came up to him. He might be short of breath, broad of chest and prone to walk with a roll, as if he was still upon the deck of one of his ships, but the sight of him brought a happy smile to Adam's face.

"Captain Mimms, sir! This is a most pleasant meeting. I was even now puzzling how I might be able to find you. How are you? What are you doing in Norwich?"

"Ah, Doctor. It is not until I try to overtake you that I am made to recall the many years that lie between your age and mine. Pray stand awhile. As usual, you have many questions, but I have not breath to answer even one for a moment." Indeed, the old man's face was beaded with perspiration and his breath was laboured. Adam was at once concerned for his friend's well-being.

"A thousand apologies," Adam said. "Had I realised it was you I would have been more attentive to my pace. Now ... stand there a moment. I will find a chair and you shall be conveyed in comfort to my mother's house where I am staying. I will walk alongside you, but you must promise not to speak more until we are safely inside."

A chair was summoned and they came to Mrs Bascom's house

together. Adam's mother and Miss LaSalle had just returned from the cathedral, so warm greetings were exchanged on all sides. The two ladies recalled with pleasure meeting Capt Mimms at Adam's house in Aylsham. The Captain, ever ready with a suitable compliment, praised the elegance of the house. It was, he said, exceeded only by the elegant beauty of its female inhabitants. If he had always spoken thus, Adam thought to himself, he would indeed have had a woman or two in every port!

It was fully ten minutes before Adam could get Capt Mimms to himself. He was impatient for some private words. The older man had already said he could not stay more than a half hour at the most, for he was to travel on that afternoon to Yarmouth.

"My sons wrote that they would send a carriage to wait upon me at three o'clock," he said. "I was only abroad to help fill my time until then. When I saw your back hurrying away from me, I called out at once. You were so much in a hurry, it seemed to me. I could not have exceeded your pace, no matter if I had been twenty years younger."

"And I am indeed glad that you did," Adam said. "It is too long since we have met. I also have need of your help, if you will give it."

"Given, Doctor. Tell me only what you need."

"I am engaged in ... another mystery, you may say. The mystery of how a patient of mine came to be set upon and why. It was no common footpad who struck him down. He was not robbed. No, sir, it seems to me that he was chosen for some reason. I have ... some idea of what that might be ..." Adam was choosing his words to avoid giving Mr Wicken's secrets away. "... but I need to trace the movements of a man who probably went to places where I may not go with decorum or safety."

"You need someone to make enquiries in the rougher parts of this city."

"That is correct. Do you know of anyone who might be reliable?

"Indeed I do, Doctor, and it is a happy chance that has brought us together. I should have been at home, taking my ease, yet I am summoned by my sons to hear yet another tale of woe about our business. When things go well, they are indulgent towards me. They say I am an old man and need not think about business matters, for they have all in hand. But when things go wrong, they are quick enough to remind me that I am the principal shareholder and should give them whatever help I can."

"And are matters so amiss?" Adam said. "You are a man of substance, sir, engaged in what I have always assumed to be a profitable trade. I do hope no ill has befallen any of your ships."

"No ... not yet, I am glad to tell you. But matters do not go well in our world. Any war brings a blight on trade, save for those commodities whose price rises most when nations must arm themselves. The damned French privateers are nuisance enough at the best of times. Now they throng around our coast to do us harm and steal our goods and ships. Swarms of them are pouring from Dunkirk to harry us as best they may."

"And they succeed?" Adam said.

"Sometimes. The King's Navy has greater demands upon its strength that it can meet. In peacetime, our government is swift to reduce the number of ships held at readiness, claiming the need for frugality in all things. Many sailors are discharged and must seek other work or starve. Now there is a panic to find enough Jack Tars to man a wartime navy. The press gangs are out in all the larger ports. Of course, they do not want anyone. They seek only experienced sailors. Thus no one with practical knowledge of the sea and ships can walk in his own streets without fear. The sailors in my ships carry letters of exemption from impress, Doctor. But do the press gangs honour them? By God, they do not!"

Adam tried to bring him back to the main point. "Now, you say you know someone who may help me."

"Ah, Doctor. You will encourage me to ramble. Yes, I do, if you will accept two people, for these men are always together."

"Of course I will, if you recommend them."

"Let me explain. One of them – he calls himself Peg and nothing else – served under me for many years, until a Spanish privateer took aim at us and fired off a cannon. The ball took off the poor man's leg. Thus he is no longer fit to go to sea and must eke out a living ashore. But he is sharp, loyal and knows this city better than most."

"He is my man then. And the other?"

"Some time ago – I do not know when exactly – Peg came across a man being harried by a crowd. The poor fellow is slow in his wits and speaks little, which was why the crowd had set upon him. Men ever fear what they do not understand, Doctor. Peg was angered by such a show of cruelty and rescued the man from the mob. They have been together ever since."

"A brave act, sir. Few would try to baulk such a crowd of their prey."

"Brave indeed – though Peg did have two pistols to help him. The other man is also something of a giant, with the strength of several men. Once his confusion at what was happening was lessened, he took up one of his attackers and threw him a good twenty feet away. The rest fled on the instant."

"And what is this giant amongst men called?" Adam asked.

"Peg calls him Dobbin, Doctor, since he is of the size and strength of a cart-horse. Yet, like many such, he has a most peaceable temperament unless provoked."

"Can you send these men to me, Captain?"

"I can and will. Once I have reached Yarmouth, I will send Peg a message via the carter. Will you be here at your mother's house?"

"Alas, I must return home tomorrow, then make a journey to London after that. It would be best for them to leave word how I may contact them on my return."

"Very well. That is what I will write. But we have talked too much of me and of serious matters. How are you, young friend? Do your affairs go well?"

"Well enough," he said. "My practice is thriving and I am pleased to say that my family are all in good health and spirits. My brother, Giles, is now a major in the militia, I believe. He stalks around his estate surveying the terrain like a general about to mount a campaign."

Capt Mimms laughed. "Like I did once upon a time," he said. "Oh, not a general, of course, but an admiral. As a young man I often enlivened the dull periods of my watch with imaginings. I saw myself leading a veritable armada against the French – or the Spaniards, or even those Yankee dogs."

"You would have made a formidable admiral," Adam said.

"No, no. I was a good enough sailor and merchant, but I had no real taste for leading men to their deaths, however good the cause. You, sir, will one day be outstanding in your profession. Of that I am certain."

"You are too kind," Adam said. "Some days I feel as if I have scarcely begun to grasp anything about medicine. Then my head aches with so much to understand! When I was young, Capt Mimms, I longed for nothing more than to become a physician. Now that I have achieved that goal, I sometimes ask myself whether it was worth it."

"Balderdash! Of course it was. Never have I met anyone better designed by Nature for his profession than you, Doctor. Be of good cheer, sir. We all suffer from difficult times, but it does no good to take them to heart. Do not be like my sons, who mope and complain and fret about their business. No, any man of sense would be stirring all his efforts to turn adversity into opportunity for profit. Be guided by me, for I have sailed through good seas and bad and found benefit in both. Take this confounded war. It will cause loss for sure. But there has never been a war that did not also produce fine profits for those with the courage and willingness to seek them out."

"I will take your words to heart, believe me," Adam said. "Now, may I call for some more punch?"

"No, doctor, though I thank you for your kind thought. Dear me, you have delayed me for too long, sir. The fine clock on your mother's mantel tells me I must be upon my way at once. My sons' carriage will be forced to wait and we will not reach Yarmouth before dark."

"Then I will tell Ellen to call for a chair. Where must you meet your sons' carriage?"

"Not far away. At The Maid's Head, where I stayed last night. I still just have time to walk there."

"But you shall not," Adam said firmly. "Grant me the indulgence to be concerned for you as a doctor as well as a friend. A gentle stroll will do you naught but good. To move in haste, then subject yourself to a lengthy journey ... those are not to be recommended for any man of your years. Nay," Adam held up his hand, "your protests will be in vain, so you need not utter them. But when do you return to Holt? Can you make time to visit me in Aylsham along your way?"

"Indeed I can, and will much look forward to such a pleasant meeting. Look for me in perhaps a week or ten days. If I can, I will send word ahead."

And so, with many good wishes and compliments on both sides, the two friends parted. The captain went to the door, where a chair awaited him. Adam to his room to make sure he should not appear at dinner for a second day in such a disordered state as the last time.

"So ..." Peter Lassimer, the apothecary, said. "What wild-goose chase has your mysterious Mr Wicken sent you on this time?"

As usual, Peter and Adam were seated in the compounding room behind Peter's shop in Aylsham's High Street. Adam had returned from Norwich the night before. Now, immediately after breakfast, he was back with his friend, eager to learn how his practice and patients had fared in his absence.

"Well," Adam said, "he has given me a most perplexing patient. Let me describe his condition as best I may, for I would be grateful for your thoughts. My own are few enough. But first, how goes my practice?"

"Excellent well, since you left it in the charge of such an accomplished man of medicine."

"Be serious, Lassimer, I beg you," Adam said. "Stop fishing for compliments and tell me in plain words what has transpired and who called upon me in my absence."

"Fear not," Peter replied, grinning at Adam's nervousness. "The only urgent cases were the poor old widow Morston, who I fear is not long to remain in this world, and a servant at Lord Suffield's house. For the widow, I could do little enough, save give her the same draughts that you have to ease her pain."

"True enough," Adam said. "She is – or was once – a fine woman, though much reduced in circumstances, I fear. She will insist that she must pay me for what little I can do, though I would give my services happily. It is her pride, I fear. She hates the idea of accepting charity, however much deserved. Still, I make sure always to temper my charge to what I believe she can pay and not stint herself in other ways."

"That will I do also. Though, since the fees of an apothecary are so much less that the demands of any physician, I do not doubt she will manage without much hurt to her purse. She knows not what draughts I gave her, so will not suspect any abridgement when the charges arrive."

"And Lord Suffield's servant?"

"No more than a bad cut upon the arm. I cleaned the area and wrapped his arm in a bandage with an ointment against any poisoning of the blood through the wound. So long as he is free from such an outcome, I think he will do well enough."

"And no other patient asked for me?"

"Only ... who was it? Oh yes ... some person from a house near Cromer. Windham, I think his servant said he was called ..."

"Windham? William Windham, the member of parliament?" Adam was on his feet at once. "What did he want? Was he upset at not finding me at home?"

"Whether he was upset or no I cannot tell, since I spoke only with his servant." Peter's wicked smile should have told Adam he was being tormented a little.

"But ... I mean, what ...?"

"Peace, my friend. Peace. Mr Windham is in London, I believe, on the business of helping to govern this land. And a sorry mess he and his friends look to make of it. No, Bascom, it was not he who needed your services but his butler. He, I believe, is often tempted to sample his master's port and has the pains of gout to bear as a result. As I informed the servant who had gone to your house, you were like to be back sometime this week and would attend to the butler as soon as might be convenient. In the meantime, I prescribed a plain diet, strict abstention from any drink other than small beer and a daily dose of a herbal preparation I gave the man. That should be enough to punish the butler for his thieving ways."

Adam breathed a sigh of relief. To deal with the greater gentry was profitable. Yet it too often brought the need to respond on the instant to any sickness in their household, however minor. Nor were such people at all prompt in settling their accounts. Still, he could not afford to gain a reputation for haughtiness in his dealings with them.

"You have my most profound thanks for helping me in this way, Lassimer. I only wish I could repay my debt in like manner, but I am near certain to be away in Norwich many more times in the coming months. I will need to ask for your assistance again in this way."

"You know it will be given, Bascom, and given almost without question. Note that 'almost'. There is a condition to my help."

"Tell me," Adam said. Payment for Lassimer's time would not be a problem, given Wicken's deep pockets. A more personal demand might be harder to accept.

"You must tell me all that goes on with this vexing case of yours," Peter said. "I may not experience such adventures as you do, but you know I love to hear of them." Peter paused, then continued. "Before that long face is translated into rambling about not being able to speak much of your dealings with Mr Wicken, let me say that I understand. A good deal of your last mystery too contained secrets that were not yours to share. Only, I pray you for the sake of old friendship, share all that you can without breaking your word or imperilling your conscience."

"You have my word on that," Adam said. "Well ... as I said some time ago, much of what Mr Wicken has asked of me is a medical matter. That I can tell you about openly and will be glad of your insight. Put plainly, I have a patient who is suffering a catatonia. All I know is that he has received a strong blow to the head. He has also been over-working and may be of a melancholic disposition in his natural state."

For several minutes, the two men conversed in the complex, technical terminology of the time. Each spoke of imbalances of humours, the effects of a concussion on a mind already weakened by melancholia nigra and a host of other medical terms. At length, Peter sat back to consider his diagnosis.

"This is a field in which I am more than happy to own you my superior, Bascom. However, of one thing I can be sure. I know of draughts well able to produce the most dangerous and troublesome effects upon the mind. However, I know of none that would produce symptoms quite like these. The immediate cause of his problem, I judge, is the concussion. Beyond that, only time will tell."

"I agree," Adam said. "This young man carries with him no reputation for carousing or going out upon the town. Indeed, from such as I know, he is most studious and rarely strayed from his room for days on end. My money too is on the blow to his head."

"A concussion is a chancy matter," Peter agreed. "I have heard of men who walked and talked normally for days after a blow like that, then, on a sudden, fell down stark dead."

"This man was, I believe, severely melancholic before the assault."

"All the more likely then that the two things together have produced a severe reaction. I presume you do not know the cause of the blow."

"That is Wicken's territory. I believe he is sending two experienced constables from London to seek out the answer and investigate the murder ..."

"Murder?" Peter cried. "You mentioned no murder before. Is your patient dead? I know grand physicians like yourself have a reputation for endangering their patients, but that cannot be it. It would bring all mysteries to an end."

Adam grinned. "No, my patient is not dead. This is another man. A messenger, it seems, sent from London to ... well, that is no matter. A messenger who arrived, delivered his message and then disappeared until a few days ago. His lifeless body was then pulled from the river."

"How was he murdered?"

"He had been struck several times upon the head, then thrown into the water, it seems."

"Struck like your man?"

"I suppose. Though there may be no connection ..."

"Of course there must be," Peter cried. "Two men, both linked to Mr Wicken and whatever strange matters he is involved in? No, I do not ask. These men are attacked in the same city at almost the same time, and you say there may be no connection?"

"I do not know."

"So ... what will you do to find out?"

"Nothing. It is not a matter for me. Did you not hear? Wicken has sent two constables ..."

Peter interrupted in exasperation. "Who will do no good. Especially with matters in the city as they stand now."

"That is what Miss LaSalle says too," Adam said. "But with city matters standing how? I have just come from Norwich and all appeared normal."

"That is because you walk around with your head in the clouds and your eyes shut, Bascom," Peter said, quite unaware of the ludicrous image he had painted. He settled down to inform Adam of the realities of life as he might a child. "The constables will do no good because none will tell them anything. They are from London, so will be as conspicuous in Norwich as two bulls in a herd of sheep. Even more, they are government men. No one will wish even to be seen speaking to such creatures."

"But why?"

"Have you neither eyes nor ears? Do you not know how unpopular this new war is amongst the artisans and shopkeepers of Norwich? How much they understand that those who are zealous to fight do so from only the basest motives: profit and power? Trade must suffer, Bascom. When that happens, the poor feel the first pain. It is the rich who profit from wars."

"But ..."

"There are no 'buts'. Listen! I do not endorse all that the French have done. Like all who set out upon a new path, they have made many foolish errors and shed a good deal of innocent blood. Those who are guilty of acts of barbarism should pay the price. But are not their hearts in the right place? Do they not seek a constitution the equal of what ours was, before these jackanapes in government swayed our noble king to follow the wrong path? No ... even a better constitution perhaps. There are many in Norwich – in this county, even in this little town – who are certain we will never enjoy prosperity without rule by parliaments elected on a universal franchise."

"In Aylsham?"

"Why not? Do men here not have brains the equal of those in Norwich, or even in London?"

"But to discuss sedition ..."

"No sedition, I assure you. We are all loyal subjects of his majesty and lovers of our country. We abjure violence of all kinds. It is by argument and persuasion that we hope to sway the men to demand a reformation of our means of government."

Adam was dumbstruck. "I never knew you felt like this," he said.

"You never asked me," Peter replied. "Nay, we can all get along well enough, even the most ardent Whig and the most loyal supporter of our present ministry. Are we not all loyal Englishmen? Only let us have the freedom to argue and debate. That is what angers me. The government have acted to stifle all debate, rather than face us and seek to convince us they are right."

He looked at Adam and softened his tone. "But I see I have startled you," he said. "Take no notice. It is still your old friend here and I have not changed my spots. What I say is nothing to support revolution. Why, even some of the gentry themselves, like Mr Coke and the great Mr Charles Fox, would tell you much the same thing. Our government seeks to scare you, not I. Look to France with an eye free from prejudice and you will see what I mean. Some there are our enemies indeed, but not most. Like the good weavers and other artisans of Norwich, the majority of the population of France fear the disruption to trade that war brings. Aye, and high taxes and many good men killed too. The rich rarely suffer from war; the middling sorts, the tradesmen and the poor always do. That is why none will speak the truth to your Mr Wicken's constables. You will see that I am right in due time."

"You might be." Adam sounded dubious. Lassimer's vehemence had surprised him more than the content of his remarks.

"Wait ... I was so carried away by my own thoughts I almost missed something far more important. Did you not say that Miss LaSalle had told you the same thing ... that none will speak to Mr Wicken's men?"

"I did, I suppose."

"You suppose! Now we come to the meat. You have involved your mother's lovely companion in your wild adventuring!"

"She involves herself," Adam protested. "She treats me as you do: as source of exciting tidbits on which to exercise her mind. Indeed, she has now appointed herself my lieutenant in this matter."

Peter threw back his head and roared with laughter. Indeed, it was several moments before he could compose himself enough to speak again.

"Bascom!" he cried at last. "What an idiot you are. Any sensible man would be overjoyed to have such an accomplished and lovely creature helping him."

"How do you know she is accomplished? You have met her but once."

"I know she is lovely from that one time. I deduce she is accomplished because you would have sent her packing if her mind was ordinary. Then you would have said so, not confessed she is helping you. Either that or, fearing to provoke me to tease you, you must have stayed silent. Now you admit the situation, it is clear she has begun to enter your affections and you long to speak of her."

"You go too far, Lassimer. I will admit she is a fine woman ..."

"Hah! You speak of her as if she were a horse! 'Fine woman' indeed. Out with it, Bascom. I will not let you leave until you tell me the nature of your feelings for her."

Adam sighed like a stage lover. "Very well. But you are the idiot, not I. Miss LaSalle does possess a quiet beauty, I admit. Not the showy magnificence of the supposed darlings of the *ton*. The kind of beauty that consists in wonderful eyes, hair that shines, an unblemished complexion and a figure suitable for a sculptor to relish ..."

"My, my," Peter interrupted, " I have never known you poetic before. This is serious!"

"Hush!" Adam said. "I will not repeat myself. Yes, Miss LaSalle is beautiful – or I judge her so – but she is far more remarkable in the quickness and power of her mind."

"Fiddle-de-dee to a woman's mind," Peter said. "It is a woman's body that you can grasp and where you can kindle such a fire as will leave you breathless."

"As I suppose you do regularly."

"As often as I can. There is no finer way to pass this life. But pray continue with your recitation."

"No, I am done. Miss LaSalle is accomplished and of a quick mind. That I own. Yet I did not ask her to assist me in this matter and I am still uncertain that she will be of great use – though she has made one or two helpful suggestions thus far."

"So, what news we have here! You have another mystery – quite a complicated one, as it seems to me – and you now have a beautiful young woman to assist you. I have always enjoyed your company, Bascom, but you may be sure I will relish it even more from now on."

ADAM DID NOT LINGER with Peter after this exchange, for he had much to do and needed to leave for London the next day. Yet it seemed he was fated to have no time for anything. He had scarce returned to his own house when his brother, Giles, arrived at the door.

"I thought I might find you away, brother," Giles said, once they were seated in the parlour. "I know you have been with mother in Norwich much of late. How is she?"

"Well, I am pleased to say. You are right that I have been staying with her several days. I have a new patient there whose needs were such that I had to remain close by. Thankfully, he too seems to be recovering. Yet now I must travel to London as soon as I may. I have spent little time in Aylsham of late and will be away a good deal even when I return."

"I sense you are involved in another mystery, brother. How do you find them?"

"Everyone accuses me of seeking out mysteries. I do not. Nor is this anything other than a medical matter. A young man was hurt and I was called to attend upon him. That is all."

"No, brother," Giles said, "that is far from being all. I may be a dull country squire, but even I can see no one calls a physician from Aylsham to treat a man in Norwich without good cause."

"Please, brother. Let us speak of other matters. How goes life at Trundon Hall? How is Amelia and your children?"

"All are well, thank God. I do not spend as much time with them as I would wish at present. Like you, I am often abroad or wrapped up in other matters."

"Concerning your estate?"

"Nay, that runs well enough. It is the government that demands my time. It is not yet six months that I have held the position of a magistrate in these parts. At first, I thought it more an honour than a burden. That was before His Majesty called out the militia at the close of the year. Now my days are filled with swearing-in new recruits and completing returns to the Lord Lieutenant of the number of men available. Worse than that, I was foolish enough to accept a commission as a major. I imagined pomp and riding at the head of a fine body of men. What I have got is drudgery and constant problems with discipline. I tell you, these local men will never cause the French anywhere near as much trouble as they are causing me."

"Is the trouble so great?" Adam said.

"Aye, great enough," Giles replied. "Norfolk has ever been a county noted for following its own path. Yes, and quarrelling with all in authority too. There are many in these parts affected by the words of Tom Paine and those like him. I do not say they would become rebels outright, but they are like enough to riot when matters are not to their taste."

"Even here, brother?" Adam said.

"Even here. Let me give you but one example. Three days ago a mob attacked the mill in Gressington. It seems the word has gone about that millers are hoarding grain in the hope prices will continue to rise. It is also said that large amounts of grain are sent abroad from Yarmouth, despite our own people suffering want from the high price of bread. Most of this is no more than fear of bad times ahead, of course. Yet there is truth in it. Some millers will hoard grain, if they believe they can sell it later at a higher price. Grain is being sent overseas. Harvests have been bad throughout Europe, it seems, and good British wheat and barley fetch a high price."

"Was the mill destroyed?"

"No, no. Even the mob is not quite so foolish as to destroy what they depend upon for grain and bread. They threw stones and howled their insults, threatening the miller with worse to come, if he did not at once make all the grain he has available to local use."

"Did he?"

"I doubt it. Besides, he was rescued before matters could come to a crisis. Word of the affray came to me and I hurried to bring it to a stop."

"Did you succeed?" Adam asked.

"After a time. At first, the mob turned their insults on me – a few of their stones too – but I was better prepared than they imagined. First I read the prescribed proclamation from The Riot Act. Then I instructed the two constables I had taken with me to seize the ringleaders. The mob laughed at that. What could three men do against several hundred?"

"What indeed?"

"More than they thought, brother. You see, one benefit of being a major in the militia is that I know how to call out my men in haste. Soon the mob found themselves facing soldiers armed with muskets and with bayonets fixed. I ordered half the soldiers to fire a volley over the heads of the crowd and the rest to help the constables round up their leaders. Most of those rioting fled. The leaders tried to call them back, of course. That was a mistake, since it prevented their own escape. By the end, we had near twenty men in custody. All are now in the lock-ups for several miles around, to be sent to Norwich for the next assizes. Rioting is a serious crime."

"It was as well you got there so quickly, brother. Oh, I know these men have rendered themselves felons in the eyes of the law, but I cannot help feeling sorry for their foolishness. Whatever they suffer, will not their families suffer as much or more? To be without a bread-winner usually leads to being cast upon the parish, does it not?"

"Indeed. Few seem to consider that when tempers grow hot. We can only hope that the justices temper punishment with mercy."

6

MURDER AT THE MILL

Despite his preparations, it seemed Adam was fated to remain in Aylsham. The scribbled note delivered first thing next morning by one of Giles Bascom's servants was terse. "Come at once. I have need of you. There has been a murder."

Adam sent Giles' man back at once to assure his brother that he was on his way. Then, after a more hurried breakfast than he was wont to take, Adam climbed into his new curricle and let William do the hard work of driving. It was scarce eleven o'clock when Trundon Hall came in sight and they rattled up the long driveway to the stable-yard. Giles must have set a watch for them, for he came out at once to greet his brother.

"I am sorry to call you hither in this way, Adam," he said, "but the need is great. You recall the miller at Gressington I told you of yesterday? The one whose mill was attacked by a rioting mob? A message reached me soon after dawn that his wife had found him murdered in his own mill. Shot, it seems. I sent orders for his body to be laid in some convenient place and notified our local coroner of what had been found. He sent back a message that the apothecary who acts for him in such cases is sick and unable to leave his bed. Could I find a suitable medical man to undertake the examination of the corpse required by law? Well, now he stands before me."

"But I have never conducted a post mortem in my life, brother," Adam protested.

"What matter is that?" His brother dismissed such a feeble excuse with disdain. "Did you not examine the body of the archdeacon killed only last year in that same village? Do you not have experience of the successful investigation of that murder? Who better could I find?"

"But ..."

"No more! I have seen how your eyes shine when you must deal with such a puzzle as that archdeacon's death afforded you. I fear this will be a more simple matter, but it is the best we poor country folk can provide."

"You make it sound as if you encourage people to commit murders for my amusement."

"No. You know that is not what I meant. But we waste time. Come inside and take a little refreshment after your journey. Then we must be on our way to the mill. By the way, have you finally decided to send that old nag of yours to the knacker? I noted the speed with which you came up my driveway and told myself it could not be Betty drawing your carriage. A snail could outrun her most days."

"It is a horse from the Black Boys Inn. No, Betty remains, but soon only in retirement. In revenge for you demanding I examine your dead bodies I want you to find me a new horse." Giles loved horses, so this was more a promise than a threat. He beamed in response.

"Gladly, brother. I dread to think what broken-winded, knock-kneed old carthorse our dealers would persuade you to buy. Now, inside at once. There is coffee or chocolate ready to your taste and cook has made fresh rolls."

It took less than an hour for the two men to take refreshment, then make the short journey beside the course of the River Glaven. Once, long ago, Gressington had stood on the edge of a busy harbour. Now the tides no longer reached through the clogged and silted channels that led to the sea. Some of the marsh had been enclosed for grazing, which reduced the flow of water still more. The former harbour was no more than a stretch of boggy ground.

At length they came to a fine watermill. It stood where the highest spring tides even yet drove a trickle of seawater to mingle with the clear stream flowing down the valley. Adam had been to that spot many times as a youth, seeking the sea-trout which lived in the river. They made fine eating. A good-sized fish was sure to bring him a treat from the cook when he returned.

But though much of the area looked the same as it had a dozen and more years before, Adam was at once aware of a lingering smell on the air. The mob had burned several of the out-buildings of the mill and the rank scent of their work had yet to disperse.

Giles introduced his brother to the solemn, elderly man who stood waiting for them in the mill yard.

"Good afternoon, Mr Waldram," he said. "Allow me to introduce my brother, Dr Adam Bascom. He is a physician and has an interest in dead bodies." Adam scowled, but his brother pressed on with evident enjoyment. "Brother, let me present to you Mr Henry Waldram, attorney and coroner. Mr Waldram has a practice in Wells and has made a longer journey here today than I have, if not you. My brother came this morning from Aylsham," he explained to the coroner.

"My compliments to you, Dr Bascom, and my thanks for coming such a way to help us. There is a passable apothecary in Blakeney whom I usually ask to undertake this duty. It seems he is sick of the ague. I suppose he must be sick indeed, for what apothecary would admit otherwise that he had not the means to cure himself?" He paused. "Our worthy squire says you have an interest in bodies. Are you not the physician who caused the former coroner of these parts such trouble in his own court by asking questions he wished to avoid?"

"I am, sir," Adam admitted, "though I did not do so from any bad motive."

"I am most glad to meet you, Doctor," the coroner said. "From all I heard at the time, your questions were exactly those which should have been asked. Now, shall we go within? The corpse has been laid on a bier brought over from the church this morning. I hope it will be light enough for your work. I will have candles brought, should more light be needed."

There proved to be plenty of light, since the bier stood close to both a window and a door which might be opened. Adam had seen many bodies in the course both of his practice and his training, but never one quite as damaged as this.

"Do you know what fearful weapon caused such injuries?" he asked the coroner, as he noted the wreckage made of most of the man's head, neck and shoulders.

"A short-barrelled blunderbuss, Doctor. The miller's own weapon and obtained, so his wife said, but recently as defence. Honest men need no such weapons, so you can make your own conclusions about the miller's character."

"Yes" Adam said. "I have been told certain millers in these sad times hold back a good part of the grain they receive against expected rises in the price of flour. It is also said they prefer to sell flour to the government for supplies to the fleet, or even to send it overseas where harvests have been even worse than here. Farmers and millers prosper, while the poor go ever hungrier."

"That was the reason for the riot," Mr Waldram said. "That and the undoubted presence of some few infected with radical and republican ideas. Notions courtesy of some of our dissenting preachers and that dog, Tom Paine. A good many of our artisans – blacksmiths, cobblers, wheelwrights, even shopkeepers – read the pamphlets and broadsheets they pick up in the towns. Some have bought, or been given, copies of 'The Rights of Man' and other seditious writings. Those who can read gather others about them and read aloud. Thus wicked notions are spread abroad. Ideas designed to inspire contumacious attitudes towards the king, the government and the gentry. There are even republican clubs sprung up in a few market towns, as I hear. They toast the success of the sans culottes in France and long for the same to happen here."

Adam turned to his brother. "Did you know of this?" he asked.

"Of course," his brother said. "It gives us all cause for concern. I have even had one or two agitators brought before me as magistrate and charged with stirring up riot and rebellion. If you did not live so much inside your own head, brother, you would have known of it too. But what can you tell us of this man's death?"

"He was shot, as you see. That would have killed him on an instant." Adam bent closer and peered at what little remained of the man's neck. "Bruising, I fancy," he said as if to himself. "Bad bruising. I wonder how that came about?"

"Did he perhaps shoot himself, Doctor?" the coroner asked.

"Can you show me the gun that did this?" Adam replied. "I fancy not, but I would like to be sure."

After a few moments, the coroner returned with a fine blunderbuss, its barrel maybe fifteen inches long. Though the mouth was flared, as was the case in all guns designed to fire a load of small shot, the extra width was not great. Shot fired from such a gun would take a little distance to spread out much.

Adam looked at it carefully, admiring the fine chasing around the flintlock mechanism and the superb woodwork of the walnut stock. "I have never before seen such a weapon as this," he said. "Surely it is no fowling-piece? With such a short barrel, it would not be accurate enough over any distance."

"You are correct in that judgment," his brother said. "Nor am I surprised that you have not seen such a gun before. I have seen only one, I believe, and that in the collection of an elderly naval captain of my acquaintance. These are designed to kill men, not birds, and at short range. Pirates use them, as do smugglers and privateers. The short barrel makes them well suited to being used in a confined space, such as aboard ship. Accuracy over a long distance is not needed. Loaded with a good charge of lead shot, they are fearsome."

"Indeed," Adam said. "Well, Mr Waldram. The answer to your

question is that you may exclude suicide as a reason for death. Though the damage to this man's body is terrible, if he had fired the weapon himself, I judge little of his head – or any part of his anatomy above his shoulders – would have been left. This was fired at him by someone else. At close range, yes. But perhaps from twelve or fifteen feet away."

"Murder then" the coroner said.

"Murder certainly, though perhaps not with just this gun." Adam's words caused both the other men to look at him. "May I see where the body was found?"

"Indeed you may, Doctor. It was over there, near to where those bags of flour are stacked."

Adam walked over. The bloodstains showed clearly where the body had lain. First he looked carefully at the floor. Then he looked just as carefully at a beam which ran across the room above the same place. It might have been part of the fabric of the building, or placed there to allow pulleys to be used to lift the heavy bags of flour. His brother and the coroner watched him, but neither spoke.

"Hmm ..." Adam said at last. "Well, Mr Waldram, you have a fine mystery. The miller was definitely shot in this place. You may see the damage done by those balls that missed him. But mark this – that damage is all to the floor, not the wall. It is also plain that a rope has been passed over the beam above the spot and perhaps something heavy lifted with it. Finally, mark the bloodstains."

"What of them, brother," Giles said. "Is there not enough blood for you?"

"You have hit on the exact point, brother. There is not enough blood. A man shot as the miller was, then falling here, would have bled profusely. But there is scarce enough blood here to show the death of a dog, let alone a man."

Mr Waldram's smile was grim. "Alas, Doctor, you have done what you promised you would not do. You have made my job harder, just as you did to my colleague last year."

"Not by my own choice either time, I assure you," Adam said. "What to make of these signs is not clear to me at the moment. That I expected them is, however, true enough. You see, when I examined the deceased's neck – or what was left of it – I saw evidence of heavy bruising, as if he had been strangled. Then I find a rope has been slung over this beam."

"That is easily explained," Giles said. "These bags of flour are heavy. I would expect those who must move them to use ropes and pulleys to ease the load."

"That's right," the coroner added. "You cannot make those marks into a mystery."

"Perhaps not," Adam conceded. "But for the rest, I would say the miller was lying on the floor, probably dead already, when he was shot. If his heart had stopped, the flow of blood would be much lessened. That, taken with the marks of the shot might suggest he was first strangled, then thrown down and 'finished off' with the gun shot. He was dead before that gun was fired."

"Then that is the evidence you must give at the inquest tomorrow, Doctor," Mr Waldram said. "Just the facts as you have found them and, if I ask you, your surmise as to what may have happened. You are clear that this was murder?"

"I am, sir. Most clear."

"Then that is enough. The duty of my court is to establish the cause of death. If it is murder, the jury may then give a name to the murderer, if they know it or have enough evidence to do so ..."

"Which they will not in this case," Giles said. "We may harbour dark suspicions against one or more of those who joined in the mob that came here, but we have no proof against any – yet. None of the ringleaders can be suspected. They were all in various lock-ups when this man was killed."

"True," Mr Waldram said. "Well, Doctor? Have you seen enough? Or are you about to produce another way to upset this scenario?"

Adam denied that he had any such intention, so the three of them left the room. The coroner went to the miller's wife with permission to arrange her husband's burial. Adam and Giles headed back to Trundon Hall.

Yet if his brother and Mr Waldram were satisfied with the explanation for the circumstances of the miller's death, Adam was not. Why strangle someone, probably with a rope or thick cord, then shoot him after he was dead? Not to hide his identity, since that was well known. An excess of anger? The desire for vengeance? Possibly. Why shoot him with his own gun, which he had bought for defence against intruders. What an idiot he was! He should have looked for signs of forced entry. Yet if the miller had found someone in his mill who should not be there and fetched his gun, would he not have shot them, not the other way around?

Later that evening, when he was alone with his brother, Adam asked if he knew whether there had been any signs of people breaking into the mill.

"None, so far as I know," Giles said. "But so much damage was done by the rioters that it would be hard to be sure. I dare say anyone could have entered parts of that mill without difficulty, simply by using the places where the rioters had made holes in the walls. Once inside, the rest would be reachable."

Adam asked no more. He did not wish to raise more mirth than he had faced already on the subject. Giles thought him a fusspot and had already cautioned him to give his evidence on the morrow exactly as they had agreed.

"The jury are plain men, brother. Honest farmers and tradesmen. If you confuse them with your wild speculations, heaven knows what strange verdict they might bring in. No. Stick to the facts and add no more unless the coroner asks you to. Even then, remember that his court has only to find the cause of death – nothing more. So long as you are sure it was murder, as you are, leave the rest alone. Your help I am glad of. Your speculations I would gladly avoid."

7

THE INQUEST

That night, Adam found sleep eluding him. He was lying in bed in what had been his own bedroom during the final years of living at Trundon Hall. Every inch of this room was familiar; each carried some memory of his youth. It should have felt comforting. It did not. Instead, it reminded him of days when his future seemed simple to discern and full of promise. Days when the sun always shone, the brook was full of trout and the local girls ... well, best not to think of that.

Finally, giving up on all hope of sleep, he turned his mind back to the puzzle of the miller's murder. Giles saw no mystery there, save the name of the criminal. The coroner, seeking to keep strictly to what the law demanded of him, turned his face away from whatever was not his proper concern. Only Adam, it seemed, was curious enough to remain bothered by what he had seen.

That there was a logical explanation he was sure, even if it eluded him. Once again, he laid out the facts in his mind, hoping to see some inkling of the pattern that must lie behind them.

He tried to set them in chronological order. Some days ago, a mob of angry people had attacked the mill. They had burned some of the outbuildings and tried to break into the mill itself. They claimed millers were holding back grain to increase the market price while they went hungry. But could threatening one miller in a remote area such as Gressington change that? The mill was a large one, but it could not be handling more than a part of the production of flour in the area. If that miller was holding back grain, why didn't the locals buy from someone else? There was a large water-mill at Letheringsett to his certain knowledge, barely three miles distant.

The miller had recently bought himself a gun designed to be used against people, not geese or ducks. When did he buy it? Was it before or after the riot? Where did he get it? Probably from the smugglers, Adam supposed. No local gunsmith was likely to stock a weapon like that.

Now to the murder itself. Having bought the gun, the miller would doubtless keep it to hand, though not on open display. If he had heard some person or persons enter the mill, logic said that he would go to where he kept the gun first, then take it when he investigated. Would it be loaded? Almost certainly it would. It was no time to be fiddling with loading an unfamiliar weapon when your life might at risk. Yet if the miller had the gun, why hadn't he used it? How would intruders have taken it from him – especially a single intruder? If he had not picked up the gun before encountering his murderer, how had that man known of its presence and where it was kept? He might have come upon it by chance, of course. But if he had come prepared to kill the miller in another way – by strangling, it seemed – why shoot him afterwards? None of it made any sense.

Finally there was the blood. The small amount wasn't consistent with the terrible wounds he had seen. If they had been inflicted on a living man, whose heart would have continued to pump for several moments after he had been shot, there must have been more. He had been strangled until his heart stopped, then shot.

Now it occurred to him that there was so little blood, and that so dark and clotted, that this explanation too was wrong. The miller had not been strangled to death, then shot in the head soon afterwards, in a mistaken belief that he needed to be 'finished off'. Nor could it have been a shooting done in the frenzy of the moment by attackers who sought revenge. There was only one explanation he could think of for the amount and state of the blood at the scene. The miller had been dead some time, maybe even some hours, before the shooting took place.

What murderer kills his victim then comes back an hour or more later and kills him again?

What was needed was to seek out the answers to these questions. Question whoever found the body. Who was that? The wife? Servants? What had the miller been doing in the days and weeks before he was killed? Who might have desired his death?

For a moment, Adam considered asking his brother, as magistrate, to set up such an enquiry. Then he thought better of it. It was not that his brother was lazy – far from it – or impervious to doubt. He was already overworked with that militia business and blessed with an almost total lack of curiosity. Whatever seemed the obvious solution would be enough for him. He would see no need to complicate matters by seeking out alternatives. Hadn't he already said as much by cautioning Adam not to cause trouble at the inquest as he had done before?

The coroner wouldn't act either. Adam knew that. Hadn't he explained, as if to a child, that his court's only role was to establish the cause of death? Murder was murder to him, however inflicted. Unless Adam could come up with the identity of the murderer – which he could not – the coroner would judge the rest beyond his remit. No, as things stood, any further investigation would be up to the dead man's family to start. They would hardly be likely to ask him to take part.

It must have been while turning this over in his mind and finding no solution that Adam fell asleep. He did not dream of murders, courts or anything to do with the miller and the inquest the next day. In fact, he dreamed of nothing at all and woke surprisingly refreshed. Thus, after a somewhat less generous breakfast than was his habit, he was ready to leave in good time, determined to play only his assigned role in the proceedings.

As WAS typical of country areas, they held the inquest in the largest room available. That was an outbuilding behind the inn, more often used for theatrical performances, village meetings and the like. When Adam arrived, it was set out ready. There was a table and chair for the coroner, with chairs to his left for the jury. To his right was a lonely chair for the witness. Before him, a mixture of benches and hay bales for the audience to sit upon. That audience comprised a good proportion of the villagers. Little enough happened in Gressington. A spectacle such as this would be relished and commented upon for months after.

The coroner opened proceedings promptly at ten. First he swore in a jury of nine local men. Then, having enquired whether they desired to view the corpse, which they declined to do, he opened with a brisk summary of the relevant law and got down to the business proper.

Evidence of the identity of the dead man came from one of his mill servants and was backed up by another. It seemed the coroner wished to spare the man's widow the ordeal of giving evidence unless it proved essential. She was present though – or Adam thought she was. A woman dressed all in black and heavily veiled was sitting at the front of the public area. That must be her.

Next, the coroner called a man who identified himself as Jacob Huckin, foreman at the mill. He gave evidence that he had found his employer dead when he arrived for work at 8:00 am. He and his assistants had been much occupied on the two days before, he said. First they had tried to defend the mill against the mob, then they must clear up the damage caused. On the day in question, they had hoped to turn again to the proper business of grinding grain into flour. The miller had asked them to make sure they were on time.

The coroner interrupted at this point to ask whether anyone employed at the mill also lived on the premises.

"Only the two apprentices, sir," Mr Huckin said. The coroner made a note of that.

Further questions established that Mr Huckin had noticed nothing amiss when he arrived. The mill had been much damaged by the riot, so it would be difficult to be certain nothing had been moved since the day before.

Next, the coroner turned to the finding of the body. Huckin said he had found his master lying beside the chute where the bags were filled with flour channeled from the grinding stones above. Since it was obvious he must be dead, he moved nothing and went in search of the miller's wife. He found her risen to supervise the maids doing the washing. She sent him at once to fetch the village constable. All this was later corroborated by the constable himself, a thin, shifty-looking fellow by the name of Haysom.

Moving on, the coroner called the two apprentices and questioned them. Had they heard or seen anything that night? Both denied doing so, though one said he had heard "a loud noise, like a thunderclap" sometime during the hours of darkness. He could not be sure when it was, because he had not risen to investigate. Following the riot, there had been several times when parts of the building, damaged or loosened by the attack, had fallen to the ground. He decided it must be one of those.

Now it was Adam's turn to give evidence on his examination of the body and findings on the cause of death. As he took the oath and waited for the coroner's questions, he could almost feel his brother's anxious gaze.

At the start, all he needed to do was confirm his name, residence and profession. Then the coroner asked for the basic details of what he had seen. Adam described the nature and extent of the damage and gave his opinion that it had been caused by a discharge from the weapon that was found alongside the body.

"Would these wounds have been enough to cause death?" the coroner asked.

"Certainly," Adam said. "No man could have survived such damage to his head, neck and shoulders."

"Could you estimate the distance from which the gun had been fired, Doctor?" the coroner said next.

"Perhaps up to fifteen or twenty feet. Certainly far more than arm's length."

That caused an excited buzz amongst the audience. The coroner banged his gavel and called for silence.

"The man could not then have shot himself?"

"No, sir," Adam said. "Had he done so, the wounds would have been far worse."

"Did you find anything else, Doctor?"

"I found some marks on what ... remained ... of the neck. They indicated severe bruising."

"Could this have contributed to death?"

"Quite possibly, sir. I could not be sure, since the damage to the area from the gunshot was so great."

"But these ... ah, bruises ... could not have been self-inflicted."

"I cannot say, sir, as I have indicated."

"Quite so, Doctor. Let me rephrase my question. Was there anything in these other marks which might indicate a natural death?"

"No, sir. Nothing. I would say that there is no likelihood of this death arising naturally."

"Thank you, Doctor. You have been very clear. You may stand down."

Giles must have been on the edge of his seat at that point, but Adam stuck to his promise and added nothing not strictly relevant to the cause of death.

After that, the proceedings came to a swift end. The coroner turned to the jury and told them that, in his judgment, they had now heard enough evidence to reach a verdict. The doctor's findings clearly pointed to foul play as the cause of death. There was nothing to suggest any other credible explanation of what had taken place. No evidence had been put forward to implicate any known individual or group as the author of this deed. The only possible verdict was "murder by a person or persons unknown".

The jury nodded their heads to one another in assent – some rather sadly, for they had been hoping to play a larger part in the decision. After some whispers between them, the foreman therefore declared their finding was as the coroner had said. The whole process had taken a little less than one hour.

Adam returned to Trundon Hall with his mightily-relieved brother. There he ate a cold collation to sustain him on his journey, bade farewell to Amelia and the children, and departed for Aylsham. The extra delay, though unavoidable, had been unwelcome. It was high time he departed for Norwich and London.

8

BACK TO NORWICH

"I have not been idle, Doctor," Sophia said. "I visited Mrs Hanwell twice in your absence. Your patient has recovered at least some of his wits. He now eats and ... does other things ... normally, much to the relief of the servants. He even speaks on occasions. However, it seems that he has no recollection whatsoever of the events which brought him to his present state."

"I am not much surprised, Miss LaSalle," Adam said. "A bad concussion may well cause a loss of memory. We can only hope it will be temporary."

"Mrs Hanwell also tells me that none of the servants have seen any person loitering near the house. There have been no attempts to make an entry."

"That is excellent. I worried that Dr and Mrs Hanwell might be imperilling themselves by continuing to offer Sanford a home."

"So," Sophia concluded. "All here has been quiet. What of your short period back at home in Aylsham?"

Adam smiled. "I cannot say it has been quiet. My brother has involved me in another murder."

"Another one! I do not know whether to envy you or despair of you, Doctor. Who is it this time?"

"A local miller in Gressington. Some days ago, his mill was attacked by rioters ..."

"An engrosser or a forestaller, I expect. Such business practices are much despised by the common people," Sophia said, interrupting Adam's flow.

"Engrosser?" Adam said. "Forestaller? What do those words mean?"

Sophia looked at him as a weary governess might look at a wayward child. "You do not know? No, I can see you do not. Well ... an engrosser seeks to buy as much of a crop as he may – all, if he can – to create a monopoly in the locality. A forestaller buys his entire crop from a farmer before it has been harvested, usually to send to London or sell overseas. Both actions prevent grain being sold in an open market and result in shortages. The price rises and the buyers profit."

Adam was amazed. "How come you know this?" he asked.

"Don't you mean how come you – a mere woman – know this when I do not? Because I read and take notice of the world around me, Doctor."

Adam decided this was dangerous ground. "Well," he said, "by whatever means you came by the knowledge, I am grateful. You are right. The rioters claimed the miller was selling outside the area or withholding grain until the price should rise further. Either way, they could not afford to buy the bread they needed."

"And they killed him?"

"No. They did some damage to his mill, but that was all. He died a few days after." Adam described what he had seen of the miller's death and the evidence he had given at the inquest.

"But you are not convinced?" Sophia said at once, "as I am not. From what you have told me, I believe someone strangled the man, then returned later to try to hide the manner of his death. Why, though?"

"That I cannot say. Did he believe he could make it look like suicide?"

"Who might wish that? Ah, I have it!"

Once again, Adam was amazed at the speed of Miss LaSalle's thoughts. "So what was the reason?" he asked.

"You said your brother thought there were radicals and agitators urging the mob on. Now, if it appeared the miller has killed himself in remorse for his actions, would that not make all convinced of his guilt? Would it not strengthen the argument that those who prosper must always do so at the expense of the rest? I suspect someone killed the miller by strangling, perhaps in revenge for the ringleaders of the riot being seized and held. He returned to his fellows to report his deed. Someone amongst them realised that suicide would suit their purposes better. The murderer, or another, then went back and tried to make it appear to be the cause of death."

"Possibly ..." Adam said. It was an ingenious explanation, but it did not quite convince him.

"Certainly, I would say," Sophia replied. "Do you have a better explanation?"

Adam admitted he did not.

"There," she said. "I have solved the mystery for you. Now you only need to find the one who did it."

"No. No. It is not my problem, Miss LaSalle, nor would my brother thank me for interfering. My part in the question of the miller's death is done."

Sophia looked at him steadily, her head on one side. "Do not be too sure of that," she said after some moments. "Even if my own, excellent, solution should prove false, I cannot believe we will have no more reason to investigate this matter. Still, you may leave it with me, Doctor. While you deal with Mr Sanford and amuse yourself in London, I will apply myself to the matter of the grasping miller. Your brother has not forbidden me to raise questions – and you had better not either!"

Adam felt this was sound advice.

WHEN ADAM WENT to The Close to check on his patient in person, he found Sanford propped up in bed. He was fully conscious and his normal self, save in the one respect Miss LaSalle had mentioned. He was completely unable to recall any of the events which had brought him to his current condition. His mind was a blank on the whole topic. One moment he had been taking his breakfast in the morning room; the next he had woken up in this bed, possessed of the mother and father of all headaches. He had no idea how he had come by it.

As Adam later told Wicken, "I have every hope that he may be returned to you as useful as before, given time. Yet on the specific matter of what happened to him, or the King's Messenger, or even the papers you sent to him, we have advanced no further."

Still, progress had been made. Adam was glad he would be able to give Wicken some good news at least.

He talked with Sanford a while longer though, for he was still puzzled by the man's lassitude and lack of interest in the world about him. He did not even seem to be puzzled by the attack. Surely someone who found he had been the victim of what seemed an attempt at murder would express some curiosity. Yet Sanford, on the face of things, blandly accepted the event and enquired no further.

To Adam's mind, this was unbelievable. He felt sure Sanford knew or recalled more than he admitted. Yet, try as he might, he could not confirm this suspicion.

At length, Adam had to accept he could make no further progress that day. He therefore took his leave and went back to his mother's house to prepare for the long journey on the next day. Perhaps he would have better luck on his next visit.

ADAM HAD NOT BEEN in London for many years and had forgotten how tedious and uncomfortable a journey it was. The stagecoach was crowded. The constant jolting most unpleasant. Even his fellow passengers turned out to be surly and devoid of conversation. All save for an attractive young woman who sat in the far corner away from him. She had smiled at him several times, but was too far away to engage in more than the odd fragment of conversation. He hoped to be able to move closer to her when two passengers left the coach at Colchester, but such hopes were dashed at once. No sooner had two spaces appeared than they were filled. One by a man of gargantuan proportion; the other by his equally vast wife. Adam was forced to remain where he was.

Eventually they reached their journey's end. There Adam, now tired, sore and irritated, was met by an emissary from Wicken and whisked away to an inn nearby. There he could rest and take some much-needed refreshment. What became of the comely young woman he did not know.

It seemed Mr Wicken was not able to meet with him until the next morning. The emissary – a young man with an unfortunate squint in one eye – urged the doctor to take his ease in his lodgings that evening. Unless, of course, he had a desire to visit the theatre, the opera or some other place of entertainment.

Adam did not. Being in London made him feel breathless. There were so many people, so much noise and so many smells, many of them sadly rank. He supposed the inhabitants grew used to it, but he could not imagine what it would be like to have to cope with such a crowded mass of humanity every day. What a country mouse he had become! Even Norwich oppressed him with its size these days. London was many times larger.

No, he would take the opportunity to try to catch up on lost sleep. Wicken had even gone so far as to arrange that he should have a room to himself – a rare luxury except for the rich. And though the inn was noisy at times, as all inns are, Adam was so tired he fell into a deep sleep right away. Too deep to be disturbed by the creaking of floorboards, the snoring of those in neighbouring rooms and even the delighted cries of someone enjoying the favours of a lady of the night.

9

NEWS FROM WICKEN

As promised, a chair arrived the next morning to take Adam to his meeting with Wicken. Breakfast had been substantial and the coffee excellent. The young doctor was therefore in good spirits as he was conveyed to a grand building in Whitehall. That was where Mr. Percival Wicken, Permanent Under-Secretary for the Home Department, had his office. Few knew he was the man with responsibility for organising all intelligence gathering and espionage outside the military.

More fine coffee was provided when Adam arrived and he was seated in comfort in Wicken's room, while the two men exchanged pleasantries. It took Adam several moments to come to terms with the palatial surroundings. Wicken was clearly a man of even greater importance than he had imagined.

Once they turned to business, Wicken expressed himself delighted with all that Adam had done about Sanford. He was especially pleased that the man was once again conscious and taking notice of his surroundings. Only the amnesia spoiled the picture.

"You say he remembers nothing?" Wicken said. "That is a great nuisance. Will his memory return, do you think?"

"I do not know. This is a most delicate stage. The loss of memory itself is proof of that."

"But is such a loss unusual?"

"Not in itself, I think. What is odd is for it to be so complete. Many people who suffer concussion cannot recall the details of the event which caused it. A bad fall from a horse, for example, or a carriage oversetting. Yet such blankness is usually restricted to the event itself. In Sanford's case, he seems to have lost the memory of several days – perhaps a week or more – before the assault itself. I am not sure what to make of that. It may be his mind protecting itself from events still too painful to think about. It may be that the mechanism of memory itself has been damaged by the blow to his head. Only time will tell."

"Time again!" Mr Wicken exclaimed. "It is what I have least to grant. Yet I will be guided by you, Bascom. You have not failed me yet."

Adam was not too pleased by the last remark. He did his best, but he was most uneasy that an important man like Wicken should depend on him so completely. He therefore pressed on before Wicken could make any greater demands.

"He may simply need rest," Adam said. "Even if he recovers his memory, he must not over-tax his mind. He cannot at once recommence the work he was doing. That I must forbid. Let him return to it gradually." Wicken pulled a face, but said nothing. "He has a bad concussion and I have yet to determine whether the melancholia that affected him before has passed or not."

"I suppose you are right," Wicken said, "yet my need is sore."

"Not half so sore, I warrant, as Mr Sanford's head," Adam replied, grinning. "Only be patient a while longer." He paused, unsure whether to share his unease that Sanford might be hiding something. It was all so vague that he said nothing at this stage. Wicken had enough worries.

"You at least have made a little progress," Wicken said." I have made none. The two foolish constables I sent to Norwich returned with nothing to show for their time or efforts. No one would tell them anything. Indeed, according to their account, after a few days they began to feel so uncomfortable they felt they must leave. No one offered them violence. Yet they feared it was not far away, should they continue with their questions."

"What will you do?" Adam asked. "Will you close the investigation?"

"By no means," Wicken said at once. "To kill a King's Messenger is a most serious offence, bordering upon treason. I cannot let it drop. I pay these men to do a job and I expect them to do it, not come running home at the first sign of trouble."

"I hear Norwich is somewhat turbulent at present," Adam said. "Maybe that is what they sensed."

"Norwich is always turbulent. Your county is known for the pig-headed, contrary, undisciplined nature of its inhabitants, Bascom. They are eager in little save to have everything their own way."

Adam had to smile at that. "It is your county too, I think," he said.

"Indeed it is, as some here are fond of reminding me whenever I take issue with them. Did you know that Norwich is referred to as "that Jacobin city" by many in this government? In some ways, the name is well justified. There are far more opponents to the present ministry amongst its voters than supporters. My spies also report the county is alive with radical clubs, societies and groups of every kind. We do what we can to suppress the worst of them, but they are like weeds in a flowerbed. Where you uproot one, two more grow."

Adam had never thought of his home like this. It was true that Norfolk people were renowned for going their own way. True even that the better class of people had a reputation for being over-fond of resorting to law on the smallest matter. But he had never thought it a nest of radicals in the way Wicken suggested. But then, Tom Paine hailed from Norfolk. His inflammatory books were the main inspiration for radicals and revolutionaries of all kinds.

Wicken continued. "With all the unrest the place seems to breed, my people in the county are fully occupied. However, I did not ask you to make the journey here just to tell you about faint-hearted constables. I need you to know more about the situation of young Mr Sanford." He paused. "Need I rehearse how secret this is?"

"You need not."

"Some two years ago, we discovered – I need not explain how – certain messages and papers of a secret nature were falling into the hands of our neighbours across the Channel. It seems a French spy in this country was sending them to his masters via an address in Rotterdam. Who the spy was, we still do not know. Whoever he was, he was damned cunning! However, we were able to trace the source of the material he was sending to someone amongst the King's Messengers."

"But ..."

"Let me finish first, I pray you. Then I will be happy to entertain all the doubts and comments you wish to raise."

Adam subsided.

"We thought on one occasion we had found the traitor," Wicken went on. "We were sent an anonymous letter pointing us to a messenger called Amos Tugwell. However, someone must have warned him, for he fled before we could lay hold of him. We have not found him either. Probably in France long ago."

Adam opened his mouth, then thought better of it.

"Either there were two traitors, Bascom, or we lit upon the wrong man. The same spy has recently begun to send more material to a fresh address, this time in Amsterdam. The devil has become more cunning. What he sends, he now sends in cipher. That was what was in the package that went to Sanford and arrived, as we believe, on the day he was assaulted. If he could decipher enough of these messages, he might uncover some clue to lead us to the traitor in our midst. For example, if we knew which messages were being read by the spy, we could trace the person who had handed them over. We too have become more wary. Now we keep a careful note of which messenger bears each package."

Wicken paused for a moment. It seemed to Adam that he looked more drawn and weary than before. The whole business must be bearing down upon him.

"Now, it seems, that hope is lost. Worse, we must assume that someone knew what was sent to Sanford on that day. To my mind, the attack on Sanford, the murder of the King's Messenger and the disappearance of the package point to the same conclusion. It was done to prevent us deciphering and reading enough of those papers to discover the identity of the spy and his helper." Another pause. "Now I am finished and you may say what you will."

"All I was about to ask was whether the King's Messengers know the contents of the packages they carry," Adam said.

"By no means! They are given a kind of leather pouch, already sealed. All they are told is where it must be delivered and to whom."

"So how does this traitor extract the documents without the one who receives it knowing what has been done?"

"I do not know."

"But you are sure the source of information to the spy is one of the messengers?"

"Yes, as sure as I can be of anything in this matter ... for various reasons."

Adam tried to think of some helpful suggestion. He failed. Still, he had one more matter to clear up.

"You are sure that this particular package reached Sanford?"

Wicken shook his head. "I'm not sure, but it seems so. The precentor's servants told me that a letter or package came to the house that morning and was passed to Mr Sanford. I assume that it was this one. It is just possible that the messenger was killed and his pouch stolen before he reached The Close. But if so, why attack Sanford?"

"Because he is a threat in any case. If your spy sees him as one who might decipher his messages, he would wish to eliminate him. That might also explain the man who loitered about the house when Sanford returned there."

"But he is safe now?" Wicken was anxious.

"I believe he is and will continue to be. No one has seen any sign of persons loitering nearby. No one has been reported watching the house since the first two sightings; when Sanford was found on the doorstep and the next day. Mrs Hanwell is a most zealous guardian. I would not envy anyone who crosses her."

"We could have Sanford moved."

"Familiar surroundings are best to aid his recovery."

"I suppose that is correct. Well, Bascom, once again you have my thanks." Wicken made as if to ring a small bell on his desk to summon someone to escort Adam from the building.

"If I may," Adam said quickly, "I will presume a few minutes more on your time. There is another matter that puzzles me. It is not connected directly with Sanford, but it may have a bearing on the aggression your constables claimed to have felt against them. Can you grant me but ten more minutes?"

"I will grant you whatever time you need, Bascom. Once before I dismissed your concerns as unworthy of my attention. Fortunately, you continued regardless, or I would have been shown to be the greatest fool in Christendom. I will not make the same mistake again."

With that permission, Adam told the story of the riot at the mill in Gressington and the murder of the miller a few days later. To this he added a summary of his concerns about the state of the body and what he had seen at the mill itself. When he had finished, Wicken sat in thought a little while before making any comment.

"Well, Bascom," he said, "it's a deuced odd affair indeed. Does your brother not agree with you?"

"My brother is a plain country squire. He is also much burdened with work due to the calling out of the militia. If someone comes forward with evidence of who might be the murderer, he will be as diligent as any magistrate – more than most, I believe. He would definitely attempt to bring the malefactor to justice. Until then, he will wait and rely on the simpler explanation. He thinks someone from the rioters came back and enforced their own brand of justice on the miller."

"Yet you tell me that all the ringleaders are held awaiting appearance at the assizes."

"All my brother knows of; all his men could secure on the day. There may be others, more cunning, who acted to set the riot in motion, but made sure they were not present. Another friend of mine has told me there are several gatherings of men of republican and radical mind throughout the county."

"Your friend is correct," Wicken said. "All thanks to ready access to seditious and inflammatory pamphlets – to say nothing of the rantings of dissident preachers. Much of England is in a state close to open insurrection. People like yourself, men used to rational argument, seek to persuade those holding to a different opinion. Amongst small shopkeepers and artisans, the talk is less of ideas and more of action. They try to force the government into agreeing to the changes they wish for."

Adam felt lost amidst this talk of rebellion and sedition. He did not agree with all the government did – far from it – but he did believe in a basic loyalty. Could not rational men produce reform without resorting to the kind of violence raging across France?

"Why pick on millers?" Adam asked.

"The poor think only in simple terms of taking the harvest, grinding the grain and using it locally. That is not how markets work in these sophisticated days. Grain and flour may be purchased from many sources. Some is brought by ship from as far away as our former colonies in the Americas. Our merchants and millers export grain to the countries of Scandinavia, to the Low Countries, to Prussia even. We used to sell a good deal to the French, though that trade has stopped. Add to that the vast size of London, which must buy all its grain and flour from beyond its boundaries. No, sir. Today's Norfolk millers are as like to sell their products to the Danes or the inhabitants of London as use them to provide bread for people in the same village."

"Yes, I see how that type of trade is necessary. They also make more profit that way, I suppose."

"Yes. Especially if there is talk of bad harvest and shortages. To that extent, your Gressington rioters have some truth on their side. I do not know whether that particular miller held back grain to force up the price, but I know that many do. Some form cartels for the purpose. Others act as engrossers or forestallers."

Thanks to Miss LaSalle, Adam did not need to confess to any ignorance of such terms.

"The trouble is, Wicken," he said, "I am not convinced this miller's murder had anything to do with the riot. At least, not directly."

"Why? What caused it then?"

"I do not know. Nor can I find out more. My involvement is over in any formal sense. It is hard to say exactly what makes me think as I do. There is the gun ... the nature of the wounds ... even the space in time between riot and murder."

"But you believe the simple answer is insufficient." Wicken said.

"Yes. It may be a just local affair. It may, however, point to the presence of men sent to our shores to stir up trouble wherever they can ..."

"... And it may have some bearing on who, in that same county, was persuaded or instructed to kill a King's Messenger and assault a man working for me. A man whom no one should have known about, unless they are engaged in espionage themselves." Wicken looked grim. "I do not like this reasoning of yours, Bascom. I do not like it at all. What it leads to smells to me of treachery and conspiracy. Yet I am most glad that your sharp eyes and keen mind have been at work. I believe I told you once before that you have a natural gift for this kind of investigatory work. Now you have proved it again. Maybe I should take over your medical practice while you assume my duties here."

"You might make a better country doctor than I do," Adam said. "Sometimes I doubt whether I should be engaged in such work."

"What rubbish, sir! Just because you look more widely than a good many of your colleagues, and think more deeply about what you see, that does not make you less of a healer. To my mind, it makes you a better one. Now, my friend, are there any other 'puzzles' you wish to leave with me? Or have you destroyed my peace of mind sufficiently for one day?"

"I do not mean to add to your burdens," Adam said, sounding contrite.

"That I am sure of, or I would hardly invite you here. But enough of that. You must be eager to return to Aylsham. From what you tell me, you have not slept in your own bed for many nights past. I have made arrangements for you to be carried home by a government post-chaise. You will be accompanied by two postillions and two extra men as guards. That way, you may travel through the hours of darkness in safety. Ah yes ..." He took a fine pocket-watch from his waistcoat and looked at it closely. "It is just about noon. If you start within an hour or so and stop for dinner at, say ... St. Albans ... you should be in Aylsham by early afternoon tomorrow."

"With your permission, I should like to return to Norwich first. That way I may visit Sanford again before I turn my attention for a while to what I have neglected most: my poor practice."

"Norwich, then. Perhaps in time for a late breakfast. I assume you can hire a chaise from there when you are ready to move on?"

"With ease," Adam said, "and I thank you most kindly for your thoughtfulness in this matter. The Norwich Machine is ... well, some say better than it was, but still far from a comfortable way to travel."

"No indeed. And do not fear that I will neglect to seek out what information I may about your murdered miller. All I ask is that you also share what you find with me. My whole duty here is based on having sound information. Yours will be sounder than most."

The two men thus parted on the best of terms. With regard to Sanford, Adam could do little more until the man's memory had improved. If Wicken fulfilled his promise and provided some answers about the miller, that problem too might move nearer a solution. Then he might at last be able to address the backlog of medical duties and chores that were building up around him.

ADAM ARRIVED in Norwich even earlier than Wicken had predicted. He had delayed for only a modest meal in St. Albans and the government postillions were skilled in the rapid changing of horses. He had them leave him at the Maid's Head Inn in Norwich, where he knew he could get what he wanted most: a substantial breakfast. To eat heavily during a journey was not something he advised for others, nor did himself. The constant jolting along the road prevented the proper operation of the stomach. Coach passengers who indulged too heavily in food or drink were apt to suffer a violent indigestion. Some, he had read, even died when their hearts failed under the strain. Now his own travelling was over, at least for that day, Adam could satisfy his hunger without fear of the consequences.

Breakfast over, Adam once again visited Dr Hanwell's house. Mrs Hanwell had taken charge of Sanford's nursing from the start and still appeared to be enjoying herself hugely. She assured Adam that she would ensure Sanford rested as much as possible. She would also report the man's progress at regular intervals via Miss LaSalle. Adam could relax.

Thus, with all complete and Sanford appearing to be on the mend, at least in body, Adam went to his mother's house. It was time, he thought, to return to Aylsham and normality. He found Mrs Bascom in her parlour sewing, in company with Miss LaSalle.

"Back again?" his mother said. "How was your time in London?"

"It is not a city I much relish," Adam said. "It is too noisy and crowded. All in all, I am pleased to be back here. May I beg a room for one more night? We travelled through all the hours of darkness, which made for speed but gave me little opportunity for sleeping."

"I did not think the stage arrived in Norwich this morning," Sophia said. "If I am correct, it came yesterday and will do so again tomorrow. It is not a daily service."

"I came by post-chaise," Adam said somewhat smugly.

"By post-chaise? That is an expensive way to travel. And you also said you came through the night, which would make it most dangerous too."

"I was given an escort," Adam replied.

"Did you arrive in time for breakfast, my son?" his mother asked. "I am sure the housekeeper could find you something ..."

"Indeed I did arrive in time to eat. I ate breakfast at The Maid's Head. After that, I went first to The Close to see my patient, who seems to be recovering. If his progress remains good, I may be able to take up residence at home again and not burden you more with my presence."

"Are you so eager to leave us, Doctor?" Sophia said archly.

"Peace, Sophia. Do not tease so." Mrs Bascom said. "My son has to make his way in the world. He cannot always be at your beck and call. I am glad to see him whenever he is able to visit. As are you, I think."

"It is always a pleasure to have company, Mrs Bascom" Sophia replied, all demureness.

"So, your Mr Wicken provided you with an official escort back home," Mrs Bascom said. "He must value you greatly. Were you able to tell him all he needed to know?"

"Only some things. There are one or two matters yet that are not clear to my mind ..."

"Please tell us," Sophia interrupted. "Your son is a veritable blood-hound, Mrs Bascom. Give him but a sniff of some strange event and he is off on the trail in a moment."

"I am not on the trail of anything," Adam replied, trying to sound detached.

"Well, time will tell, Sophia, will it not? Long experience of my second son has taught me this. His protestations of distant interest in puzzling events are best treated with scepticism."

"Indeed, madam," Sophia said. "Though I have known the doctor for scarce twelve months, I too have learned that. Once his curiosity is aroused, he is as inconstant in his claims of detachment as most men are in their protestations of affection."

What that had to do with anything was more than Adam could see, though his mother seemed to grasp some profound meaning in the remark.

"I am not aware that he has made any such protestations of late, Sophia. Are you?"

This innocent remark caused Sophia to duck her head and break out into a sudden spasm of coughing. She refused all aid, however.

"You have a poor opinion of men, Miss LaSalle," Adam said, when the coughing had all but ceased. "However, that is no matter. It is true that the death of the miller at Gressington puzzles me a good deal. I have asked Mr Wicken to find out what he can, but I have few hopes that he can give it much attention. The poor man is frantic with work and looks quite drawn."

"A most interesting man," Mrs Bascom said. "Would you not agree, Sophia?"

"Most interesting, madam."

"Too old for you, I judge, even if he is not already in possession of a wife."

"Madam!" Sophia's blushes had returned in full measure. "You cannot believe I think of all men I meet as potential husbands."

"Only some then."

"None," Sophia said firmly. "I have told you many times that I do not expect to be other than I am. Now who is the tease?"

"When next you see him, please give Mr Wicken my compliments, Adam, and say that I hope to make his acquaintance again some time. In the meantime, it is a little while since we visited Giles. What do you think, Sophia? Would you judge it is time to go to Trundon Hall again?"

"It must be more than a month since our last visit," Sophia said. She had recovered her composure.

"Then I will write to Giles and suggest we visit him on Monday week, if he finds that convenient. I suppose Miss LaSalle and I may find refreshment at your house on our way there or back, Adam?"

"Of course. I will be delighted to receive you both. However, I must give my attention wholly to my practice for a while. It might be best to delay your visit to Aylsham until your return from seeing Giles. If you stay at Trundon for … what? a week? … you could perhaps stay with me for a day or two before coming back here."

"Perhaps we might. I am growing old and Miss LaSalle needs company nearer her own age. Is that not so, Sophia?"

"Your company is quite sufficient, Mrs Bascom, I assure you," Sophia said.

"Pish! Well, I will leave you two together and prepare myself for dining. Do not let my son detain you too long, Sophia. You too need to change your clothes in good time."

Once they were alone, Adam told Sophia the gist of his conversation with Wicken. The matter of the spy was fresh news to her and her eyes shone with excitement.

"It is like an adventure story, Doctor. How lucky I am to live under your mother's roof! There can be few lady companions who have the privilege of associating with persons such as yourself, engaged on such fascinating work."

"I should rather say unlucky, Miss LaSalle."

"Not at all, Doctor. Now, I have much to consider. To me, the matter of the miller is of greater importance than either you or Mr Wicken judge it to be. As for the spies, discovering who is the traitor should take precedence over all else. Indeed, it ought to have been no great matter, had it been attended to promptly. I expect much time and effort was wasted on that silly letter. It was obviously a hoax."

"How do you make that out?"

"Unmasking a traitor is too important to be handled in such a way. The man who thinks he knows who it is would speak out plainly and expect a substantial reward, not send an anonymous note. No, Doctor, your Mr Wicken was getting too close to the culprit and had to be distracted. It is only sad no one had the sense to warn him it was a false trail."

Adam would dearly have loved to argue the point with her, if only to dent her irritating confidence in her reasoning, but he could not. She was most likely correct in her conclusion.

"I had not looked at it like that," he said softly.

"Had you not, Doctor? Maybe you should have ..." She stopped on a sudden and hung her head. "Alas, what a silly, vain creature I am. I promised not to taunt you and here I am doing that very thing. Take no notice of me, I pray you. It is but nervousness that I will say something stupid that makes me act thus. I will go to my room now. Good afternoon, sir. I believe you take a chaise from The Maid's Head shortly and so will not be here for dinner. Permit me to wish you a pleasant journey."

With that, she left the room, causing Adam to feel even more puzzled by her behaviour than before.

10

THE BARONET

It had been Adam's most earnest hope after his return from Norwich that he be left in peace to catch up with the business of his practice. It had been sorely neglected of late. Worse, it would decline altogether if he kept setting his patients' needs aside in favour of Mr Wicken's demands. It was not to be. The very next day, a servant came from Mr Jempson's house to enquire if Adam would be kind enough to call at noon. Miss Jempson wished him to meet someone desirous of his services as a physician.

Mr Jempson, a wealthy Quaker merchant, was a person of great importance in the little market town of Aylsham. He had moved to Aylsham less than six months ago, having much new business at Lynn and wishing to leave behind the noise and bustle of Norwich streets. Now he lived with his only child, his daughter Elizabeth, in a fine, new-built house perhaps a quarter of a mile from Adam's own.

In keeping with Quaker values, his house was of modest size and constructed in a plain style. There was none of the exterior ornamentation beloved by most of the gentry. No grand, sweeping steps up to the main entrance. No pillars framing the door, nor pediment above. Its architect had tried to avoid all bombast and grandiosity. Only the beauty of its proportions and the quality of brick and stone proclaimed it no ordinary gentleman's residence.

Mr Jempson and his daughter had been particular friends of Adam since he had rescued the elderly merchant from highway robbers. There could be no question of refusing their request to call, however busy he might be.

Adam arrived at Mr Jempson's house at noon, as arranged, and was shown at once into the parlour. He had expected to be greeted by the master of the house, but found only Miss Jempson present. She was sitting beside another lady near the window. A cat was curled on her lap and she stoked it with one hand. Its purring was to be a background to all their conversation, blending with the gentle tick of the fine clock on the mantle.

"Good morning, Doctor," she said, acknowledging his formal bow with a slight inclination of the head. "Thank you for answering my call. My father will be sorry to have missed you. He has been called away on most urgent business in Lynn. Like you, I imagine, he is much occupied with business matters in such dark times as these. We can only pray that the hand of Providence may protect us from harm and bring us safe to haven at last."

Her companion gave a most unladylike snort. "I suppose you believe that Providence may do such a thing, Elizabeth. I do not. We must deliver ourselves or perish. Is that not so, sir?"

Adam was startled. He had been watching Miss Jempson's cat – an addition it seemed since he had last paid a visit. It sat with its paws held in a neat muff shape and its head resting on its mistress's bosom.

Adam much envied that cat. Miss Jempson seemed to him even more serene and beautiful than he had remembered. The hand that was stroking the ginger fur was slim and of a fine shape. The bend of her neck made him ache to place his lips upon it. Even her voice – gentle, rich and unusually deep for a woman – brought small quivers of delight to his spine.

What was the matter with him? The other day in Norwich his mind had been filled with the most unsuitable imaginings about

Miss LaSalle. Now, once again, he must keep a tight hold upon himself, lest he betray the shocking thoughts that arose in him.

Realising he had been silent too long, while his eyes never strayed from the cat and the young woman across the room, Adam spoke up hastily.

"Um ... Perhaps so, madam."

His prolonged gaze had clearly not gone unnoticed. The two ladies exchanged knowing glances. Then Miss Jempson introduced her companion: Lady Alice Fouchard, the wife of Sir Daniel Fouchard, Baronet. She it was who had need of his medical expertise. At least, her husband did. Sir Daniel, it appeared, was a very sick man.

Startled by the news that the lady seeking his advice was not just an aristocrat, but a grand one, Adam looked at Lady Alice properly. She must be of a similar age to Miss Jempson, but there was little similarity beyond that. Where Miss Jempsons' manner and looks were soft and domestic, Lady Alice had the fine bone structure of the true aristocrat. Adam judged she must be taller than most women, though slim in figure. She dressed as befitted her station, of course, yet it was the woman herself who drew attention, not the clothes. A mass of rich blond hair framed her face below an elegant hat and her eyes were of a most piercing blue. She might well serve as a model for a painting of Britannia, so commanding was her presence.

"I know so, sir. Now, enough of such pleasantries. My dear friend Elizabeth has been singing your praises in such exalted style that I determined to try your value for myself."

"Do not frighten our guest, Alice," Miss Jempson said softly, "and do not embarrass me with thy exaggerations. Like many a grand lady, Doctor, Lady Alice defends herself when nervous by assuming a most aggressive manner. Do not be deceived. She will be kindness itself, once she feels relaxed in your presence."

"I can speak for myself, Elizabeth," Lady Alice said. "You need not treat me like some child who has forgotten her manners."

"Need I not?" Miss Jempson smiled. "Forgive me. Thou knowest I love thee well. Perhaps thou shouldst simply tell our good doctor what has brought thee here."

Lady Alice accepted this gentle rebuke without further remark. Indeed, when next she spoke her voice had lost some of its sharp edge. Now she sounded only saddened and weary.

"My husband is much older than I am, Doctor, and has been ill for some time. Indeed, he was not a well man when we married. It appears we may have but little time together, for his other physicians have all but given up. Death could come at any time. Indeed, it would be a most blessed relief from his suffering. Why a supposedly loving God should make him endure such torments, I cannot tell."

"My father would say it is not for us to question the ways of Providence," Miss Jempson said.

"Your father is a saint," Lady Alice replied. "I have long known that I am not."

"Do you know what ails him, my lady?" Adam asked. "What do his physicians tell you?"

"Little, sir. The principal one is an old fool who wears a musty wig and has no remedy for anything beyond bleeding. That I will no longer allow. My husband has little strength as it is. Being bled seems to rob him even of that. I have told Dr Pettigrew the next time he bleeds my husband will be the last time he sets foot within my house."

Adam had heard of Dr Pettigrew, though they had never met. Once he had been revered for his medical skills. Now he must be seventy-five years of age, if not more. Like many physicians of his time, he had been trained to view sickness as the result of an imbalance in the humours of the body. It seemed his views had not changed.

"Has he not told you the nature of your husband's sickness?" Adam asked.

"Some foul growth or cancer in his stomach. Whatever it is, it causes him terrible pain; pain I can scarce bear to see him suffer any longer. That is why I am here, Doctor. Miss Jempson has told me that she believes you may be able to lessen that pain. I do not expect you to cure my husband. Both he and I are well aware that he is beyond mortal help. But, I pray you, if you know how, release him from the agonies that tear at both of us every day."

There were tears in Lady Alice's eyes as she spoke, and in Miss Jempson's too. Both ladies looked towards Adam with such hope that he could have cried also. He knew how powerless he was like to be in the face of such a disease.

"My husband has had a full life," Lady Alice continued after a moment. "His only regret is that he has no heir, despite marrying four times. Two children were indeed born alive, but neither lived beyond their fifth year. I was his last hope and I have failed him. Perhaps the illness was upon him already when we married. Now his title and lands will go to a distant relative. Although our marriage was arranged by my family, as such things are, I have come to love my husband dearly."

"Are you also of the Society of Friends?" Adam asked.

"No, I am not and bear allegiance to no church or sect," Lady Alice replied. "Miss Jempson and I met through mutual friends and discovered a liking for one another. She is my rock in these dreadful circumstances."

"Lady Alice was born far away in the county of Hereford, Doctor," Miss Jempson added. "She is a member of the old Norman lineage of the Scudamores. Several of her relatives are peers of the realm. Others are senior clergy of the Established Church – indeed, I think more than one are bishops. However, the bulk of her husband's lands lie hereabouts."

"Hush, Elizabeth," Lady Alice said. "My father may have come from noble blood, but he has precious little money or lands these days. You might say my husband bought me, sir. Yet if he did, I have had the best of the bargain. The few estates that made up my dowry were of little consequence. Yet my husband has treated me with the most gentle consideration and care and insisted I enjoy all that his wealth can provide."

"Let us speak of money no more," Adam said. "Lady Alice. It is my judgment that you would have me speak plainly."

"Your judgment is correct, sir."

"Then I must tell you that we physicians have few remedies for pain. Those we do have are but coarse instruments. They blunt the pain, but cloud the mind as well. I must also tell you that a great use of them, as might be indicated here, has been known many times to shorten life."

"I thank you for your honesty, Doctor. What you say does not surprise me. As to shortening life, I believe my husband would come near to blessing you for shortening his, since it is nought now but suffering and misery. Nevertheless, I would have you ask him yourself."

"That I will do," Adam said. "When may I visit your husband? Until I have examined him, I must talk only in generalities."

"Will you come today?"

"I will. How far off is your house?"

"Scarce five miles. It will take you perhaps forty minutes to be there."

"I will come at four, if that will be convenient, my lady. First I hope to consult a good friend of mine who is the apothecary in this town. His views I trust and I know him to have greater skill and knowledge with the compounding of medicines than I do."

"A physician and an apothecary who are friends? You amaze me, sir. I thought those two professions were always on bad terms."

"Not in this case at least. We have known each other since we were students and he has helped me many times. Once again, my lady, let me stress that, while I promise you that I will do my best, I will not offer you false hope. What you tell me makes me think your husband's pain may be more than I can lessen much. I will try, but can promise no more."

"All that you have said makes me believe that Miss Jempsons' praise of you was justified, Doctor," Lady Alice said. Now she rose from her chair to bid him farewell. She was indeed as tall as him, though slender as a young horse. "You are the first doctor who has treated me as an adult human being and not as that inferior creature, a mere woman. I will look for you at four."

LATER THAT DAY, as he made his way up the drive to Mossterton Hall, Adam wondered if he had ever seen the house before. It lay far from the road, surrounded by thick woodland. Anyone driving along the road itself might see gates and an entrance, but no more. Even when he had turned through the entrance and travelled many yards further, he could see no sign of buildings. The driveway was edged with substantial oak trees which hid much of what lay to either side. All that appeared to his right was an area of rough heathland, with yet more woodland beyond it. To his left was an open field, dotted with sheep. It too rose a little from the roadway, until it ended in yet another dense line of trees. He had made his way another quarter of a mile before he had proof that there was any actual habitation ahead.

The county of Norfolk is not blessed with good building stone. There is flint of course, but that is of little use save for rough walls and barns. What stone there is is soft and too easily weathered for building. A gentleman who desires a grand home must build in brick. So it had been since the days of Good Queen Bess, and so it would remain. Some had used local clay to make good bricks, where it was suitable. Some used brick from the Low Countries, brought in as ship's ballast.

Mossterton Hall did more than use Flemish bricks. The curved gable ends and the hipped, tiled roofs, showed whoever designed it had studied the work of Dutch architects, not the Roman and Italian styles popular in Adam's day. It had most likely been built when Dutch King William and Queen Mary had been England's monarchs. Maybe its owner of a hundred years ago had wished to show loyalty to the new, protestant succession.

Lady Alice must have set someone to watch for him. After he had left his carriage with a groom and allowed a solemn footman to lead him into the house, she came into the entry way to greet him in person.

"Forgive me, Dr Bascom," she said, "if I do not at once offer you refreshment after your journey. My husband has been in much pain this day. Whenever that is the case, he falls eventually into an exhausted sleep. I try never to wake him after until he is ready. He has so little relief from his suffering I am loathe to bring him to wakefulness unless I must. With your agreement, I will take you to him at once while he is still conscious and able to speak with you. I have told him of your coming."

All this while, she had been leading him through the grand entrance hall towards a fine set of stairs beyond. As he glanced around, the signs of wealth were obvious. Old-master paintings adorned the walls. There were fine statues and rich plasterwork. Yet none of these elements were carried so far as to be ostentatious. While it was obviously the house of a rich family, its owners must also have been men of elegant taste.

At the top of the stairs, Adam's host led him to the right and along a corridor lined with family portraits. Some were stiff figures with Elizabethan ruffs about their throats. Others, more recent, were by the most fashionable portrait-painters of the day. Men like Sir Joshua Reynolds, Mr Gainsborough and Sir Peter Lely. All depicted persons accustomed to wealth and power. It was almost intimidating.

After some thirty paces, Lady Alice stopped beside a closed door and beckoned him forward.

"This is where my husband spends his days, Doctor," she said. "Let us enter quietly, in case sleep has come to him already. If it has not, I will introduce you and withdraw. To be plain with you, I can no longer bear to see more of his agony than I must. When you are ready to leave, please pull the bell-rope beside the bed to call a servant. They will bring you to where I will be."

With that, she opened the door with the most touching care and peered around it. What she saw must have satisfied her, for she pushed the door open with some vigour and stepped inside. Adam followed her.

To his surprise, the room was full of sunshine. In most sick-rooms, he found a most profound gloom, as if the sadness of the family needed to be reflected in darkness about the patient. Here, in contrast, all was light and airy, even to a small bunch of fresh flowers placed on the table beside the bed. Only when he looked at the man who lay propped up in that bed did the full horror of his condition become plain.

That it was a man was clear, but nothing about him spoke of anything but death. His skin was of a most unhealthy pallor, drawn around his head and face so tight that it seemed but the slightest covering for the skull beneath – a skull that must soon be made even more visible by worms and decay. On his throat, the skin hung in folds. He must once have been a solidly-built man, even a strong one. Now he was nothing but bones draped in the final, feeble trappings of life. Only the eyes still showed a certain fierce attention, though the whites were yellow and bloodshot. They remained fixed on Lady Alice as she bent towards the bed. It was if her husband was cherishing every last image of her his brain could register, before death snatched him away from her for ever.

"This is the doctor I told you about, my dear. His name is Dr Bascom. I have asked him to see if he can offer you any relief from your pain."

"Only death can do that – though he will not come, Alice." Sir Daniel's speech was husky, and his breath laboured. Yet there still remained enough in the tone to suggest the fine speaking voice he had once possessed. "I beg of you, do not let me be subjected to yet more bleeding or cupping. They do no good. I am dying and there is an end of it."

"I will not, dear husband, I assure you. I have already made that plain to Dr Bascom. But he has told me he might yet be able to offer something of use to you. I believe him. Will you not at least hear what he has to say?"

There was a long pause, while Sir Daniel's whole body stiffened in what must have been a tremor of agony great enough to rob him of the power of speech. Then he spoke again.

"For your sake, I will, for I know how you fret about me," he said. "Come closer, Doctor. My voice is not strong enough to reach far. Besides, I would like to take a good look at you. Ah ... so young. Still, that does not signify. Dr Pettigrew is near my age. Yet the years have done little to enhance his skill or his ideas. Sit, sir. There is a chair by the bed. Alice, my dear, do you leave me so soon? I suppose you must. My condition torments her almost as much as it does me, Doctor. I love to have her near me, yet cannot bear to see her so wretched as she is when she in my presence."

"She loves you deeply," Adam said. "Of that I am sure, Sir Daniel. She would stay if she could."

"I know, I know ... well, Doctor, what now?"

"Sir Daniel," Adam began. He had dreaded this moment. "It is my way to be as honest with my patients as I judge each can bear. From all I have heard, I believe I can be entirely honest with you. Will you allow me to speak thus?"

"I will, and welcome it."

"Then I must tell you at once that I can see no hope of preventing that end which must come to us all. I will not insult your understanding with false promises; nor add to your sufferings with treatments that I am sure must fail."

Sir Daniel said nothing, but his eyes never left Adam's face.

"The best I can do – and that is not certain – is to seek to lessen your suffering until the end comes. Unfortunately, no physician has much to offer as effective remedies for pain, save those which will dull your mind and cause you to sleep."

"You tell me what I know already, Doctor. Others have offered to bring me days of oblivion and I have refused. I saw your surprise as you came into this room to find the curtain drawn back and shutters wide open. It should not have amazed you. Before too long, God willing, these eyes will close for ever. Until then, I would see as much of the sun, the sky and my beloved woods as I may."

"Nor will I take those from you, even if you permitted it," Adam said. "Yet when darkness comes, none of them can be seen, and the hours of night are often the worst times for the suffering that sickness brings."

Adam paused again. It seemed to him essential to choose the right words for what he must say next.

"This is what I propose. I will provide a medicine that will bring you oblivion, but only for the hours of darkness. You may leave it aside during daylight hours, then take again when the night comes. For the period when it is light, I will see whether another, different medicine may bring you sufficient relief. It will dull your pain, but not take it away. Its virtue is more that your mind will be clear and your vision undimmed. Is that course of treatment something you can accept?"

"You say this daytime medicine will but dull the pain, not take it away?"

"That is correct."

"But that I will be clear-headed and alert."

"Indeed so."

"Then," Sir Daniel said, "I accept and that right gladly. I like pain no more than the next man, Doctor."

"There is but one more warning I must give, Sir Daniel. The medicine I will give you to take at night is strong. Stronger than I would use in other cases. It is my belief that taking it may well shorten your life somewhat. I cannot be sure, but it is a danger. If I give it to you, it must be on the understanding that you are aware of this and accept it of your own free will."

Sir Daniel smiled. "I do so, Doctor. What matter if my time on this earth is lessened by a week, a month or even more, so long as what time I have left is passed in less torment than at present? Give me your medicine, sir."

"I will summon a servant and have what I need brought here, Sir Daniel. I have the medicine itself in my bag, but it needs to be given in a little brandy to be most effective."

Adam rose and pulled the bell-cord. When the servant came, he asked that a small decanter of brandy be brought, together with a suitable glass. The servant nodded and withdrew.

"I do have one request to make of you, Doctor," Sir Daniel said, after the servant had left. "Before I take your draught, will you sit and talk with me a little while? I pass so much of my time alone that to do as I ask would be a great kindness. There was a time when my wife sat with me for hours. Now, I fear, her sadness will not allow her to stay with me for more than ten minutes. I still crave human companionship, sir. There will be none where I am going."

"I will sit and talk with you gladly, Sir Daniel. My work for today is ended. Beyond wishing to reach my home again before dark falls, I have no other reason to hasten away. What shall we talk of?"

"Not the state of this terrible war, sir, nor of politics at all, by your leave. Such words tend to drive me into a passion, which cannot be good for me. No ... I have it ... tell me of some present case you have that is testing your mind. I have no medical knowledge, I am afraid, but I love a good puzzle."

Thus it was that Adam sat by the dying man and explained the puzzle of the assault on Sanford and the death of the King's Messenger, Toms. At least, as much of it as he was free to. Perhaps half-way through his narrative, the servant returned with the brandy and a glass. Adam measured out the double doses of laudanum and valerian mixture and dropped them into a glassful of brandy. He left the glass by the side of the bed. Only when he had finished his tale did he persuade Sir Daniel to drink.

"It will not work at once," he said. "Perhaps ten or fifteen minutes must pass before sleep will come to you." Many times during his narrative Adam had seen that terrible stiffening and shuddering that indicated another bout of pain, though Sir Daniel had born all without a sound. It would be too cruel to allow that torment to continue much longer.

Sir Daniel lay back on his pillows and closed his eyes. "A fascinating puzzle indeed," he said. "I will turn it over in my mind as much as I can. One thought, however, comes to me at once."

"Tell me, please," Adam said. "I have no useful thoughts of my own."

"I believe it may be of some use to you," Sir Daniel said. "If not, you are free to disregard it and set me down as in my dotage. It is this. When two events happen in the same place and near enough at the same time, the temptation is always to assume they are connected. Even worse, that they are but two parts of the same whole. I would

counsel you to recognise that for what it is: an assumption only. The
two assaults you have mentioned may be connected, but they may
well stem from different causes. Unless you think over both these
possibilities, you will find yourself looking for a link that was never
there."

ABOUT HALF AN HOUR LATER, Adam drove back home to Aylsham. He
had left the medicines with Lady Alice and instructed her carefully in
their use. He would not have Sir Daniel's death on his conscience,
however much the man longed to leave this world. The man was
already deeply sedated before he left, but he assured Lady Alice the
effect would not last more than eight or ten hours, if that. During the
day, she must see he took three or four good doses of the double-
strength tincture of willow bark Peter had prepared. It would dull the
pain, but it would not bring unconsciousness.

Now he turned once more to the problem of Sanford. Sir Daniel
had given him sound advice, Adam thought. What if the murder of
Toms and the assault on Sanford were not connected? He could
hardly believe it was the case, yet he must admit that neither he nor
Wicken – so far as he knew – had any evidence to prove the link. As
Sir Daniel had noticed at once, they had simply assumed the link was
there. But what could account for the events if they were not
connected? Two days had passed between Toms arriving in Norwich
and handing over his package to Sanford and the fatal evening.
Sanford would have been working on his attempt to unravel the
coded message or messages during that time.

What had Toms been doing?

Wicken said Toms had been told to wait and bring Sanford's work
back to London. Had any one asked how he had spent those last
forty-eight hours of his life?

What fools they had been! Adam at once resolved to write to
Wicken the next day and seek some answer to that riddle. Wicken
said his two constables had gone back to Norwich. They surely could

find out something of Toms' movements, if they did not know already. Once he and Wicken had that knowledge, they would have a far better notion of how to view later events. Either to stay with their belief the two assaults sprang from a single cause, or set it aside and look at each one as standing alone.

Thus it was that, despite all the surprises of that day, Adam reached his home in something closer to his normal high spirits. This did not go unnoticed by either Hannah, the maid, or Mrs Brigstone, the housekeeper. If both attributed it to the wrong cause, few could blame them.

"I warrant it was meeting Miss Jempson," Hannah said. "She's a beautiful lady, for all that she's a Quaker." She stared at the ceiling, her eyes dreamy with thoughts of fine clothes and elegant manners.

"Don't be such a great lummox, girl," Mrs Brigstone said. "The master would never marry a dissenter. Besides, them Quakers to my certain knowledge only marries amongst themselves. No, 'tis not her who puts the spring in the master's step. Perhaps it's some other lady. His mother has many friends amongst the aristocracy and gentry. Norwich is full of rich women and I dare see she knows many of 'em."

"But wouldn't they be married?"

"And you think that counts for anything? You haven't been around the houses of the gentry as I have, that's plain. Why, some of them fine ladies 'as more lovers than you and I 'as ever 'ad good dinners."

"But I always thought the master such an upright and moral person, Mrs Brigstone. Surely he would never have any part in such goings on?"

"The married ones might 'ave daughters, mightn't they? What about the widows? That Mr Lassimer, the master's friend, is a holy terror when it comes to lonely widows, as I 'ear tell."

"Would the master think like that too?"

"I never yet met a man who was proof against temptation, young lady. I grant you the master is a fine man, but how can anyone say what he would do if a beautiful woman smiled at him in that special way."

"What special way?" Hannah was bewildered.

"Gar! You knows I don't doubt, girl. That way that says 'come to bed with me', as plain as if it were written down and held under the man's nose."

"I ain't never looked at anyone like that," Hannah protested. "I wouldn't know 'ow either."

"You will," Mrs Brigsone said darkly. "You will. All us women be born with that knowledge. All it takes is the right man and the right time and you'll try your luck, same as any woman will."

Thus it was that, when all had retired and Hannah lay in the dark, she started twisting her face and trying to imagine what look might tempt a man to try her virginity. Meanwhile, Mrs Brigstone dreamed happily of days long past. Times when every haystack seemed put there especially for her to lead Tom, or Dick, or Harry into the most delicious temptation. Only Adam, who had caused such turmoil in the minds of his staff, slept without dreaming at all. Though he would gladly have dreamed of Miss Jempson or Miss LaSalle, if he could have brought it about.

11

A TIME OF CONFUSION

Adam was never an especially early riser. The previous day had been more tiring than usual and it was after nine before he left his room. Then, freshly washed and shaved, he made his way into the dining room to take his breakfast. The sun that had made the world look so cheerful the day before had gone. One day of shining at a time was enough. Now the house had that dismal look that went with thick clouds and the threat of rain.

There was no sign of Hannah with his breakfast, but Adam was in no hurry. The carrier must have been to Aylsham that morning. Hannah had left a copy of The Norwich Intelligencer newspaper of two days ago on the table for him. Adam picked it up and began to read in the fashion typical of many, skipping over serious matters and seeking out amusing diversions.

What his eye lit upon was no diversion, though it came low on the page and had not seemed of great importance to the editor of the paper. It was a report of a riot in Norwich:

"On Tuesday last, at about seven o'clock in the evening, a most serious riot took place in this city. A hue and cry went up that two government spies had been discovered. In but a few moments, a large crowd assembled,

vowing to seize the spies and eject them from the city altogether. The men identified had taken refuge in an inn near to the Market Place, and the landlord tried valiantly, first to reason with the leaders of the mob, then to defend the men with his own person, but he was swept aside. The two were taken and dragged into the Market Place to the joy of the whole crowd. There they were set upon and beaten most cruelly, while certain elements of the mob cried out that they should be hanged. However, before it could be seen whether this ultimate act of cruelty would indeed be inflicted upon the men, a group of constables arrived; and though they could not by any means wrest the victims away from the hands of the mob, they succeeded in dispersing the mob and preventing immediate murder. The two victims were taken up and borne away to find medical help. Both were alive, but their wounds were such as to cause those who carried them to fear for their lives.

That such an act of barbarism should take place in our fair city is cause enough for shame, but until some aid be available for those who have lost their employment due to the current state of war with France, the number of idle people loitering about the streets will not decrease. It is much to be hoped that the Mayor and Aldermen will petition His Most Gracious Majesty for help in this matter.

At the last moment before this paper was printed, it was learned that both victims, who were from London, claim to be constables of the Bow Street Court. They have survived their ordeal thus far, though with broken bones and bruises about the body. It will be some days before they can be returned to their families. Meanwhile, they are being cared for by well-wishers."

Two constables! Mr Wicken would not be at all pleased at this turn of events. What could it mean? Were there those in the city who had also guessed why the constables had come? Men who had somehow been involved in the assault on Sanford and the murder of Toms, the King's Messenger? The constables had told Wicken before that they had felt threatened. Now it seemed threats had turned into action.

It was while he was musing over the possibilities and producing more questions than answers that Hannah came in with his break-fast. Adam looked at her quite absently, seeming to consider her in some detail from head to toes, but actually seeing nothing. Unfortunately, this produced an entirely false impression on the girl. That was thanks to her conversation with Mrs Brigstone the day before. Maybe she had given her master that 'special' look, the girl thought. If she had, it had been without her knowledge. Perhaps it was natural to her. Could she have power over men she had never imagined?

Somewhat flustered by this thought, she returned to the kitchen. There she decided, on an impulse, to share her thoughts with the housekeeper.

"Master was looking at me funny this morning," she said. "Like he was considering doin' something. He looked at me all over, from head to toe. It made me sort of embarrassed and excited at the same time. I wonder what's got into his head, Mrs Brigstone?"

The effect of this question was not at all what she had expected.

"Hannah Neston!" the housekeeper said. "Has you been giving the master the eye, you little strumpet? Has you been trying to egg him on to something he'll regret? You ought to be ashamed of yourself! I thought yesterday you had some wicked idea in your head, but I never thought you would be so shameless as to act on it."

"Me?" Hannah was annoyed that her innocent question had produced such an angry response. "I ain't done nothing. 'Tis the master who's eyeing me up, not the other way around."

"If he is – and I can scarce believe it of the man – it will only be because you've been leadin' him on. Well, it will be the end of my time here if it's true. I won't stay in a house where the master uses the maids for his night-time pleasure. It isn't decent! Hannah, Hannah. What has you done?"

"Nothing, I tells you. Nothing at all."

Mrs Brigstone ignored this disclaimer of guilt. Instead she continued in the previous vein, working herself up into a fine state of indignation. "I thought you was a decent girl, Hannah Neston, not some flibberty-gibbet like most of the girls around 'ere your age. I can see I'll need to keep a close eye on you. Next thing I know, you'll be sneaking off with the delivery boys what comes here. Probably hopin' to do 'eaven knows what disgusting things behind the washhouse."

"Behind the washhouse?"

"It would serve you right if the master did come up behind you one day an' tip you over, pull up your skirts an' 'ave his way with you, right there. You'd soon learn what it's like for a girl to be used as some rich man's plaything, then thrown aside to starve or walk the streets."

This was too much for Hannah, whose eyes blazed with fury at such unfairness from a woman she had thought her friend.

"Well if he did, at least he'd show some sense. He'd never try to make a plaything of you."

Her reward for this insult was a stinging slap across the face and a mouthful of curses she had never imagined Mrs Brigstone even knew.

"'Ere!", Mrs Brigstone said at last, her own face now twisted with rage and indignation. "I got the master's coffee ready. Get out of my kitchen and take it to him. Just that, mind. Don't go flaunting yourself in front of 'im, or whatever you've been doing. I'll be watching you, Hannah Neston. Start playing around and one of us will have to leave this house, you or me. I don't believe the master ever looked at you like that. It's just your filthy mind. Go on! He'll be waiting."

When Hannah came back into the dining room with the coffee, Adam was alarmed. The girl had clearly been crying and there was a fierce, red weal across her left cheek.

"Hannah?" he said. "Are you alright? Have you hurt yourself? Come sit here and let me see."

The thought of what Mrs Brigstone would think if she saw the master touching her cheek was so terrible that Hannah fled at once. She could not be persuaded to leave the privy, where she hid herself, for some time after. Meanwhile Adam called Mrs Brigstone and inquired the nature of the problem.

"That girl's a bit overwrought, sir," his housekeeper said. For all her railing at Hannah, she could not bring herself to get the girl into trouble. Nothing had happened and it was likely all in her mind anyway. She must be, what, seventeen now? A difficult age, the older woman thought. Not a child and not quite a woman either. "Stepped on a broom left lying on the kitchen floor and the 'andle upped and hit 'er in the face. I reckon it's ... you know ... that time ..."

Adam did know, being a doctor, but it still embarrassed him to have Mrs Brigstone draw his attention to it.

"Very well, Mrs Brigstone. If that's all it is, tell her to go to Mr Lassimer and ask him for an ointment to soothe the bruising. He can send the bill to me." With that, he dismissed the whole matter from his mind.

Mrs Brigstone did not. For the next several weeks she kept such a close watch on Hannah that the girl considered giving in her notice. Only the sure knowledge that she would find it hard to find such a good position in any other household in Aylsham kept her from doing so. As for 'special looks' – and men in general – she decided to avoid both, if all they brought her was such trouble.

ADAM'S THOUGHTS about the riot in Norwich were proved correct sooner than he thought. His breakfast over, he decided to walk down the street to Peter Lassimer's shop and dispensary. There he hoped to indulge, if he could, in one of their lengthy discussions of the ways of the world in general and Adam's latest puzzle in particular. Yet he had gone no further than his own front door when a man rode up on a large horse. That he carried a letter from Wicken was plain. No one else Adam knew had use of the King's Messengers. And such this man must have been. He had the royal arms on his saddlecloth and a horse much too fine for ordinary folk.

Adam took the letter from him and returned inside. Letters from Wicken were never of the kind that might be set aside to be read at a time of greater leisure. If he had written, it must be to seek action on some point.

As always, the letter was brief. Wicken must have set down his thoughts as soon as news reached him of the riot in Norwich and the two men hurt there. They were, of course, his men. Now he was more than angry about their treatment. He had instructed the local magistrates to investigate, but had little faith in them. He wanted Adam to find out all he could and write to him on the subject as soon as possible. How Adam was expected to do that, Wicken did not say. He clearly did not concern himself with such trifles. The man was so used to issuing orders and having them obeyed on the instant he had forgotten he was not addressing one of his hired men.

That matter over, Wicken immediately changed the subject of his writing. His local spies had discovered Toms had spent time in several Norwich hostelries, looking to hire a chaise to take him out of the city. He seemed to know where he wanted to go, but not the route to be taken. Since he was pressed for time, he did not want to risk getting lost along the way. All they could discover of his destination was that it was somewhere northwards, towards the coast. They could not even be sure whether he had managed to get the vehicle and driver he wanted.

For the moment, Wicken added, he was forced to wait on events. He had neither more men to send to Norwich, nor the time to come himself. Finally, since by the end of the letter he had recollected to whom he was writing, he made a most humble and gracious appeal for any information Adam might be able to provide.

As Adam later reflected, this request gave him all the permission and encouragement he needed – which was little – to involve himself in a new puzzle. What it omitted were suggestions on how he might go about it, and access to the resources needed. Still, he need not be held back by such problems. Already an idea was forming in his mind. He would recruit the people he needed himself. Then he would set them to seek out information in Norwich with far less visibility and upset than Wicken's constables had caused.

He was not allowed to think about this new task for more than a few moments either. He heard another knock at the door, muffled voices, and Mrs Brigstone telling someone to wait for a reply.

It wasn't a fresh call for his help, but an urgent request that he should visit Mossterton Hall at the first possible opportunity. Sir Daniel Fouchard was asking for him. Lady Fouchard too was most desirous of seeing him as soon as might be convenient. Since this sounded ominous, Adam decided he must set aside all other plans for the day and go to Mossterton at once.

"Tell the person who brought this message I will be on my way as soon as my chaise is ready, Mrs Brigstone," Adam said. "Then ask William to have Betty harnessed and between the shafts as quick as he can. Has Hannah gone to see Mr Lassimer?"

"She 'as, Master."

"When she returns, send her back again with a message for Mr Lassimer himself. She is to ask him if it will be convenient for me to call upon him at ... what is the time? ... say two hours at least ... between three and four this afternoon. If it is not, tell her to find a time when it will be. Is that clear?"

"It is, sir. Shall I prepare you some vittles for your journey?"

"No time, I fear. Still, I'll not starve after that excellent breakfast you made for me. Now, be off and set all in motion. I have only to get my medical bag and a coat and I will be off too."

12

BACK AND FORTH

Adam may have been in a great hurry to reach Mossterton when he set out some fifteen minutes later, but Betty was not. She was not accustomed to being taken from her comfortable stable and hustled into her harness with so little ceremony. As a result, she decided to sulk – a skill she had polished to a fine edge of perfection. This involved refusing to go faster than a moderate walk. Added to this were sudden stops to express unreasonable fear of some harmless object by the roadside. Finally there were continual cold looks delivered in Adam's direction over her shoulder. Had she been the temperamental and spoiled mistress of some great lord, she could not have put on a better display. It was all injured innocence oppressed by unreasonable demands.

As a result, it took near fifty-five minutes to make the journey to Mossterton – a trip that ought to have taken thirty at the most. Adam arrived in a state of simmering fury. Had there been a knacker's yard nearby, Betty would never have made the journey home again.

Adam was greeted at Mossterton Hall by a cheerful-looking butler. His experience of that breed had been limited thus far to the sour, supercilious and usually alcoholic variety. This was a most pleasant change. With a cheery smile, the man informed him that Sir

Daniel's orders were to take the doctor to his room as soon as he arrived. Later, when the two of them had finished their 'little talk', Adam was to ring for a servant. That servant would conduct him to Lady Alice. After that, the broader smile implied, Adam's fate was in the lap of the gods.

On entering Sir Daniel's room, Adam was struck once more by its lightness and airiness. Just as yesterday, the shutters were open and the curtains pulled back as far as they would go. Weak sunshine flooded into the room. He fancied one window was even open to a small extent. He could smell grass and sheep and the faint tang of the sea from afar off.

Sir Daniel was propped up in bed, frail as ever, but possessed that morning of an energy lacking the day before. As Adam moved towards him, ready to begin his examination, he raised one hand and pointed to a chair set ready by the bed.

"Sit, Doctor," he said. "Let us not waste time with the usual rigmarole of examination. Thanks to you, I had the first night of unbroken sleep I have had in months. It has brought me a small return of life, which I do not intend to waste on unnecessary trifles. Sit, sir!"

Adam sat.

"I knew your father," Sir Daniel continued. "Not well, but I knew him. A most companionable and cheerful man, but the worst estate manager and the most reckless with money of any man I met. To be frank, it was a wonder his fortune lasted as long as it did. All gone now, I suppose?"

"Not quite, Sir Daniel," Adam said. "My elder brother, Giles, is squire at Trundon Hall. My father's early death deprived us of a most loving parent, but it saved us from utter ruin. In the five years that have passed since, Giles has proceeded a fair way along the path towards restoring the estate to some kind of stability."

"You're a younger son then? One of those who must make their own way in the world?"

"That is so. I have no taste for soldiering or sailing the seas; nor any for becoming the rector of a dull parish and devoting my life to the raising of bees, the study of rocks, or publishing books of turgid sermons. I had no money to begin a business. Doctoring or the law were all that was left."

"No, my friend – I hope I may call you that – you do yourself no justice with such remarks. You did not choose medicine, even as a last resort. It chose you."

"It is a hard task-master, Sir Daniel."

"Life is a hard master, Doctor, whatever profession or calling we follow. Look at me. I inherited great wealth. Over the years, I have added to it a good deal. I should have been able to end my days quietly, looking out across my acres and smiling upon a brood of children who would share all I had achieved. Life has decreed quite a different end. Four times I have married, Doctor. Four times I was lucky enough to find a wife who regarded me with affection and planned to rear my children. It never happened. One went to her grave childless and two died in the effort of bringing new life into the world. None of my offspring, few as there were, reached their fifth birthday. Now my fourth wife is to become a widow at two and twenty."

There was nothing to be said that could mitigate such a catalogue of woes. Adam sat silent.

"The bulk of my estate is entailed on the next male heir, so title and most of the lands will pass to a most stupid fellow, Doctor," Sir Daniel went on. "A wastrel, as I hear. The son of a cousin of mine who takes after his father – a fool who blew out his brains after he had been caught cheating at cards. Another futile attempt to win back a little of the fortune he had wasted at the tables. Such is the idiocy of families like mine. Still, I have taken care that my wife should block my nephew from getting his hands on his inheritance right away. She has the right to live in this house, and manage this estate along with the other trustees, until she dies or marries again. As you have seen, she is young and healthy. She may even outlive him." Sir Daniel produced a wheezing laugh that ended in a burst of coughing.

When he had recovered, he waved Adam back to his seat and continued his relating of the future as he expected it to be.

"Alice will be rich enough in her own right, of course," he said.

"She will get back the lands she brought to me on marriage and have a good portion besides on which to live. All the lands I have added to this estate, here and elsewhere, are mine to leave to whomsoever I wish. It is only the Mossterton estate proper that must go to that young puppy of a nephew, along with the baronetcy." Another burst of coughing.

"Sir Daniel," Adam interrupted. "I pray you not to exhaust yourself. I have no doubt that you have taken the greatest care over your bequests. These are matters to discuss with your attorney, not with me."

"Yes ... my attorney ... need to call him here." The sick man's strength was starting to fail him.

"Have you taken a dose of the other medicine I had made up for you, Sir Daniel? The one for use during the day?"

"Not yet. I felt so well, you see ..."

Adam rose at once and crossed to pull the cord that would summon a servant. When the maid arrived, he sent her to ask for her master's daytime medicine, with a small glass of port wine into which it could be mixed.

"As I told you yesterday," Adam said to his patient, "it will dull your pain, nothing more. It has a most bitter taste, I fear, which is why I usually tell patients to take it mixed with a little sweet wine. Then you must rest, sir. I am most glad to see you somewhat recovered, but you must not imagine this respite is anything more than temporary."

Sir Daniel looked up at Adam and managed a faint smile. "A wise warning, sir. Some say those who are dying are granted some clear sight of the future they will not see. Do you believe that, Doctor? No, I can see that you are as great a sceptic as all the medical tribe. No matter. I will say my piece all the same. Any one can see that you are a fine doctor. Perhaps only a dying man can see that you will, in time, be a great man as well – far greater than your father would have been, even if he had not squandered his money. Let your brother take on the role of squire. You are destined for much more important things."

"Hush, sir," Adam said. "Look, here is your medicine. Drink it down. Yes, I said it would taste bad. I will pour just a little fresh port wine into the glass to take the taste away."

The maid had waited to remove the dirty glass, as Adam thought. However, her real reason was to deliver a message.

"My mistress asks me to bring you to her, sir. That is, if you have finished speaking with the master here."

"We are finished, Molly," Sir Daniel said. "I have no more strength for today. Will you come again soon, Doctor? Please say that you will. I have so few people to talk with. A fresh face is worth a thousand pounds. Nor have I forgotten that puzzle of yours we talked about. You must tell me how it progresses and I will use such brains as I have left to assist you in untangling it, if I can. It has already occurred to me to wonder whether that messenger fellow – the one who ended up in the river – had any links to this area before he came to Norwich the last time. Did he have relatives to visit, perhaps? That might show where he went while he was in these parts. No, I must not delay you here further. Be off to see my wife, doctor. She is not a patient woman and it will not do to keep her waiting ... come again ... I beseech you to come again soon ..."

Adam promised that he would. For nearly all the rest of the baronet's short stay on this earth, Adam strove to make daily visits. It held Adam in Aylsham when he longed to be elsewhere. Yet who was to say that it did not, in the end, prove one of the essential elements in solving the mysteries he was grappling with?

Adam found Lady Alice seated in a small parlour, with a book open in her hand and a drowsy kitten purring on her lap.

"Forgive me if I do not rise to greet you, Doctor," she said. "This little tyrant has only just tired himself enough to fall asleep. Thus he graciously lets me read without demanding all my attention be directed to him. How did you find my husband?"

"Somewhat recovered, my lady, I am glad to say. A solid night of sleep has done much for him. However, he must be careful not to exhaust himself. As I have told him, this state is but a respite, not the beginnings of a recovery. He has found already that his strength is far less than he hopes it may be."

"Have you agreed to visit him regularly? He was most anxious on this point. For what they are worth, I will add my own entreaties to his, sir. I do my best to keep him amused, but I am only one. It is all I can do to keep my own fears at bay. Besides, he needs masculine company as well."

"I have promised your husband I will come as often as I can, my lady."

"That is kind. Let me be honest with you, Doctor. When dear Miss Jempson pressed me to call you, I agreed only for her sake. I had no faith that her enthusiastic description of your ability was more than some … partiality. Doctors have come and gone from this house in numbers without doing any more good than a flock of sheep – save that sheep would not send disgraceful bills of account afterwards."

"It saddens me that you have come to such a low estimation of my profession, my lady," Adam said. "There are some indeed who promise much, while their eyes are dazzled by their estimation of how much they may look to gain from a rich family such as yours. Thankfully, they are but a minority. The rest of us do what we can. What hampers us is a lack of sure knowledge and an even greater lack of the tools to effect recovery."

"Nay, sir. Do not seek to defend them, nor include yourself within that number whose good intentions mask their weak abilities. I am delighted to discover for myself that all Miss Jempson said of you is true. Indeed, she told me but half of the truth. In one day, you have accomplished more for my husband that all the others did in months of visits. One day!"

"My lady, do not estimate my abilities so high, for so I must surely cause you even greater disappointment than would otherwise be the case."

"Fiddlesticks, sir! I speak but the truth. Nor it is your abilities I am praising, great as they may be. It is you – your character – that has made the difference, Doctor. You are the first who has troubled to sit with my husband and talk with him as two men together. You are the first who has promised to return for further conversation, even though you know that nothing will put off the inevitable. The first who grasped that, when a cure is impossible, all efforts should be directed to making my husband's death as easy as it can be."

Her eyes were shining. Whether with the vehemence of her speech or with tears for her husband's death Adam could not have said.

"I do not have the power to thank you enough, Dr Bascom," she went on. "Nor will I ever have, though I live to be a hundred. And not just for what you have done for my husband, sir, but what you have done for me as well. I too slept last night for the first time in weeks. This morning, I have been able to sit here, with this little darling for company, looking out at the world with some hope that my nightmare is ending."

"My lady ..." Adam began.

"No, sir. I will bid you good day at once, lest I say more than I should and more than propriety will allow. Come again soon, very soon. My husband will be most glad to see you ... and so will I." With that, she rang a small bell set beside her chair and the maid returned in an instant. The speed with which this happened seemed indeed to bear out Sir Daniel's remark that it did not do to keep the lady waiting.

"Dr Bascom is leaving, Molly. Please show him out. Farewell, Doctor. Once again, I offer my poor thanks for all you are doing for my husband."

ADAM KNEW that Peter Lassimer would be eager to know the effect of the compounds he had made up for Sir Daniel. He would also wish to catch up with news of Adam's other activities. The next morning, therefore, as soon as he had completed his breakfast, he made his way to the apothecary's shop.

Although the calendar suggested spring must be advancing, the heavy clouds and constant drizzle gave the lie to such optimism. People hurried along the street, trying to avoid the mass of puddles and the clinging mud. None stopped to pass the time of day, for who would linger outside longer than they must in such foul weather? Adam found himself continually moving to one side or the other. First to pass some lady with her head held low to avoid the wet, then a servant sent to fetch some necessity and mightily upset to be thrust outside. A few banged into him and hurried on with a perfunctory apology. One even omitted this act of politeness. By the time he reached Peter's shop doorway, Adam was soaked through, bruised and in a generally dismal mood.

Pushing inside, he found Annie at the counter. Her habitually cheerful face was clouded like the day outside. She greeted him with no more than, "Himself is in the compounding room, Doctor. You know the way." Then she turned back to some small task she was doing, leaving him to take off his own coat and hang it on the coat rack in the corner. Finally, Adam entered the compounding room, after giving a quiet knock on the door. Something was much amiss. It made him nervous.

Peter was head-down, absorbed in making small pills on the board he had for that process. Yet when he looked up, his face was cheerful and his manner quite normal.

"Bascom! I thought you might be here yesterday, but you did not come. Sit down, man. What dreadful weather we are having. Wait but a moment and I will be done with this task and can give you my full attention."

"Thank you," Adam said. "I intended to visit you yesterday, but I was called urgently to Mosterton Hall."

Peter looked up sharply. "Not bad news, I hope. Your receipt for that opiate was strong, but it should not have proved fatal."

"Nor did it," Adam replied. "Fear not, friend. I was called there to hear good news, not bad. It seems Sir Daniel spent a quiet night and awoke much refreshed. He is still in pain, of course. Still I have good hopes that the tincture of willow bark you made up for me will assist during the day. I found I was there to receive somewhat embarrassing thanks from husband and wife."

"I hope you made mention of the skilled apothecary who made up the medicine for you."

"Indeed I did, and bear their thanks to you also. We both stand high in their estimation – at least at present."

"And will remain there," Peter said. "Do not be such a pessimist! Well, that is most satisfactory. And what other news do you bring me from all your running to and from Norwich? I gather you made yet another appearance at an inquest in Gressington. I swear you attract murders, Bascom. All is quiet here for decades. Then you arrive and two men are murdered in that wretched little village within twelve months. Now, my friend. Sit there and tell me all, for I am agog for news. Forgive me if I do not call Annie to bring coffee for a while yet. She is not best pleased with me and is like either to throw the coffee over me or put some foul-tasting herb in the cup."

"Yes," Adam said. "What ails that girl? When I came in, she scarcely acknowledged me."

"She is leaving me, as I believe I told you was likely. Having failed to tempt me into a proposal of marriage, she is off to try her luck elsewhere. You know ..." He assumed a knowing expression and looked Adam up and down in the manner of a butcher considering a fat bullock. "... I thought at one time she might even set her cap at you."

Adam spluttered and turned an interesting shade of pink. "Me, sir? I assure you I never gave her the least encouragement of that sort. Never! Why, I scarcely looked at her."

"No? I suppose not, when your eyes have been engaged in surveying more tempting fare. How is the lovely Miss Jempson, by the way?"

Adam's complexion grew even more pink. "Miss Jempson?" he said. "Why, well enough, I imagine."

"I expect you imagine other things as well. No matter. Then there is the delightful Miss LaSalle. All these visits to Norwich must have given you ample opportunity to improve your acquaintance with her. And now Lady Alice Fouchard too, another young beauty. I declare you are a magnet to the ladies of these parts."

"Lady Fouchard is married!" Adam gasped.

"Indeed. But that seems never to be much impediment to members of the nobility. Besides, before long, she will be a widow, and a rich one at that. I suppose that thought has never crossed your mind?"

At last, Adam had himself under control again. Peter delighted in teasing him, but this had gone too far.

"It is in poor taste, sir, to make a jest of a husband's death. Sir Daniel is a fine man. I have no doubt his wife is deeply attached to him, despite the large difference in their ages."

Peter had the grace to look contrite at this rebuke. "Forgive me," he said. "I meant no harm, as you know. It is just that sometimes you sit in this room looking solemn as an owl and I cannot resist the temptation to tweak your tail feathers. However," he continued, the grin returning to his face, "neither Miss LaSalle nor Miss Jempson are spoken for. So ... which one will you marry?"

"Neither, I imagine," Adam said, as sternly as he could. "So let us leave my affairs alone for a while and turn to yours. Annie seems sad enough to be leaving you, yet you are cheerful as any grasshopper on a June morning. Explain yourself, Lassimer."

"There is nought to explain. Annie is not sad, she is angry because I am not more upset at her news. If you knew anything about women, Bascom, you would understand that. It is one thing to announce you are leaving and be begged to stay, and quite another to be wished God's speed and a happy voyage. Her pride is hurt by my refusal to play the role of the jilted lover."

"Could she have expected it?" Adam asked. "She must have known that you have ever treated women as a bee treats a flower. You flit from one to the next, interested only in what attraction they hold for you."

"Expected it? Probably not. Hoped for it, wanted it? Very much so. Men always over-estimate their attractiveness to women. Women – especially pretty women – easily assume all men will be dazzled by their charms. To find otherwise is a bitter blow."

"Did you not find her attractive?" Adam said. "I always thought her unusually pretty in face, figure and manner."

"Hah!" Peter cried. "At last you admit it. I knew you had cast your eyes over her and liked what you saw. Oh, not as a wife. She was a fool if she ever thought that. You will marry for money and breeding, like all members of the gentry. But a pretty, willing mistress to warm your bed would be another matter."

"Lassimer," Adam said in a warning tone. "We are not all as lascivious as you. Well, if Annie is upset because you will neither marry her nor grieve at her loss, I suppose the widows of these parts will rejoice."

"As many do, when I chance to call. For heaven's sake, Bascom, do not be such a puritan. Enjoy life. It comes but once. I have told you before those fits of melancholy you are prone to are due to your unnatural abstention from the pleasure of the bed."

"And will doubtless tell me again," Adam said. "Enough! You asked for news of my patient in Norwich. He is recovering slowly. He knows his own name and where he is, but he cannot yet recall anything else."

"So you have nothing to report on that subject?" Peter said. "No matter. Let us turn instead to the murder of the miller of Gressington."

"I have little that is new on that either," Adam said. "I wish I understood more about the circumstances of the attack on his mill. To do so might give me some insight into why anyone would want to murder the man."

"It is as well that I can help you then," Peter replied. "First, yon miller was a most unpopular man, with a well-deserved reputation for greed and dishonesty. All millers are suspected of some such failings. He was known to be privy to every trick of his trade: adulterating the flour, giving light weight and cheating both farmers and customers. In these uncertain times, you can be sure he was holding back grain to increase the price. His kind ignore the need of local people in favour of the better prices to be found in London or overseas. To my view, it is a wonder his mill was not attacked before."

"So the riot was against an unpopular, dishonest miller, who was guilty of all that was alleged against him?"

"I would say that was so. I do not hold with violence, but I cannot bring myself to condemn men driven to extreme measures by such as the Gressington miller."

"Even murder?"

"No. That I will not lay at their door. For a start, all the supposed ringleaders of the riot were in custody, so must be innocent. For the others, why kill the man? Why risk the gallows? To riot is to make a public statement, hoping to cause those about the area to take note of your grievances. Some may want to cause damage to the property of those they judge guilty. That is so they will share the pain and repent of their ways. But murder undertaken in stealth accomplishes nothing but the death of one man. It is a crime of cold hatred, not anger."

"You may be right," Adam said. "So who might hate the miller thus?"

"Any number, I suppose. He cheated many. Still, it takes a good deal of hatred – or a mind used to violence – to kill in cold blood. I would look to the smugglers in these parts. They are hard, vicious men, well used to death. That miller was known to be in league with a good many of the smuggling fraternity. He hid their contraband at his mill and transported it, concealed within sacks of flour and grain. It is also said he acted as a place where those who wished to use the smugglers as a secret way into or out of England might hide until the arranged time."

"So why would they kill him ... the smugglers, I mean?"

"If he cheated them as he did others, they would kill him for sure. They would also kill him if they suspected him of betraying them. There could be several more reasons. Feuds between groups. Too many captured loads whose loss was thought to be the miller's fault. The temptation to help himself to a portion of the contraband before sending it on its way."

"This seems most sound reasoning," Adam said, "but do you have any evidence to back it up?"

"Evidence?" Peter replied. "How could I? Can I go to the leader of the smugglers – even if I knew who that was – and ask him to tell me whether anyone killed the miller on his orders? No, if such as the smugglers are behind this murder, you will never have evidence of their crime."

Adam was disappointed, for he knew Peter's words to be the simple truth. To blame the smugglers seemed an excellent solution. It might also account for the miller's purchase of the gun to defend himself. Stealing from the thieves? Betrayal even? It all made sense. Was the miller one of Wicken's spies? Would Wicken have told him if he was? Well, he would worry about it no more.

"I thank you for these thoughts, as always," Adam said, "but I must go now. I have too much neglected my patients and my practice, and I fear that neglect is not yet at an end. I have promised to visit Sir Daniel as often as I can. He is lonely, as well as in great pain. His wife tends him with great devotion, but she is but one person to talk to. I have done all I can for him as a doctor. Now I must do my best to help him as a friend as well. But one thing, before I leave ..."

"Your curiosity would make a cat ashamed, Bascom," Peter said, smiling. "Very well, ask what you will."

"Are you truly as free from sadness at Annie's departure as you claim?"

"Of course not, but I will never tell her so ... and nor must you. You know how fond of her I became. I even offered to teach her enough to deal with those who come to the shop to buy simple remedies. She seems to have interpreted that as a hint at marriage. She was a good servant and a pleasant face to look upon beside me on the pillow ..."

"So you did bed her!" Adam said. "I knew you would."

"Of course I bedded her – and she was as eager for it as I was, believe me. Nor did she come to me a virgin. No, Bascom, she has treated me badly and I will have my revenge by smiling upon her as she leaves."

"A poor revenge," Adam said.

"Yet all I will take," Peter replied. "I have written her a fine reference to give to a future master and agreed to pay her in full to the end of the time we agreed when she came to me. I do not think she will stay in Aylsham. My guess is that she will go to Norwich in search of her fortune. I only hope she does not fall into the hands of the wrong people there. They will convince her that her path lies smoother through the bawdy-house than an honest kitchen. Many a country wench has taken that route and lived to regret it."

"You speak truly," Adam said. "Well, you can do no more for her. Though I cannot applaud your small revenge, I will not betray it. I have no doubt some lonely widow will soon put a genuine smile back on your face."

"As I have said often enough, that is a remedy you should try, Bascom."

"Now I truly must go, or you will be seeking to sell me some of your quack medicines as well as your immoral advice. Farewell, my friend. I will be sure to visit you again as soon as I have more gossip to give you."

"See that you do," Peter called after him. "And do not forget my advice, moral or not. You need it."

13

PROGRESS AT LAST

I t seemed to Adam that he was destined never to have the time free to deal with his medical practice. No sooner had he arrived home than he heard a banging on the front door and Hannah came to find him.

"Captain Mimms begs your pardon for arriving unannounced, Master," the girl said. "He asks if you be able to spare him a little of your time."

"Show him in here," Adam said. Pray God this would be a brief visit. If not, he would have no time to spend on the needs of his patients or to make his daily visit to Mossterton Hall.

As Hannah turned away, he added, "When you have done that, bring us a jug of punch and glasses. By the way, how is the place where the broom hit you?"

"The broom ...? Oh, yes ... the broom, of course. Better, thank you, Master. I went to Mr Lassimer as you told me. He looked all over my face and neck most carefully – in case there was any more damage, he said." I wager he did, Adam thought to himself, and took the opportunity to look down the bodice of your dress at the same time. Hannah was a well-built young woman. Peter would be more than happy with what he found beneath the fabric.

"Did he give you anything to help the pain?" Adam said.

"Oh, yes, master. Some ointment. Wonderful good it is too."

"Excellent," Adam said. "Now away with you and show Captain Mimms in here as I said."

Hannah bobbed a shaky curtsy and hurried off, relieved to have been asked no more. Despite all her resolutions on her future conduct around men, she had found Peter Lassimer's careful questioning much to her taste. The gentle touch of his hand on her cheek had also been far more arousing than was good for her new state of moral rectitude.

Capt Mimms came in with that rolling walk that denotes a man who has spent long years at sea, and the frank and open gaze of one whose mind is alert and whose conscience is clear.

"Good morning to you, Captain Mimms," Adam said.

"Good day to you, Doctor," the old man replied. "My most humble apologies for arriving in this way. Truth is I intended to send word ahead of me and forgot." He tapped his head where the large bald patch was edged with a stubble of snowy white. "Mind is failing along with the body. What happened to your maid? Someone slap her face?"

"I believe she stepped on a broom and the handle sprang up and hit her," Adam said.

"Believe that and you'll believe anything. Someone caught her a fair blow, I'd say."

"Well, it was not me, sir. I hope this day I find you well."

"Fair enough, given a following wind and twenty fathoms beneath the keel, Doctor. Said I would call on you on my way home to Holt. Now here I am, and glad to be away from Yarmouth. I told my sons they must either do without my advice, or at least meet me in Norwich. Those confounded roads are harder on an old man's bones than the worst gales I ever met in the North Atlantic. Make me take a carriage to Yarmouth and I ache for a month."

"Do you wish me to see if I can ease your discomfort?"

"No, no, Doctor. It's not too bad. I just enjoy a complaint now and again. That seems to lessen the pain by itself. No, what I wanted to speak to you about is that affair of the miller in Gressington. If the Norwich papers reported it truthfully, you examined the body and gave evidence at the inquest."

"That is true enough," Adam said, wondering where this could be leading. He hoped the old sailor was not about to spring something on him that would upset Peter's useful thoughts about the smugglers. He had only just begun to dismiss the idea of the miller's death as an unsolved murder. He had no wish to begin again.

"A good deal of turmoil and upset in Norwich at the moment. Yarmouth too, despite that mayor being so proud of dealing with the mob last year without calling in soldiers. Most of the gentry believe these riots are all to do with the price of food. The harvest last year was a bad one. This year's is likely to be little better. Always some unrest when people start to go hungry, you see. I remember in ... when was it? ... sixty-six? sixty-seven? Anyhow, some thirty years ago now ..."

Adam interrupted. While he knew he must allow Mimms to explain his point in his own way, he could not risk a long digression into events before he was born.

"Is it not the shortage of grain causing the trouble then?" he said. "Take that riot at Gressington two days before the miller's death. That was said to be due to want of flour at prices the labourers and the poor could afford."

"Maybe, sir. Maybe. I'll not say it wasn't. But what I've heard is that there are dangerous people about in these parts – republicans and radicals. Men infected with the disease that's destroying France. Agitators too, sent from France to stir up trouble. They find passage with the smugglers hereabouts, then wander about trying to weaken our resolve to fight. Irish, most of them."

Adam was becoming lost. "You think that radicals and those who support the ideas of the French revolutionaries are behind these riots? Not our own hot-heads? Nor just men driven to desperation by poverty and need?"

"All of those," Mr Mimms said. "But you draw me off the point, doctor." Adam grinned at that, but said nothing. "What I am trying to tell you is that this miller who was murdered was in league with the smugglers and the radicals as well. I shouldn't be surprised if he was even in league with the French. I heard say people have seen lights shown from the top of his mill, with other lights answering from out at sea. Our whole coast is infested with French privateers, Doctor. My sons tell me those devils seem to know when a group of merchantmen is setting out for the Baltic or northwards to Newcastle. Aye, where they are leaving from and by what tide as well. Then they lie in wait off shore and pounce. Captains used to be able to ransom their ships and cargo. No more. Now any ship as is captured is sailed for Dunkirk, the cargo sold, the ship used by the French, and the crew held as prisoners of war."

"And the miller's role in this?" Adam said, desperate to keep to the point.

"Didn't I say? Thought I had. My information is that he may even be the secret leader of one of the bands of smugglers who use the coast about here. Not all their leaders go to sea. Some stay on the land and deal with the transport and sale of the contraband brought ashore."

Oh Lord! That was another source of confusion to add to the mix. If the miller was a chief of the smugglers, they would hardly have been behind his death – unless there was treachery in the group. It would explain how he came by the smugglers' gun, of course, but nothing else.

"This is all most interesting, Capt Mimms," Adam said, "but we lack enough information to be certain which explanation may be the true one. However, just for the moment I am more exercised by some pressing questions that concern a patient I have in Norwich. I think I did mention him to you. A young man who was attacked somewhere, but managed to reach safety, though with his mind much disordered."

"Did you mention him? You may have done. Seem to remember something like that. Staying somewhere in The Close, as I recall."

"That is the one," Adam said. "Now, what I need there most at the moment is information. When last we met, you said you knew two men who might be willing to do a little nosing around for me amongst the poorer sort in Norwich, did you not?"

"Of course! So I did. Why didn't you remind me before, Doctor? You shouldn't have confused me by asking all about that chap in Gressington. I know just the men to help you. Peg and Dobbin. Good fellows who served under me many a year when I was still a ship's master. Poor old Peg lost part of his leg in a fight … but didn't I tell you this before?"

"You did, Captain. And you said you would contact them on your return to Norwich."

The old man hung his head. "Quite went out of my mind, I regret to say. Penalty of age. Always forgetting things these days. But when are you next in Norwich, Doctor? I'll send word to them to come to see you, if you'll but tell me where and when."

Adam thought of the effect a visit from a peg-leg sailor and a man with the size and intelligence of a horse would have on his mother's household. "I must go again to Norwich next week, Capt Mimms," he said. "Say Tuesday. Tell them to meet me in some suitable inn there."

"The Maid's Head, I suggest, doctor," the Captain said. "That's a suitable place for a gentleman like you and not too grand for Peg and Dobbin. Indeed, as I recall now, it's where the two of them have found work, for they can no longer go to sea. That will be an excellent place to meet. Tuesday then. What time?"

"Tell them to be there at noon, if you will. Now, sir. I am most obliged to you for calling on me. It's always a pleasure to talk with you, but I must not delay you further. You'll be wishing to be on your way home to Holt before it gets dark."

"Quite right, Doctor. Why, look how the time has flown. You really should not keep me here so long when you must know I have only a little time to spare. Still, I don't say that I don't enjoy talking with you, even if you do have a tendency to ramble off the point. Discipline, sir, that's what you need; a disciplined mind like mine. No point dancing around what matters most and running off after red herrings when there's full gale blowing towards a lee shore and sandbanks in the way. Got to be clear and decisive. I'll be off then."

By the time Capt Mimms left to continue his journey to Holt, more than an hour had passed. It was now too late to set out for Mossterton Hall in his own chaise, as he had intended. The old horse, Betty, would not be pleased to be taken out of her stable. Nor would she relish a trip to Mossterton and back without a decent time between journeys to rest in the palatial stables they must have there. Taking her into account was not a matter of sentiment. When she didn't want to work, she did all she could to be awkward. She would stop at the edge of the road to eat some delectable titbit only she could see. She would dawdle up slopes and sometimes refuse to climb them at all. She shied at the slightest sound or movement within fifty feet of her. Worst of all, she walked so slowly you felt weeks would pass in the shortest journey.

Still, he had made a promise and no horse would make him break it. If he sought a riding-horse from The Black Boys Inn, he could ride to Mossterton to see Sir Daniel, if only for a few minutes. Tomorrow he would make up for it by spending a good amount of time at the man's bedside.

Adam had grown fond of Sir Daniel. He was also coming to believe human contact was as much the cause of the man's improvement as the physic. Faced with a dying man, most people instinctively drew back or kept away. Maybe it took a physician well used to death in its many forms to stand his ground. The man within is unchanged, even if his body is collapsing into the ultimate decay.

Adam's irritation at the way his plans for the day had been thrown into confusion soon faded. He sent William to get a horse and set out some twenty minutes later. Along the way, he could think over what to do next. The weekend was approaching and he had much to complete before he could return to Norwich. If he went to Mossterton Hall again in the morning, he would have time in hand to visit one or two of his most important and local patients on his way home. Not so long ago, he had wished for nothing more than a break from routine visiting. Now the thought of it cheered him immensely.

As Adam was about to leave, someone else came to his house, but this time to the back. A delivery, probably. Certainly nothing to concern him.

In that he was wrong. After less than five minutes, Hannah came to say the visitor had been one of the servants from Trundon Hall, who had come on the matter of a new horse. Adam's brother sent word he had found exactly the animal needed. It was a strong young mare, placid in temperament and in sound health. Just four years old, the servant told Hannah, with that deep chest that always indicates a good wind. Since such animals were ever in demand, Squire Bascom had bought it on the spot. Now all that was needed was for Adam to send someone to collect the beast. Her name, it seemed, was Fancy.

Adam was delighted at the news, for old Betty had become a sore trial to him. He was tempted to send William, his gardener and groom, to Trundon Hall the next day. On reflection, however, he decided Monday would be best. There was no question but that he must keep old Betty until the end of her natural life or William would never forgive him. Horse and man had formed such a bond as existed between few married couples. Adam had not the heart to demand that it be broken now. No, Betty could stay in her accustomed stable and William could clean and freshen the spare stable for the new horse, Fancy. That would take him a good part of the weekend. Then he could go to Trundon on Monday on Betty and return riding the one animal and leading the other. When Adam went to Mossterton in the morning, Betty would have to do.

Adam's final plan was to take the Monday post chaise to Norwich from the Black Boys Inn. He would visit Sanford first, at the precentor's house, spend some time with his mother, meet Peg and Dobbin, make a final check on Sanford and return on the Thursday chaise. After his return to Aylsham, he could visit Sir Daniel again on Friday.

Greatly satisfied with these thoughts, Adam rode on. When he returned home he would take pen and paper and write at once to his mother to warn her of his arrival. He would also send a short note to Wicken with what little fresh information he had found.

THE NEXT MORNING saw Adam back at Mosserton Hall once more, as he had planned. When Lady Alice greeted him, a single glance at her face told Adam of her husband's state. The old man was both weaker and more troubled with pain. As he examined him, Adam noted the laboured breathing, the rapid, irregular pulse and the clammy feel to his skin. He was glad that he had taken pains to visit yesterday, even though it was so late. Glad too that today he was not pressed for time. He settled down by Sir Daniel's bedside to do what he could to ease the baronet's last days with conversation and human companionship.

Sir Daniel clearly knew his situation. He did not press Adam for false hope or demand more medicines to relieve his discomfort. Instead, he seemed delighted to be able to reminisce about his life. He recalled the good times and triumphs past and laughed at many of the woeful mistakes and setbacks that had once seemed so terrible.

It did not take him long to wear out his meagre strength in this way. When his breath came in yet more ragged gasps, he sank back into the pillows to rest and asked Adam about his own future plans.

"As to my future, Sir Daniel," Adam said, "I must confess myself uncertain."

"Then you are as all men, Doctor," Sir Daniel said, his voice weak now, but his mind as sharp as ever. "We plot and plan and declare we will do this or that. Yet all lies in the hand of chance – or Providence, if you prefer."

"That has been my experience already," Adam said. "When my father died, we feared his poor management of our lands must ruin us. Yet fate – or Providence – took a hand and one of our uncles, who was a most prudent man, died childless. The greater part of his wealth passed to my brother and allowed him to settle my father's debts. Thus he became squire of Trundon Hall without all those mortgages to weigh him down. He had no reserves, but at least he had no debts either."

"A most fortunate turn of events, Doctor. Yet, as a younger son, you must have known since your youth that you must make your own way in the world."

"I did. My poor father had hoped to make some provision for my future, but in that he failed as he did in so much else. Once again, it was my uncle's bequests that saved me. He left me just enough to pay to qualify as a physician. Thus, like my brother, I found myself entering my future path in life free from debts, but without anything more, save what I could earn for myself."

"You should count yourself lucky," Sir Daniel said. "Many a man who has embarked on his profession with ample money in hand soon founders. Want and need are great spurs to ambition and diligence. Without them, it is easy to become content with mediocrity."

"My good fortune went further than that, sir," Adam replied. "Last year, I became involved in the mystery surrounding the death of the Archdeacon of Norwich. I will not bore you with the details, for you must have read something of the case ..."

"Indeed I did and found much of interest in it."

"Through that circumstance, my name came to the notice of a good number of people in Norwich and roundabout. Many have since used my services as a physician. I had expected to struggle to establish a practice. Thanks to my notoriety in that case I soon had all the work I could manage ... and more."

"Yet I sense you are still unsatisfied, Doctor. Does your ambition stretch so far that you hope to reach the heights of your profession without toiling up the lower slopes?"

"By no means, sir. What bothers me is whether I am suited for that profession at all."

"Then set your mind at rest, Doctor. Never have I met anyone more clearly designed by nature for the care of the sick," Sir Daniel said. "No, it is not that. I would say that what troubles you is far worse."

"Worse, sir?" Adam said. "What can be worse that having spent a good part of your life qualifying for a skilled profession, then coming to doubt whether you are suited for it?"

"Realising you are destined for greater things, Doctor. Feeling afraid of the burden this places upon you. That is what is worse. I can sense something in you that may well foretell where your life will take you."

For several moments, the old man's strength failed him and he lay back against the pillows, his eyes closed and his breath coming in feeble sobs. Even so, he waved away Adam's attempts to urge him to rest. At length, he spoke again.

"No, Doctor. I will have an eternal rest soon enough. This is important and I must say it. Never be afraid of greatness, my friend. Embrace it. It is true that it may demand far more of you than the life of an ordinary man. But if it is your fate nothing less will bring contentment. You are discontented now with your life as a country doctor for that reason. It demands too little of you, not too much ..."

Sir Daniel's earnestness of speech was too much for him. He was forced to stop by a severe bout of coughing which took several minutes to pass.

"One more thing, Doctor – and this too is a serious warning. In the short time given us to talk together – which I deem a most cruel trick by capricious fate – I have found you to be a conscientious and serious young man. Do not take life too seriously. Do not do that, I beg of you. Nothing is certain in anyone's future but death. Enjoy yourself while you can, sir, lest, like me, you find your life snatched away before you are ready to leave it."

Sir Daniel could say no more. He dropped back against his pillows exhausted and fell into a fitful kind of sleep, too thickly laced with pain to do him any good.

Nor could Adam speak to comfort him, for his eyes filled with tears and his throat was too tight with held-back emotion to allow him words. After a long moment, he took Sir Daniel's hand. Thus he sat for maybe ten more minutes, allowing his tears free run at last. That was how Lady Alice found him when she came into the room. At once she left again, withdrawing as silently as she had come, save for the sound of her own quiet weeping.

∾

ADAM DID NOT NORMALLY VISIT patients on a Sunday, but Sir Daniel's state the day before had left him deeply concerned about the man's welfare. He could not put off his return to Norwich. Yet his heart told him he must not leave before satisfying himself he had done all that he could to ease the baronet's passing.

Adam arrived at Mossterton just before noon in a state of great trepidation. He was mightily relieved to discover that his patient had spent a quiet night. Indeed, Sir Daniel seemed to have found a new lease of energy from somewhere. His breathing was far less laboured and his voice had returned to something of its old strength.

For a while, the two men talked of pleasant trivialities and old memories. Then Sir Daniel leaned forward a little and, taking Adam's hand, turned so that he might look full into the young man's eyes.

"If you are willing, Doctor, I want you to make me a most solemn promise. No, wait. You must hear first what it is that I wish you to do. I know that I have little time left and must make use of it wisely. That is why I have summoned my attorney to come here early tomorrow morning. I believed that I had done all I could to ensure that my dear wife is properly provided for after my death. I see now that there was one most important omission."

Adam waited. It seemed to him that this was a private family matter and he felt embarrassed that Sir Daniel was speaking to him of it.

"My wife has a good mind and is a highly capable woman. I'm sure you will have noticed that. Even so, it is hard for a young woman to be alone in the world – especially one with a fortune at her disposal. In my will, I have appointed executors and trustees for my estate. Besides, as I have already told you, the bulk of it is entailed and will pass to my nephew. What I have not done is to appoint a guardian to assist my wife in handling her own money matters. That I will do tomorrow. Those are but cold, financial arrangements. She needs a guardian who is more than that. She needs a careful and devoted friend. I wish that friend to be you."

"Me!" Adam was startled.

"Yes, you, sir. I can think of no one better fitted for the role."

"But ..."

"I must ask you to trust me in this, Doctor, for I have neither the time nor the energy to convince you with arguments. Nor will I try to bind you to our arrangement through any legal processes, even if I could. All I ask is your promise, man-to-man. Will you give it?"

What could Adam say? The look in Sir Daniel's eyes, full of quiet pleading, tore at his heart. To refuse would be utterly despicable.

"Yes, Sir Daniel," he said quietly. "I will do as you ask. You have my promise."

After that, Adam thought Sir Daniel had fallen asleep, for he had fallen back onto his pillows and his breath came, not evenly, but less raggedly than in his waking state. He therefore rose as quietly as he could and prepared to slip out of the room. But, just as he was turning away from the bed, the old man's eyes opened and he spoke in a remarkably strong voice.

"There's something I almost forgot, young sir. That would be a pity, since it seemed to me when I thought of it to be most pertinent to the puzzles you are grappling with. Now, how does it go ...? It was such a long time ago that I last heard it. Ah, yes. That's it. *Non estia multiplicanda est sine necessitate.* You understand the Latin?"

"I do indeed, Sir Daniel," Adam said. "It's sometimes known as Occam's Razor. Elements should not be increased – or added, would be better – without it being necessary. If you must choose between two likely explanations, chose the one that is simpler."

"That's it," Sir Daniel said, his voice sinking again and his eyes drooping with fatigue. "Don't introduce characters you don't need. *Non estia ...*" His voice was barely a whisper now, then died into nothing.

"I must go and let you rest, Sir Daniel," Adam said. "Tomorrow I leave for Norwich, but I will come to see you again on Friday, when I return." But whether the dying man heard, it was impossible to tell.

Adam left the room with his own thoughts in such a tangled jumble that he feared meeting anyone before they had time to recover. Now, as luck would have it, as he stood waiting by the front door for a footman to bring him his hat and coat, he saw Lady Alice coming towards him.

"Well, Doctor?" she said. "Is all well between you?" Adam did not know what to say. Maybe she sensed his dilemma. Maybe she had never expected an answer. Either way, she continued without waiting for him to speak. "Have you given him your promise?"

"I have, my lady," Adam said. "Nor will I forget it."

"I do not doubt you," she said, "and nor will he. It was indeed a happy day that brought you into our lives, sir. You have brought peace to my heart as you have to my husband's. Will you come again tomorrow?"

"Alas, my lady, I cannot. I must go to Norwich for a few days. I have commitments there that I must attend to. I hope to return by Friday and will come again then."

"I understand, Doctor. You cannot be entirely at our beck and call. Let us hope you will come in time. Farewell then ... and please, hasten back, as soon as you can." With those words, she turned and walked away, allowing Adam to make his escape.

ADAM WAS SO DISTRACTED that evening, and ate so little at dinner, that Hannah mentioned it to Mrs Brigstone when she took the plates back to the kitchen.

"I reckon master be sickening for something," she said. "He didn't eat near anything for 'is dinner. Just sat there, all quiet like, staring at the wall. D'you think he's thinking on someone special, like? Some fine lady?"

"That wild imagination of yours will get you into trouble some day, my girl," Mrs Brigstone said. "Don't you go imagining things about the master. Man like him – stands to reason. He's got a lot on his plate. I expect he's thinking about some patient. He went to see that Sir Daniel Fouchard again today, so William told me. They do say the poor old man is dyin' a most painful death. That'd be enough to put any man off his food."

"It must be terrible troubling to be a doctor," Hannah said. "Imagine having all those people dying on you all the time."

Mrs Brigstone was indignant. "What d'you think you're saying now, my girl?" she said. "The master cures people. He doesn't kill 'em. You just watch your tongue, or the main thing you'll have to worry about will be my hand around your ears again. Now, get back to your work! Have you lit the fire in the master's bedroom? Put the kindling ready for the morning? Master has to be up early. He's leaving for Norwich. He won't want to be trying to get himself shaved, washed and dressed and eat some breakfast with you messing about with the fires."

"Yes, Mrs Brigstone. All that's done."

"Have you cleaned all the knives?"

"I'll do that tomorrow, Mrs B."

"You'll do it tonight! I got plenty of other things to keep you busy tomorrow, and the next day, and the day after that. I'll put a stop to your imaginings. Right, get them knives done now, then off to your bed. No reading either. We're not made of candles to be wasting them on you frettin' over some silly story."

"But parson says I must read all I can," Hannah protested. "If I don't, I'll never be good at it. That's what he says."

"He didn't mean some silly romance," Mrs Brigstone objected. "He meant an improving tale or some verses from the Bible."

"But words is still words," Hannah said.

"It's reading those kind of words that makes you answer me back," Mrs Brigstone replied. "You're so sharp you'll cut yourself, see if you don't. I've half a mind not to give you a candle at all. Make you go up them stairs in the dark."

Hannah shuddered. "You know I don't like that," she said. "I'm afeared of the dark. Old house like this, probably there's ghosts."

"Stuff and nonsense," Mrs Brigstone said. "I've been here more years than you and I ain't never seen a ghost. Be off with you! And make sure you get all the rust off them knives. I've seen what you calls 'cleaning' afore."

14

DISCOVERIES

Adam disliked getting up while it was still dark. Indeed, he was never keen to get up at all. He liked to start the day as gently as he could, then fortify himself for what was to come with a hearty breakfast. However, the chaise from The Black Boys Inn departed promptly at six-thirty. That meant passengers joining a morning stagecoach from Norwich had time to breakfast at one of the inns or coffee-houses. Though Adam was not travelling beyond Norwich, he had to keep to the same schedule.

The morning was cold and damp, with a bitter wind blowing from the north-east. Exactly the kind of day that everyone living in Norfolk soon came to dislike. 'A lazy wind' the old-timers called it. Blew right through you instead of taking the trouble to go around. A wind off the frozen lands far to the north, crossing nothing but empty sea on its way to trouble folk with rheumatism and the ague. The four passengers huddled into their coats and hunched themselves against it. There would be no cheerful conversation along the way.

Adam's mood matched the weather. He had slept badly, as he usually did when he knew he had to rise early. The long, empty hours had given him far too much time to ponder the happenings of the past few weeks. Why on earth had he ever agreed to involve himself again in Wicken's problems? All it did was make his head ache and show him to be an even worse investigator than he was a doctor. He was still no further forward in finding out what had happened to Sanford and Toms. And as for the miller at Gressington ... if he had any sense he'd forget all about it, as he was sure his brother had already.

Thus it was that he reached Norwich sunk further into melancholy than he had been when he started. Indeed, he was so miserable and angry with himself he denied himself a proper breakfast. He took a single dish of hot chocolate before setting out to walk the few hundred yards to The Close.

Naturally, at such an hour the precentor's household had not even risen, so the walk was wasted. A good start to the day! He might, if he had been thinking sensibly, have gone to his mother's house. Even if she were still in bed, her cook would have welcomed him into the kitchen and made sure he had good food to eat. That, of course, would have prevented him from wallowing further in the bog of self-pity which had claimed him. Instead he strode up the slope from Tombland towards the castle on its mound. Then he wasted an hour and six pence on terrible coffee in a place called "Lampson's". Most of its customers were blear-eyed shopworkers about to start their day. There were also several young men who looked as if they had been up all night. Adam assumed they were trying to sober themselves enough to remember where they lived.

SOON AFTER NINE, Adam returned to Dr Hanwell's house. There he found Sanford sitting in a chair in his bedroom. He was already fully clothed and looked as if he had been freshly shaved. So much seemed normal. Many an invalid, when he begins to feel better, has the urge to leave his bed and start life again. To wash, dress and at least sit up in a chair. Maybe read a book or talk with a visitor.

Had Sanford decided to take up his life again? Perhaps. Much of his appearance would fit that pattern. Yet there was no book in his hand; no newspaper lying nearby, no writing materials. Until Adam had come in, he seemed to be quite alone, just staring at the wall in front of him. He did not even turn his head to see who had entered.

"Good morning, Mr Sanford," Adam said. "I'm glad to see you up."

Sanford said nothing.

"How do you feel, sir?" Adam tried to keep his voice as normal as possible. "Does your head ache? Do you feel dizzy or sick?"

Sanford stirred a little, but still did not turn his head. "None of those," he said, his voice dull and lifeless. "Nor, before you ask me, do I remember anything more than I was able to the last time you came."

"You have had a bad concussion," Adam said. "Such an injury may take some time to heal. Until then, it will be best to rest as much as you can."

"Rest ... Yes, rest is what I need. A long rest." Sanford's voiced tailed off and he resumed staring at the wall.

"Well, not too long I hope. You should be able to be out and about again quite shortly now, though I cannot yet sanction you returning to the work you were doing. That, I think, would be too demanding at this stage. Besides, you still seem somewhat low in your spirits."

Still silence. Then Sanford said, "This is indeed an evil world, Doctor. How can anyone be cheerful in the face of such great wickedness? Dark and hateful things flourish, while all that is lovely is snuffed out."

"Come, sir," Adam said. "Things are not as bad as that, surely? It is true that we are at war again, but we have fought the French many times and always come out the victors. I do not doubt we will do so again. Why do you not take a turn in the garden? I see no problem in that, so long as you wrap up well against the cold. There are at last some signs of spring. That alone is enough to make any man feel more cheerful."

"You are like Mrs. Hanwell," Sanford replied. "She comes and fusses over me, when I would far sooner be left alone."

"Mrs Hanwell is a fine woman," Adam said. "She has nursed you with great devotion, though she had no obligation to do so. If she fusses, it is because she is concerned about you, as I am."

"You think me ungrateful, Doctor. That is not the case. I merely say that I would prefer to be allowed to live my life in my own way."

"And what is that way, Mr Sanford?"

Throughout their conversation, Sanford had never looked at Adam once. His gaze had remained firmly on the wall before him. Now, still without turning his head, he said, "Do you have any specific reason for being here today, Doctor?"

Adam was startled. Such an odd thing to say. "You are my patient, sir," he said at last. "I come to satisfy myself of your progress."

"Then I believe you are finished. My progress is as you see, sir. I have nothing more to tell you about what happened to me. I'm sure you have other patients who need your attention. You would be doing both myself and them a great service if you left me."

Adam's natural anger at such a curt dismissal nearly overcame him. How dare this man treat him like a servant, to be called or dismissed at will!

"Very well," he said. "I will leave you, if that is what you wish."

And never return, if I had my way, you ungrateful, ill-mannered puppy, he said to himself.

Yet once he was outside the room and making his way back downstairs, his anger ebbed away, to be replaced by curiosity and concern. The last time he had seen Sanford, the man had been pleasant enough. What could have happened to change this? Was it true that he could remember no more of the assault upon him? He said he could not, but that proved nothing. Was the melancholy that he had suffered before the attack returning in even greater measure? Melancholy patients often resisted all attempts to help them. For a physician, it was one of the most frustrating aspects of a frustrating condition.

Maybe Mrs Hanwell could offer him some useful information? She had spent a good deal of time with Sanford and may have observed the change coming on. Adam looked around for some way to summon a servant, but found none. Not until he had made his way back to the entrance hall did he encounter a young maidservant, busy with some dusting. At once he dispatched her to enquire whether Mrs Hanwell was about and could spare him a few moments.

WHEN SHE RETURNED, the maid conducted him to the parlour, where Mrs Hanwell was waiting.

As briefly as he could, Adam told her of what had passed between him and Sanford. Then he asked her if she too had become uneasy about their patient.

"He said he could remember nothing more of the events of the past," Adam told her, "yet I am not sure I believe him. On the last occasion I was here, I might have done. Then I would have said that he had not only lost his recollection of the assault upon him, but also the melancholy that preceded it. Now that melancholy has returned in full force. Something has brought about the change, but I do not know what, and he will not tell me. Can you help me at all?"

"Perhaps ..." Mrs Hanwell spoke with obvious deliberation. "But it would be only my opinion. I have little direct experience of such a terrible state of mind. But there is something new. During the last few nights, Mr Sanford has suffered the most terrible nightmares. Twice or more each night he has called out in his sleep and raised the whole house with the uproar. Yet he himself does not wake ... or not at once. When he does finally wake himself, he will not speak or explain, though the tears upon his face are eloquent enough."

"Can you make out what his calls are?" Adam said. "Are they words, or just cries?"

"No, they are words and clear enough. 'Sally' is what he calls out, over and over again. Just that. 'Sally'. Though once I thought I heard him say, 'Lost'."

"Lost?" Adam said. "What can that mean? A lover? Has some young lady turned down his proposal of marriage? Did he give his heart to Sally, only to be rejected?"

"No ... " Mrs Hanwell said, "I would not judge Mr Sanford to be suffering the pangs of unrequited love. More some overwhelming grief." She paused, uncertain whether to speak further.

"Please continue," Adam said gently.

"You will think me foolish," she said. "As a little girl, I had a pet cat whom I loved as only a lonely child might. We seemed to spend all our time playing together. It even suffered me to dress it like a doll and carry it about. One dreadful day, I woke to find the cat nowhere to be seen. My nurse would only say it had been taken to heaven. Only years later did I discover that the poor creature had been found hanged in the stable yard. It was the victim of the most despicable behaviour by one of the grooms."

"Humankind are the cruellest of creatures," Adam said. "You must have been heart-broken."

"I was. Desolate. I cried for days. I would not eat. I could not sleep. Eventually, sheer exhaustion forced me to sleep and a kind nurse managed to tempt me to eat a little. My father brought me a new kitten, yet it was not the same. My grief ebbed away in time, but I never forgot the incident. Even now, I can scarce tell you of it without being overcome with grief. Many years later, I discovered my father had taken his horse-whip to the groom, then dismissed the wretch without a reference. Had I been able to lay my hands on the man, I would have served him as he served my darling Mopsy."

Adam had little doubt that she meant exactly what she said.

"From that time forward, I determined never to give my heart and risk such hurt again. Until I met and married, that is. My husband and I married as many do, Doctor. Our families determined on the match and saw we were introduced. Then, finding one another amiable enough and feeling sufficient attraction, we agreed to marry. Yet once we were wed, my dear husband always treated me with such kindness and respect that I cannot help but love him. If he were taken from me, sir, I believe I might for a time behave as Mr Sanford does. In my opinion, that poor young man is suffering the misery of a most cruel loss. Though whether Sally be sister, lover, child or pet, I cannot say."

Adam, against all propriety, found himself leaning forward and taking Mrs Hanwell by the hand. He could not stop himself; nor could he speak at first. He looked into her face and saw, behind the lady of maturity and status, that same little girl whose dearest friend had been snatched from her.

Then the moment passed and he removed his hand. "Not child, I think," he said. "Sanford is not married. Nor have I been told that he is close to any woman. Sister, perhaps ... or beloved pet. Thank you for telling me this. I am sure he finds these nightmares and dreams most painful, but they are a sign that his mind is trying to cope with whatever has happened to him. How do you find him otherwise?"

Once again, Mrs Hanwell considered her reply fully before she spoke. "On the surface, well enough. But there is much that makes me uneasy. It is as if he is always playing a part. Our Mr Sanford is, I would judge, a person much given to secrets. When he first began to recover his wits, what we saw was the true person. That is so no longer. Dr Bascom, I am certain he recalls far more than he has admitted to you or to me. How I guess this I cannot say, but I am convinced that it is true. He may well know who this Sally is, though he claims he does not. I do not believe him, sir."

Adam thought her words were likely true. Mrs Hanwell seemed fierce and outspoken, yet much of her own manner was a mask long worn to protect a most perceptive and sensitive nature. He now felt sure that Sanford was concealing whatever he had remembered about the last few weeks. Still, knowing the man's work and contact with secret matters, that was not surprising. Should he assume this reticence was any other than the habitual wariness of a man used to staying silent about much of what he saw and knew? What if it were more than this? Mrs Hanwell's impressions were making him wonder anew. Maybe he ought not to dismiss his unease too lightly.

"Go on please, Mrs Hanwell," Adam said. "I think you may well be right in what you say. Have you observed anything else about our patient? Anything else that may account for this lowering of spirits and the signs of returning melancholia?"

"Well, doctor," the Precentor's wife replied, "I ... Yes, I would say I have. Not when he thinks I am watching, of course. Then he is ... not cheerful, never that ... but amiable and calm at least. But these terrible dreams and night-time terrors must indicate some turmoil within. If I come into his room suddenly, perhaps without him hearing my step, I always find him staring at nothing. It is as if his sight is all turned inwards to places none but he can visit. Oh dear! You will think me a silly, over-imaginative old woman; the kind who jumps at every shadow and suffers the vapours on a regular basis."

Adam laughed. "Never that, I assure you. Never that. You have been of great help to me, Mrs Hanwell, and I thank you. Please keep attending to Mr Sanford's moods carefully and tell me what you observe. And, if there is any sudden change, send word to me at once. I will be at my mother's home for the next few days, then back in my own house in Aylsham. Oh ... I also suggested to him that he should take some brief walks in your lovely garden, provided he wraps up well. Perhaps the fresh air and an occasional sight of the sun may improve his mood – if the sun ever does consent to appear. Where the spring has gone this year I do not know. "

WHEN ADAM finally arrived at his mother's home, he was feeling tired and downhearted. He was sure Sanford had remembered a good deal of what had happened to him – maybe even why – but for some reason he had determined not to tell anyone. Was that due to the return of severe melancholia? Adam could not be sure even of that. So far as he could see, his way forward was blocked. All he could do was sit down and write a suitable letter to Wicken, giving him the latest news, poor though it was. He half-considered suggesting they give up.

He had scarcely seated himself at the desk in the small parlour and spread a sheet of paper before him when Miss LaSalle came into the room. So great was his distraction that even the sight of his mother's pretty companion failed to stir him.

"Ah! There you are, Doctor," she said. "We wondered where you had hidden yourself. Your mother asked me to find you and request that you come and join us in the parlour to take some coffee."

"I have a letter to write," Adam replied. "Perhaps when I have done that ..."

"Please, Doctor," Miss LaSalle said. "Your mother is quite worried. You have barely spoken to either of us since you arrived. I think she fears she has upset you in some way. I have tried to convince her that could not be the case, but she insists that I bring you to answer for yourself. Although it is not my place to comment on your behaviour, I do feel that you might try to show a more friendly face to the world."

"Perhaps I might," Adam irritated now, "if the world showed a better face towards me."

"Why should it, sir? I'm sure the world has more to worry about than the opinion you hold of it. It has always seemed to me that the world is much like a mirror. Scowl at it and the face you see scowls back. Smile and it will assume a more cheerful visage in return."

"I did not know you were a philosopher, Miss LaSalle," Adam said. He knew he was being disagreeable, but he could not help himself.

"Are not all women, doctor? Else they could never cope with the way men treat them. Now, please stop trying to annoy me and do as I ask. I promise I will give you many more opportunities to vent your bad temper in my direction if you wait but a little."

Adam was defeated. If she persisted in responding with such wit and good humour to his truculence, he might as well give in. Yet he was still sulky enough not to want her to see his change of mood.

"Oh, very well," he said, sighing mightily. "If I must ..."

"Indeed you must, sir. Now come along and stop behaving like a small boy whose playthings are taken from him. Reassure your dear mother that you are not annoyed with her or I will be angry with you. Like the cat you think I am, I assure you I can bite and scratch with a will, if provoked."

With that, she stood aside to allow him to precede her through the doorway – and to conceal the way she stuck out her tongue at his back, once he had passed.

It took Adam some minutes to convince his mother that he was simply feeling dull and disheartened and she had done nothing to upset him. Just when he felt that was all cleared up, she started again in an another, unexpected direction.

"Sophia?" she said, in the tone she had always used when Adam was still a mischievous little boy. "Was it you, then? Did you say something to upset my son?"

Miss LaSalle seemed too bewildered to speak.

"Really, mother!" Adam said. "What nonsense have you dreamed up now? Of course Miss LaSalle hasn't said anything to upset me. How could she? She is always politeness itself in her dealings with me. A paragon, in fact." The lie slid so smoothly off his tongue he almost believed it himself. Miss LaSalle's sudden start, and the look of total amazement she sent in his direction, pleased him enormously. That will teach you, he said to himself. At once his black mood dissolved as if it had never been.

"Very well. If you say so," Mrs Bascom said. "In that case, the problem must be you, which I should have realised in the first place."

"What problem do I have?" Adam said. Had they both gone mad?

"I have no idea," his mother replied, " but if I am not the cause of your odd behaviour, nor Miss LaSalle, you are the only other person here. So it must be you. Anyway, stop it at once, whatever it is. We are both agog to hear how matters have progressed with that patient of yours – Mr Blandford."

"Sanford," Adam said, shaking his head. "And they have not progressed at all. Physically, he is recovering. In his mind, he is going backwards. I also think that, for some reason I cannot fathom, he is concealing a good deal from me. It seems likely he has recovered some, perhaps all, his lost memories, yet he chooses to deny it. Unless his attitude changes, I can see no way in which we can ever know what happened to him. Nor discover what part he played – if any – in the murder of the King's Messenger."

For a few moments, all were silent, then Miss LaSalle said, "And you are sure no one else can help you with information on that matter?"

"Well ... not sure," Adam said. "How can I be? I know of nobody else who was present or saw anything."

"Have you sought out such a person?"

Miss LaSalle's simple question hit Adam's mind like a cannonball striking a barrel of gunpowder. It exploded in his mind and left him speechless. It had never occurred to him to seek out witnesses. He had simply assumed there was no one to be found.

Sir Daniel's words came back to him. 'When two events happen in the same place and near enough at the same time, the temptation is to assume they are connected. I counsel you to recognise that for what it is: an assumption only.'

What other baseless assumptions had he made? What else was unclear to him only because he was too dull of wit to sense possibilities beyond the obvious?

"Dr Bascom? What have I said? Have I upset you in some way?" Miss LaSalle's voice, edged with genuine concern, broke through Adam's fog of confusion.

"Upset me? Of course not. Miss LaSalle, I declare that you are as clever as you are beautiful. A genius!"

"Watch out, Sophia," Mrs Bascom said. "When a gentleman declares you to be clever and beautiful in the same sentence, you may be sure it is because he wishes to persuade you of something you had best avoid."

"Your son has never before said I was beautiful, madam," Sophia said. She sounded both wistful and bemused.

"Don't let it go to your head," Mrs Bascom replied. "I have long experience of his peculiar ways. He is full of praise because something you have said has set his mind off in a new direction. You are admirable because you served to stimulate his thoughts, nothing else."

Adam chose to ignore all this comment about him. His mind was churning around with such speed that he had neither the wish nor the energy to deal with anything else.

"Yes! Yes!" he said. "Of course. Seek out witnesses. Must be some.

No one does anything in this huge city without being seen. An advertisement in the newspaper perhaps? With a reward."

"An advertisement?" Miss LaSalle said, abandoning her attempt to draw out the pleasure of being called beautiful for any reason whatsoever. "The people you most need to reach will not be reading the newspapers. The reward is a good idea I grant you."

"I will not have a ragamuffin band of loiterers, ne'er-do-wells and others of the labouring classes coming to my door in search of a reward," Mrs Bascom said. "Mention money to people of that sort and you will have hundreds making up all kind of tales to claim it."

Adam subsided, crestfallen. They were right, of course. The kind of people who might have been loitering somewhere in the vicinity of the Bishop's Bridge after dark would probably be illiterate. None could afford to buy a newspaper either, or enter a coffee-shop to read one. Once again, Miss LaSalle came to his rescue.

"Indeed, madam," she said. "Such a thing would never do. But if Dr Bascom knew of someone who might spread word around amongst the right people. Someone who would undertake to send him only those with genuine information ..."

"Miss LaSalle," Adam cried. "Once again you have proved the sharpness of your mind and I congratulate you ..."

"Not on my beauty though," the young woman said softly.

"What? Oh ... that too, I expect," Adam said. "No ... tomorrow I have arranged to meet exactly the persons who may be able to assist me. Two former merchant seamen ..."

"Not here," Mrs Bascom said at once. "You surely do not intend to invite common seamen into my house, former or otherwise."

"No, mother. Not here. At an inn."

"I am glad to hear it," she said. "Well, we will expect to hear the outcome, especially since it has all been Sophia's idea. Now, what else have you been doing since last you were here? I have heard enough of people of the lower sort."

"Well, mother, I have another new patient. Sir Daniel Fouchard. Miss Jempson was kind enough to introduce me to his wife, Lady Alice Fouchard, who has asked for my help. Poor Sir Daniel is close to death, I fear, but I am doing what I can to ease his pain, for none can save him."

"Sir Daniel Fouchard," Mrs Bascom said. This was much more to her satisfaction. "A baronet, I believe. An older man with a young wife. I imagine Lady Alice is a fine person."

"She is, Mother, for she dresses in the height of fashion and is a most elegant and lovely person besides that."

"Elegant and lovely ..." Miss LaSalle said faintly.

"Indeed," Adam said. "She must be but a little beyond her twentieth year. She has a fine figure ..."

"Fine figure ..." Miss LaSalle said, more strongly this time. "And I suppose this Miss Jempson also has a fine figure and is of considerable beauty."

"Miss Jempson is a Quaker," Adam said.

"And may not Quakers possess such attributes, sir? Or are they reserved for those owning allegiance to the Established Church ... as I do?"

"Miss Jempson is a young lady of great beauty, Miss LaSalle, since you press the point. She has fine eyes and a most delicate complexion ..."

"Well, madam," Miss LaSalle said, interrupting Adam's litany of praises for Elizabeth Jempson. "I see you were right to warn me not to take your son's compliments to heart. It seems he is enamoured of every woman he meets who is less than fifty years of age. Even Quakers."

Adam stared at her in astonishment. "But you asked me," he said.

"It was well I did, Doctor, else I might have been deceived. With your permission, madam, I think I will go to my room. It is time I changed for dinner."

After she had gone, Adam turned to his mother in bewilderment. "What did I say?"

"I cannot understand how you have reached almost to your thirtieth year and remained so ignorant of women, my son," she said. "I am sure it is none of my doing. Perhaps if you had older sisters ..."

"What?"

Mrs Bascom leaned forward and patted her son's hand. "Never mind, Adam," she said. "One day, God willing, a woman will be willing to take you in hand and address your education in the ways of our sex. This is not a task a mother can do." She paused for a moment in reflection. "God send her great strength though, for I fear she will need it. Now, I too must retire and so must you. I understood you had a letter to write. Then we must both change for dinner. And do be prompt when the dinner-gong is sounded. You fall into some dream and keep us waiting more often than not. So … off with you to your letter. If you complete it quickly, you may even be in time to send a servant to catch the last collection of the day."

The letter that Adam now wrote to Mr Wicken was not the one he would have composed but half an hour earlier. Then he felt defeated. Now, though he explained the problem with Mr Sanford and his frustration with that young man, he went on to add that he had good hopes of discovering the truth about what happened though different means. Then, on an afterthought, he added a postscript asking Wicken to enquire whether any knew of someone called Sally, who might be important in Sanford's life. It was a long shot, but it might be his only hope.

Finally, he washed his face and dressed carefully in appropriate clothes, then sat in the chair beyond his bed to await the sound of the gong. This afternoon, at any rate, he would prove his mother wrong about his attention to proper behaviour.

15

PEG AND DOBBIN

A t the appointed time next day, Adam seated himself in a quiet corner of the main room of The Maid's Head Inn, a glass of porter before him. He did not have long to wait.

The two men who came through the door had to be the ones he was due to meet. The first to come in was a small, wiry man, wearing the faded blue clothes of a seaman. His hair was covered by a grubby cap and his face such a mass of lines and weathering that it could have passed for an engraved map of the world. The fact that he used a stick to support him and had a wooden leg confirmed the identification.

Behind him followed a true giant, well above six feet in height and broad as a church door. He too wore faded seaman's clothing, which strained over his arms and thighs and scarcely met at all over his massive chest. This was a carthorse of a man, slow but immensely strong and, if his face was any indication, as quiet and placid as all such beasts tend to be.

They were clearly well known in this inn, for those in the room waved or greeted them with a few words. Yet even while seeming to be engrossed in such greetings, the little man had picked out Adam in the corner. Now he came over and nodded respectfully, remembering at the last moment to stretch up a hand and pull the cap from his head.

"Morning, sir. I'm thinkin' you'd be the doctor Cap'n Mimms told us to seek out here."

Adam agreed that he was and invited the two to place their orders with the serving wench, then come and sit with him. The sight of Dobbin trying to perch on the stool provided nearly caused Adam to burst out laughing, but he managed to restrain himself in time.

"Thank ye kindly, Doctor," Peg said, when he too had settled himself and tasted his ale. "Landlord here has a good brew and makes sure to give full measure. With all the coaches which begins and ends their journeys here, I'm thinking 'e must make a good livin'. Now ..." another pull at his ale, "... the Cap'n says you got a job for me and Dobbin' here. Afore you starts to explain, Doctor, I'd better tell ye that Dobbin is a bit slow in his wits. For all that, he's as good a man as walks on this earth and a fine friend to 'ave alongside in any fight. Just you tell me what you wants and I'll make sure Dobbin understands."

"I want to trace a man," Adam said. "A stranger to these parts. In fact, the man they pulled out of the river a week or more ago now. I've been told he was in Norwich to meet with another man, who is a patient of mine. This second man was attacked and left for dead, probably on the same day as the first one – Silas Toms by name – was killed."

"Was 'e the murderer?" Peg asked.

"I don't think so," Adam said. "Toms was a big man, loud-mouthed and something of a bully, as I've been told. My patient is a scholar, not a fighter. Whoever attacked him struck him a fearful blow to the head. A blow that took away his memory of where he was and what he was doing at the time – or at at least, so he claims."

"An' you doesn't believe 'im?" Peg said.

Adam hesitated, then decided to stick to the truth. "No ... not now. I think that was the case, but I suspect he has recalled all since. Yet for some reason he does not wish to tell me."

"An' you needs to know?"

"Yes. Not that my patient is in any trouble, so far as I know. It's just that he seems so low in spirits, even to the stage of suffering true melancholy. Such people often conceal the cause of their illness. I may be able to heal his bodily hurts. Without a idea of what happened to him, or whether it was linked with the death of Toms, I can do nothing to ease the sickness in his brain."

"I understand," Peg said. "Used sometimes to get men like that after a fight at sea. During the fight, it's all noise an' smoke an' screaming. Cannons goin' off and balls smashing 'gainst the sides o' the ship. Like Hell itself it is. Afterwards, there are some who don't settle down again, like the rest o' us. I've seen men just standin', starin' at nothing an' shaking like a jelly – for 'ours after even. I've even seen some run stark mad and throw themselves into the sea. 'Tis a terrible thing to lose your wits, Doctor."

"Terrible indeed," Adam said, "which is why I want to help him, if I can. But can you ask about and try to find what this man Toms did in Norwich. He was here for several days. All I know is that he delivered a message to my patient, then was found dead in the river some four days later."

"We see'd 'im. In 'ere." These were the first words Dobbin had spoken and the sound of the man's voice made Adam jump. He had almost forgotten he was there.

"Aye, Dobbin. Reckon you be right 'bout that."

"Are you sure?" Adam said.

"Sure enough, Doctor," Peg replied. "Big, burly, loud-mouthed fellow. Strangers in these parts stand out, they do. 'Sides, he wasn't goin' down too well with the people 'ere. Treated them like fools. In the end, 'e got 'isself thrown out. But afore I goes on, Doctor, what d'you know of two men who was here not long after, also asking about this Toms? Looked like government men. We don't like their kind. Now, Cap'n Mimms 'as vouched for you, an' we'd trust him wi'out question or we wouldn't be 'ere. But who might you tell 'bout what we finds for you? Thass another matter, if you gets my drift."

"Of course," Adam said. "I'm not a government man, as you call it. Nor am I here for any purposes but my own. As for the two men you mention, I had nothing to do with them, whoever they were."

"Glad to 'ear it, Doctor. This is a respect'ble inn. No one in 'ere would tell 'em anything, but none did them 'arm either. I 'eard they was 'anging around other places – dangerous ones for a stranger to mess with – and got themselves into trouble. Those places be full of smugglers, free-traders and thieves. It don't go to turn up askin' questions and throwin' yer weight about."

"Yes," Adam said, "which is why I am asking you to help me. I doubt that Toms spent his time in the kind of places I can go into."

"No, Doctor," Peg said. "I'm sure 'e didn't. That Toms, as you called 'un, thought he could treat us like country fools. He believed 'e could go anywhere, no matter 'ow dark or dangerous. There's places in this city Dobbin an' I wouldn't go into wi'out knives in our 'ands. If 'e did, I'm not surprised 'e ended up in the river."

"Do you know what he wanted?" Adam asked.

"As I 'eard – and 'e spoke so loud as you'd 'ave to be stone deaf not to catch every word 'e said – 'e was lookin' fer someone to take 'im to Holt."

"Holt?" Adam said. "I wonder whatever for?"

"Can't answer that," Peg said. "None in 'ere would 'elp him, beyond saying as 'ow it be a good few miles away to the North. But, as I said, 'e ruffled so many feathers that he got 'isself tossed into the street outside afore 'e could press the point."

"Can you find out if anyone did take him to Holt?" Adam said. "I'll pay you fairly." He reached into his pocket and laid a half-guinea on the table. "The other half waits on your success."

The coin disappeared in an instant and Peg smiled at him. It was not a nice sight. He had few teeth and those that clung on were yellow and rotten. "Don't you worry, Doctor. Dobbin an' me will get you what you wants to know."

"Tell the man 'bout Amos," Dobbin said. It was clear he had been listening and following what was said, even if he stayed silent most of the time.

"Ah ... that were right queer," Peg said. "Dobbin's right, Doctor, an' I should've thought of that. There's a man been working 'ere, on an' off, for a few years now. 'Elps out in the stables mostly, but works as a potman in the evenin's too. Well, just afore that Toms cove gets 'isself thrown out, Amos comes in from the yard. Takes one look at Toms, turns white as a sheet and runs out faster'n a dog after a rabbit. What's more, no one 'as seen 'im since then. Just disappeared, 'e 'as."

"You said his name is Amos?" Adam said.

"Aye, Amos Tugwell. Not from around these parts, but fits in well enough. Don't know much more 'bout 'im than that."

"I've never heard his name mentioned by my patient," Adam said, "but it seems he knew Toms. Didn't like him either, by the sound of it."

"Plenty more like 'im then," Peg said. "Well, we'll be about your business, Doctor. If you can come 'ere tomorrow, same time, we'll tell you what we's discovered. An' perhaps you'll bring the friend to that golden coin you put down?"

"I certainly will," Adam said.

"Come on, Dobbin," Peg said, heaving himself up. "Let's go. Thank'ee fer the ale, Doctor. We'll be 'ere tomorrow, as I said."

"One more thing before you go," Adam said. "There's a similar pair of coins available to anyone who was on or near the Bishop's Bridge the night Toms was killed. That is, if he can tell me anything useful about what went on there. My patient may have been there too, you see. It's been suggested to me he might even have witnessed the murder. Then been attacked himself by the murderer to keep him silent."

"Ah ... I can see 'ow that might work," Peg said. "We'll put the word out, Doctor. Never fear. Reward like that will loosen people's tongues, I dare say."

"Talk to any first, will you?" Adam said. "I don't want to waste my time with the sort who will make up wild tales to earn the reward. I'm sure you'll be able to work out who might be genuine and who's chancing their arm. If you find someone who saw the murder – which I think unlikely – send them to me at once at this address. It is my mother's house, so please use this knowledge wisely."

"Indeed we will, sir. And we'll see what they 'as to say afore we lets you near 'em. A very wise precaution too, if you asks me. Right, is that it?"

Adam indicated that it was and the two men departed as they had come. Peg leading the way and Dobbin following faithfully behind him.

So, Adam thought, after they had gone. Toms had been in The Maid's Head – and probably other places – trying to find a way to get to Holt. Whatever for? No one suggested he had any local connections in Norfolk. Besides, Holt wasn't the sort of place an outsider would even have heard of. Why go there? It was fresh news anyway. As he had suspected, Wicken's constables had soon been sniffed out for what they were. No use expecting people here to tell them anything, even about a murder. The government was unpopular enough in these parts, without people's added suspicions of the Revenue. In these times of little work and less cash, the smugglers were the only source of regular work for poor men trying to keep their families alive. One night helping to shift contraband paid more that a whole week of back-breaking farm work.

And who was Amos Tugwell? Why had he bolted when he recognised Toms? Again it made no sense. Toms wasn't known to have been in Norwich before – at least, Wicken had made no mention of such a connection. That argued that this Tugwell must have come across him some place else. Toms was, by the little information Adam had, a bully, but there had been no suggestion of anything worse.

His mind full of questions without answers, Adam decided to take a walk along by the river himself. He hoped that doing so might clear his head. It wasn't an especially warm day, but there were a few signs of spring. Some of the blackthorn bushes looked as if they might soon break into blossom and buds were swelling on hawthorns and elders.

At the Bishop's Bridge, he paused and tried to work out what might have happened. Had Sanford perhaps seen Toms' murder? That might account for his distress, but not the blow to his head. And if the murderers wished to silence a witness wouldn't they have made sure he was dead? Had they been disturbed? There were few people walking this way in daylight. After dark, no one would come along here who didn't need to. It would be much too dangerous. So why had Sanford, a respectable young scholar, been in these parts – assuming he was? Meeting a whore? That was possible, but unlikely. If you had money in your pocket, girls could be found in more salubrious places than this. None of it made any sense.

Thus an hour and more passed in yet more fruitless speculation, until Adam could bear it no more. He made his way back to his mother's house to puzzle, fret and wait on events. There was little else he could do.

BEFORE GOING HOME, Adam decided, on a whim, to pay another visit to Dr Hanwell's house. He would see whether there was any change in his patient. Unfortunately, he found the young man even more melancholic than before and still denying he had any return of his memory. It seemed hopeless to prolong the visit. Adam left within half an hour. Still restless, he next called at a coffeehouse to catch up with whatever was in the London papers.

It was thus scarce an hour before the time for dinner when Adam finally returned to his mother's home. What on earth might he do to occupy himself the next day until he was due to meet Peg and Dobbin again? Not for the first time since he arrived, he wished he could visit Sir Daniel. Yet such a visit would occupy most of the day. It would not be wise to be out of Norwich so long. If Wicken replied to his letter promptly, as he usually did, there might be something in what he wrote that would need to be dealt with at once.

It was with such thoughts chasing one another through his head that he arrived at his mother's door and rang for someone to admit him. That someone proved to be Ellen, Mrs Bascom's housemaid. She was in a fine state of agitation.

"Ah, Doctor," she cried as soon as she opened the door. "You're back. High time too, if you'll pardon me saying so. I've been praying for your return this hour and more."

Adam was alarmed. Was someone sick within?

"What on earth is the matter, Ellen," he said. "Is your mistress unwell? Or is it Miss LaSalle? Both seemed in the best of health when I went out this morning."

"They are both well enough, sir. It's ... I don't know what to say ... there's this *person* in the kitchen, sir. I'm glad to say that cook and the housekeeper are both out, for I don't know what they would say about it. As for the mistress and Miss Sophia, I thought it best not to acquaint either of them with such a matter."

"A person, Ellen? Who is it?"

"A female person, sir. She says her name is Molly Hawkins and she was sent to you ... oh, bless my soul ... sent to you particularly, sir, by someone by the name of Dobbin."

Light began to dawn in Adam's mind. "What sort of female person, Ellen?" he asked.

The poor girl blushed to the roots of her hair. "A ... well ... I cannot say the word, sir. She told me she's a ... no! I cannot say it. A ... a ... a lady of the night, sir. And she says you owe her money!"

"It is not as you surmise, Ellen, so calm yourself," Adam said, laughing. "Molly Hawkins, or whatever her name is, has given me no services of that nature. Nor do I owe her money as she says. I have been seeking information about a certain event in the city and asked two people to spread the word that I will give a reward for anything useful. I imagine this young ... lady ... has come to claim it."

"She ain't no lady, sir, an' that's God's truth!" Ellen said angrily. "Now, if you'll beg my pardon for asking, will you please come at once to the kitchen and hear what she has to say? Then she may be gone before anyone else comes. The shame of it! Such as her in the mistress's own kitchen."

"Go about your duties, Ellen, and leave this to me. I did not expect anyone to come this quickly, or without prior warning. That is all there is to it. If anyone must answer to my mother for her presence, it will be me. Now, be off with you and leave us alone. She will tell me nothing if you hover in the background, full of righteous indignation."

When he entered the kitchen, Adam found a remarkably pretty girl, of maybe sixteen or seventeen years, seated beside the stove. As she saw him, she jumped up. "Are you the doctor?" she said.

"I am Dr Bascom," Adam replied. " I gather Dobbin sent you here. You have something to tell me?"

The girl smiled at him. Like most of her profession, she dressed in an approximation to the latest fashion, though somewhat ill-fitting and tawdry. Indeed, the arms that showed from the sleeves of her gown suggested the body beneath was far too skinny for what she wore. The bodice of the dress drooped over breasts far smaller that its original owner must have possessed.

"It's real warm in here, Doctor," she said. "You've no idea what warmth means to a girl like me, always on the streets. You wouldn't have a bite to eat, would you, sir?"

Adam opened the door and called for Ellen. He was sure she would not be far away. Despite his explanation, she was probably close by in case he might take it into his head to enjoy poor Molly's favours on the kitchen table. She would definitely not wish to miss the chance to report that to the other servants. The speed with which she appeared proved that he was correct.

She found some bread and butter – with a bad grace – and put it on an old, cracked plate, as one might do for a stray dog. When Adam told her to make tea, she looked at first as if she might refuse. Then the glint in Adam's eye, and the recollection that he was the mistresses' son, persuaded her to do as he asked.

Molly wolfed down the bread and butter as if she had not eaten for days, which might have been the case. The dish of tea she regarded with deep suspicion.

"What is it?" she asked.

"Tea. It will warm you inside as well as out."

"I ain't never drunk tea, sir," she said. "Don't know as 'ow it would agree with the likes of me."

"It will agree with you very well, Molly," Adam said. "Just take tiny sips. It will be quite hot at first."

"'Ot? A drink what's 'ot? Are you speakin' true?"

"Indeed I am," Adam said. "You said you like the heat. Now, sit back by the stove and I will seat myself here, at the table. Then sip your tea and tell me your story."

Molly took a tiny sip of tea, jumped at the warmth, then screwed up her face at little. "It's awful bitter," she said.

"I expect Ellen put no sugar in it," Adam said. "Here. Let me scrape a little of this cone into the dish for you. Now try it."

The expression on Molly's face after she had tasted the sweetened tea was worth anyone seeing. "I likes it!" she said in triumph. "I truly likes it. An' it warms me chest as it goes down too. Thank you, sir, thank you. Imagine me, in a fine kitchen, by a warm stove and drinkin' tea. 'Tis a true marvel."

"Now, Molly," Adam said. For all the experiences Molly must have had in her short life so far, she was still a child beneath. "What have you to tell me?"

"It's like this, Doctor," she began, pausing from time to time to sip more of the tea. "As you will 'ave guessed, I'm a whore. It's an 'ard life, it is. If I don't attract the gentlemen, I don't eat, simple as that. Trouble is, I'm too skinny for most on 'em. They gets a grip on me little titties, maybe feels up me skirt, then pushes me away and goes to find someone with a bit more flesh to whet their appetites. It's not my fault I'm thin, is it, Doctor? Some of us is made that way."

"That is true, Molly, though in your case I expect it's because you're young and half-starved as well."

"I'm eighteen, sir," the girl protested. "Been a whore nigh on four years. I got what men wants, even if it isn't what you call vol ... vol ..."

"Voluptuous," Adam said. "No, that's true, Molly. However, you haven't come here to discuss the failings of your customers. Tell me what you saw by the Bishop's Bridge that night."

"Right you are, Doctor. It were like this."

Adam sat in complete silence throughout most of what Molly had to say. Indeed, she so far forgot his presence, and the grand house in which she sat, that she lapsed more than once into the language of the street. Adam was neither shocked nor censorious. He took it as a mark of trust and even some verification of her tale. Had she been making something up, he was sure she would have been more aware of her words; more careful to tailor them to the audience. Indeed, what she related, with many digressions into comments on the coldness of the nights and the dangers of getting too far away from the other girls, was far too straightforward and predictable to be an imagined tale.

She had her 'pitch' on the roadway between the warehouses, the merchants' houses and the river, she told him. It wasn't the best pitch. Those were all taken by the more attractive whores with the more aggressive pimps. Still, it wasn't one of the worst either. There were men who sought out whores like her. Men who wanted little girls. Men who tried to work out their fantasies of deflowering virgins. She got by, but not much more than that.

From time to time, of course, she needed to piss. When that happened, she would call to the girls on either side of her to warn any interlopers off her pitch. Then she went along the river bank towards the Cow Tower. It was dark there and there were bushes where she could 'do her business'.

It was while she was crouched down in such a bush that she heard footsteps coming along the path. She saw two men, one approaching from each direction. One she described as a big, tall man; a 'bit of a bruiser'. The other was younger, smaller and had 'the look of a parson about him'. Not wishing to encounter any man in such a dark and lonely place – at least until he paid her first – she stayed put. That was how she heard and saw what took place when they met.

The big man seemed angry, she said, yelling at the other one that he should be finishing his work, not out wandering about. He said he'd been kept waiting "in this shit-house of a town" long enough and needed to be on his way.

The young man said something about not being able to make head nor tail of what he had been brought. That caused the big fellow to become even more angry, and he yelled that the other must think him a fool if he expected him to believe such nonsense. Then he demanded that 'the papers' be given to him at once.

"That seemed to make the young one real mad too, Doctor," Molly said. "He started to yell that he knew the other was a traitor and would see him hanged for it."

"Did you ever hear him call the big man by any name?" Adam asked her.

"Apart from the rude ones, you mean, sir? No ... I don't recall any ... oh, yes. Now I do. Once, just once, he called him Sly Bombs."

"Sly Bombs? Are you sure?"

"Something like that it were."

Adam suddenly grasped the truth. "Was it Silas Toms?" he said.

"That's it, sir. You got it right. Sly Toms or Bombs, like I said."

Next she had seen the two grappling with one another. The young one never had a chance. In her view, he fought like a little boy, where the older one knew how to land blows that were hard and accurate. At last, perhaps in desperation, she saw the younger man bend down and catch up a branch was lying on the ground. He swung it wildly and struck the big man a good blow on the head with it.

"He fell down, he did," Molly said. "Not fer long though. Next he's up with a roar and grabs the branch 'isself. 'Course, 'e knows what to do with it. 'E gives the younger man a right belt, full on the side of 'is 'ead. Down 'e goes, an' I starts to reckon 'e's killed 'im. Then t'other fellow gets involved."

"What other fellow?" Adam exclaimed. "You said there were only two of them."

"So there were, Doctor, at first. I 'adn't seen t'other one. 'E must 'ave been hiding in the bushes, real close to where I was havin' a pee. Fair give me a turn, 'e did, when 'e rushed out."

This third man, it seemed, must have crept up during all the shouting or been in the bushes all along. Either way, he dashed out and came up behind the big man – Adam was certain this was Silas Toms – and hit him with a cudgel he had in his hand ready.

"Just ran up behind 'im, swung that big, ole cudgel up 'igh, and brought it down – bang! – right on the top of the big man's 'ead. Big man went down just like 'e'd been poleaxed; like a bullock bein' killed by the butcher. Bang! 'Is knees gives way 'e's on the floor."

The third man didn't stop at that, though, Molly said. He seemed wild with fury, yelling and swearing and landing blows on Toms' head with the cudgel after his body lay on the ground. At last, after a good many such blows, this third man started to calm down. First he walked over to where the young one lay and looked down at him. Then he walked back to the big one, bent down and started to roll him over and over towards the bank of the river. It took him a few minutes, but in the end he managed to roll the body into the water. Then he stood up again and watched it float away.

All this time, Molly had stayed crouching in the bushes, afraid to come out in case the murderer realised what she must have seen and decided to kill her too. Next, this third man did a most surprising thing. He began feeling through the young fellow's pockets – to rob him, she imagined. He must have found something, for he fumbled in his own pocket and brought out a bit of candle and a flint. He lit the candle and seemed to be looking at a bit of paper. Then, to her great surprise, he managed to heft the young man onto his back and set off heading towards the Cathedral.

Once they had gone, she said, she dared to come out and run back to her pitch as fast as she knew how. The other girls made fun of her, asking if she'd met someone nice and had a friendly 'you know' in the bushes. She started to try telling them what she had seen, but they wouldn't listen. A man came along then and offered her sixpence for 'one up against the wall'. She tried for a shilling, but he wouldn't give more, so she took his sixpence and led him round to her usual spot between two warehouses. After that, she had three more 'takers' in quick succession – a marvellous turn of luck – so she took the two shillings and sixpence she'd earned (one man had paid the shilling) and went to buy herself something to eat. And that was that. Later, when the news of the murder broke, she decided to keep quiet.

"I didn't want to get involved, did I, sir?" she said. "No money in that. Couldn't bring back the dead, neither." She wouldn't have come today had it been anyone else but Dobbin who spoke to her.

"'E's always kind to me, Doctor. Slips me a few pence when he can and won't never even let me wank 'im off in return. Once, when me pimp 'ad knocked me about a bit, 'e saw what 'ad happened and sorted 'im out. My God, 'e near killed that pimp. But it worked. I ain't never been knocked about since."

Molly had no more to tell, so Adam gave her the guinea he had promised. Her eyes grew wide at the sight of the golden coin.

"Don't give me that, Doctor, I beg you. Anyone finds me with gold in me pocket will swear I stole it."

Adam took the coin away and replaced it with eleven shillings. These Molly quickly tucked into her pocket, saying she'd never had so much money at one time before. Then Adam took another golden half-guineas and showed it to her.

"I promised a guinea for useful information," he said. "I have given you half in silver, as you asked. If your pimp, or anyone else, sees it, you can say you had a lucky day. This half-guinea I will give to Dobbin to keep for you. Tell no one you have it. It is just for you, in case you are ever in worse need than you are today. And thank you, Molly. What you have told me has been of great use."

The girl seemed to be in a daze as she stood up, carefully checking she had put safe the coins Adam had given her. Then, at Adam's gentle insistence, she abandoned the warmth of the stove and the dish of tea – long empty now – and went back out into the cold of the late afternoon.

Later that evening, when Adam, his mother and Miss LaSalle were seated in the drawing room, playing a game of cards, Mrs Bascom had a question.

"I gather from Ellen's wild effusions, Adam, that you entertained a lady of the night – her words – in my kitchen earlier today. You even gave her bread and butter and a dish of tea. Is this true?"

"Quite true in every respect, mother," Adam said. "She had come in response to the offer of payment for information, which Miss LaSalle suggested yesterday."

"A quick response," Mrs Bascom said. "And was that all?"

"Yes, mother. I don't doubt Ellen has by now convinced herself that I spent the time in the most abject debauchery, but I did not. The poor girl, one Molly Hawkins by name, is but eighteen, thin as a rail, and suffering much from the cold. However, the information she brought was of considerable use and I paid her as I promised."

"I'm glad to hear it," his mother said. "You must always pay your debts. How sad it is that girls like that must sell themselves to earn a crust."

"She was most grateful for the warmth of the kitchen, Mother, so I did not hustle her away, as Ellen would have had me do. Poor Ellen thought you would be scandalised by the girl's presence and she would be blamed."

"Ellen is a silly child," Mrs Bascom said. "She also comes of a most godly household, which is guaranteed to fill her head with terrible nonsense. What you have told me of this Molly Hawkins makes me sad, not angry."

"It made me sad too, mother, so I will give her a little extra, to make up for the earnings she lost by coming here. I understand there is a man whom I met only today who is keeping an eye out for her. I shall see him again tomorrow and will make sure he continues to do so, as best he can."

"That is a kind thought," his mother said, "and seems to me to offer an excellent course of action. This city is full of girls like your Molly. It is impossible to stop the trade."

"It is indeed," Miss LaSalle said, "since there are so many men who take advantage of it."

Adam looked at them both gravely. He had planned on giving Peg the half-guinea to pass to Dobbin. Now he decided to increase the amount to a guinea. He had no doubt Dobbin would convince the pimp to leave Molly alone, even if he did sniff out her extra earnings. If the wretch had felt Dobbin's anger once, he'd fear to provoke it again.

Miss LaSalle spoke again. "This Molly," she said. "Was she pretty?"

This time, Adam saw the chasm opening at his feet and stepped aside.

"Yes, Miss LaSalle, she was," he said, "or as pretty as any girl might remain when she is cold, hungry, dirty, and chronically under-nourished. Pretty, as I say, but not beautiful. It takes a woman of a little more maturity to reach a true state of beauty. Many a girl loses her childish prettiness as she grows and never becomes beautiful. Certain children, who are less pretty at the start, develop with age to become true beauties after, say, their twenty-first year. I have met some like this, Miss LaSalle, so can vouch for the truth of what I say."

While Miss LaSalle tried to extract the meaning from that, Adam's mother smiled at him, saying quietly, "You are a quick learner, my son, once set on the right path." Then, more loudly, she enquired whether he was any closer to solving the mystery of Mr Sanford.

"I am almost there," Adam replied. "As soon as I have it all, I will be sure to tell you both what I have discovered."

"I will hold you to that," his mother replied. "Now, let us put an end to this card-game, for none of us have our minds upon what we are doing. Perhaps dear Sophia will sing for us, or play the pianoforte?"

16

MORE DISCOVERIES

As Adam had told his mother, he felt he had more or less solved the mystery of who killed Silas Toms. The assault on Sanford was also explained by Molly's evidence. It had indeed taken place on the same night, and in the same place, as the murder of Toms. The last blow Toms had given Sanford must have rendered him unconscious for some time. Then, suffering from confusion and memory-loss due to concussion, Sanford had either been carried back to the Precentor's house or taken close enough to make it on his own. Why had Toms' murderer done that? It seemed an odd act of mercy after such a violent attack on the other man.

Of course, it was still just a guess that this Amos Tugwell had killed Toms. Adam had no firm proof, though it was the most likely deduction, given what Peg had told him. Even so, it didn't help him understand why the man who rescued Sanford took such pains to be sure Toms was dead. Does a man who acts to rescue another from a beating – or worse – then kill the attacker in a fury and heave his body into the river? That must have been done for a stronger reason. Something like hatred or revenge. And none of this helped with the second mystery: the murder of the miller at Gressington.

Having a little time between rising and taking breakfast, Adam sat at the desk in the small parlour. There he composed a letter to Wicken. With matters as they were, it would be of little use to that busy man to burden him with a lengthy list of what was still in doubt. Instead, Adam wrote that he was on the verge of solving the question of the murder of Toms. If Wicken would but be patient, Adam would journey to London again to explain all, once the final pieces of evidence were in place. Meanwhile, he would be grateful for any information Wicken could give him on one Amos Tugwell. This man had been living in Norwich for some few years now, but must have been acquainted with Toms at some time. It wasn't quite a satisfactory letter, but it was the best Adam could do. Perhaps he would know more after his meeting later in the morning with Peg and Dobbin.

This time, the two former seamen were waiting for him when he arrived at The Maid's Head, empty tankards before them. Adam took the hint and ordered himself a glass of best porter at the same time. Then, once all had full glasses in their hands, Peg gave his report on what they had found since their last meeting.

"I gathers young Molly came to see you, Doctor. Dobbin tells me you quite bowled 'er over with your fine manners and your generosity. I 'opes what she 'ad to say was useful?"

"It was indeed," Adam said. "And while we are on the subject of Molly Hawkins, I promised I would give Dobbin some money to keep for her against a rainy day. To make up for the earnings she must have lost by coming to see me," he added, unable to keep himself from blushing a little.

Peg took the money, then winked at Adam. "Molly's a fine whore, sir. Bit on the skinny side for many, but she knows 'er trade ... as I expects you'll agree. Most kind of you to do things this way. That pimp she 'as is a grasping little toad and would 'ave all 'er cash if he could, long afore she could 'ide it away."

Adam was about to protest that his explanation had been the literal truth and he had not laid a finger on Molly. Then he reconsidered. What Peg thought was only what most men would have done. Nor would Molly have refused him if he had asked. Better to seem an ordinary man than make the two think he was trying to show himself superior to others. Besides, Sir Daniel had urged him to enjoy life while he could. It was time he put away his prudishness. Still, he was glad he had not taken advantage of Molly. To do so in his mother's kitchen was altogether a step too far!

"Now, Doctor." Adam realised Peg was speaking. "We got a bundle o' news for yer. I expect, like us, you think it was Amos Tugwell that Molly saw bashin' Toms' head in. Well, 'ere's some more things what points to 'im. As I told you before, when Amos saw Toms in 'ere the first time, 'e bolted. 'Owever, we been told 'e come back later and was askin' everyone what Toms 'ad been sayin' an' where 'e was stayin'. We've also been told Toms did a round o' several other inns, lookin' for someone to take 'im to Holt. Most o' that time, a man followed 'im around, quiet like. This man either lurked in some dark corner or came in immediately Toms left and wanted to know what 'e'd been up to."

"Was it Tugwell?" Adam asked.

"Can't say fer sure, doctor, but I reckon so. Anyhow, in the end Toms finds someone who says 'e'll drive 'im to Holt next day."

"Did Tugwell go after him?"

"Ah, you're a bright one, Doctor. Got ahead o' old Peg. Again, I doesn't know fer sure, but I reckon 'e did. See, landlord 'ere tells me 'e hasn't seen hide nor hair o' Amos since that evening Toms was 'ere. But the next day, an 'orse went missin' from the stables. Caused a bit o' a fuss, that did. Everyone blaming the other fer letting it out or leaving some door open so it could be stole. Then, bless me, but the 'orse is found next morning, all tied up safe an' well in the place 'e was took from. Now, what d'you make o' that?"

"Tugwell borrowed it to follow Toms."

"Right enough, Doctor. Amos 'ad always appeared to be an 'onest man. By my way o' thinking, 'e might borrow a ridin' 'orse, but 'e wouldn't steal one. I still can't rightly believe in 'im as a murderer."

"I wish I knew what he saw Toms up to in Holt," Adam said. "If he's disappeared we can't ask him either."

"Ah, now. Dobbin 'ad a bit o' luck there. The man who drove

Toms to Holt turned out to be a man in the city who Dobbin knows. Some sort o' relation. So Dobbin asks 'im what 'appened that day."

"Would he tell?" Adam asked eagerly.

"Sure 'e would, fer Dobbin. Seems once they was on their way, Toms asked him to go beyond Holt. Didn't even want to stop there. Offered 'im another guinea to take 'im on to some little village, right on the coast."

"Gressington?"

"Aye, thass the name. Couldn't quite recall it meself."

"The cabman took Toms there?"

"O' course. A guinea's a fair amount o' cash. Took Toms right to an 'ouse next to the mill. Waited outside perhaps ten minutes, then Toms comes out, 'appy as a pig in muck, and a bloke with 'im. That must 'ave been the miller, our man says, 'cos 'e was all dusty with flour. They shakes 'ands real cordial like and Toms 'ops up into the chaise and says to take 'im back to Norwich. So off they goes and that's an end on it."

Adam felt stunned. He had been so sure the two murders had nothing to do with one another. Yet here was a clear link, both with Toms and perhaps with Tugwell too. But if Tugwell had murdered Toms – which seemed certain – could he have murdered the miller as well? Why on earth do that? And why take no pains to hide Toms' death, yet dream up an elaborate scheme to make it look as if the miller had killed himself? Oh Lord, Adam said to himself, everywhere I turn in this affair I find more questions, but still no answers.

"Anything else?" he asked Peg.

"No, Doctor. Thass all. We'll keep lookin' fer Amos, but I'm sure 'e's well clear o' Norwich long ago."

Adam handed over the second half-guinea he had promised. Then a thought struck him.

"Just one more task, if you'll take it on ... oh, and another half-guinea for success," he said.

"Fire away," Peg said. "We're yer crew, so to speak."

"You said the driver of the chaise took Toms to Gressington, to a house by the mill. Can you find out all you can about the miller there?" He decided to stay quiet about his involvement in the inquest into the miller's death, in case that put him on the side of the authorities in Peg's mind. "It's an odd thing, but I heard somewhere that miller got himself murdered around the same time."

"Gawd!" Peg said. "I 'opes Amos ain't run mad, doctor. I always liked the man an' I'd 'ave sworn 'e weren't no murderer afore now. I finds it 'ard enough to credit 'e killed that Toms. But to kill another ..."

"The miller's death may be for quite another reason," Adam said. "It seems a group of men attacked the mill the day before, claiming the miller was hoarding grain to drive the price up. His death might be about that. I'm just curious, in case he was the one Toms went to see. I know the village a little. The only house close to the mill is the miller's own"

"Ah, I sees now. Hmm ... Thass a good way off our patch, doctor. Never been to those parts meself, nor Dobbin either, to my way o' thinkin'." Peg pondered for a few more seconds, then his face lit up. "I knows! We'll ask George Fenn, the carter. 'E goes to those parts – Holt and villages round about there – twice a week. 'E's bound to 'ave 'eard something. Good many millers been 'oarding grain, if you asks me, Doctor. Greedy buggers, all on 'em. Wouldn't be at all surprised if some poor, starvin' villager 'ad enough an' cut that miller's throat fer 'im. Yes, leave it to Peg an' Dobbin. I'll find George Fenn soon as I can and send you word." He smiled slyly. "Perhaps Molly would bring it personal like?"

"Perhaps," Adam said drily, "but I'd prefer to hear it from you direct." He wasn't prepared to take his 'man of the world' act too far. "You know where I am staying. I expect to be there until Friday, then I will return to Aylsham, where I live."

The three parted quite soon after. Peg and Dobbin went in search of the carter, while Adam returned yet again to his mother's house.

MRs BASCOM and Sophia were waiting for him when he returned, eager to know what he had discovered. Since he had given his promise on the matter, Adam settled down at once to tell all that he now knew. Both agreed that Amos Tugwell was the most likely person to have killed Toms. Yet neither could see why he should have done so.

"Tugwell must have known Toms before from somewhere," Sophia declared. "No other explanation makes sense, given his behaviour when he came upon him in The Maid's Head. He followed Toms about the city. At least, we must assume that was him. He even borrowed a horse to track him to Gressington. Maybe he discovered something there that made him wish to kill Toms."

"Indeed," Adam said. "That is my thinking as well, though I am uneasy at making quite so many assumptions on such flimsy evidence."

"So you need more, Doctor. Will your ... I know not what to call them ..."

"Peg and Dobbin? My searchers, perhaps."

"Will your searchers be able to discover the answers?"

"I do not know, Miss LaSalle. They admit their only hope is this carter they mentioned."

"Then you must go to Gressington yourself, Doctor."

"I? For what reason?"

"To investigate the miller's death."

"Nay, my brother would not thank me for that. He is the justice there. Any further investigation must come from him."

"But you have said already he takes little interest in the case."

"No, I said he has little hope of solving it. He also has many other duties to occupy his time."

"Yet now you can put him on the correct path, Doctor."

"Adam is correct, Sophia," Mrs Bascom said. "Giles is the justice there and none should interfere without good cause. So far as I can grasp all the twists of this matter, we have none. All we have is a series of assumptions and guesses lacking sound evidence. Would this girl Molly give evidence in a courtroom, Adam?"

"I am sure she would not, Mother. Nor would Peg and Dobbin. No one likes murderers, but most of the poorer folk around here fear the authorities more. No, if I made such a suggestion, they would disappear, I believe."

"So we are stuck again," Sophia said. It was clear she was angry at what she had heard.

"Not quite yet," Adam told her. "I had already thought of going to Gressington to make enquiries, but I cannot – must not – appear to be involving myself in the death of the miller. I can seek out what Toms was doing there and why, but no more. That I may be open about with my brother without fear of causing upset. First I will go home again as I planned to attend both to my practice and Sir Daniel. Then, when I have time enough, I will visit Trundon Hall, let my brother know what I am doing, and see what I can find out. Will that be sufficient for you?"

"It will," Mrs Bascom said. "No, Sophia. Please obey me in this. Let my two sons sort out between them what may be done with proper attention to the law. Great heavens! I knew Adam to be sorely afflicted with curiosity, but I declare you are as just as bad. Now, let us leave this subject and talk of other matters."

17

THE LAST DEATHS

W hen Adam woke up the next morning, it was as if he had never slept. Fragments of what people had told him were whirling around in his mind, yet none made any sense. Had Molly said something he had not recognised as important? Why was the man Tugwell following Toms everywhere? Why had Sanford called the man a traitor? What did he know that even Wicken did not?

When the truth hit him, it was as if a terrific explosion of light had seared across his brain.

Traitor! Molly had told him Sanford had shouted out that Toms was a traitor, then added curses and many other vile names. Traitor! Why had he ignored what she said? That was it! That was why Toms struck Sanford down; why Molly thought he was moving in to finish him off when Tugwell intervened. Of course!

Then another spasm of understanding produced the reason for Sanford's recurrence of melancholy and why he denied that his memory had returned.

Sanford didn't know Toms was dead.

How could he? Molly had said that he was on the ground, apparently unconscious, before Toms met his own end. He had himself examined the damage to the back of Sanford's head, so he knew she was speaking the truth. Sanford could not have returned to consciousness until after Toms' body had floated away down the River Wensum. When he did wake, muddled and confused, severe concussion had destroyed his memory of what had happened.

Since then, everyone treated him as an invalid. None would have talked to him of the murder. That wasn't a fit subject for a sick-room. So ... if Sanford had now recalled his belief that Toms was a traitor, he would wish to tell someone. But supposing he thought Toms was still alive – and had already tried to kill him to prevent his discovery being shared with the authorities? He must be terrified of leaving his current place of safety.

There he was. Caught between knowing what he had thought, and what Toms had done when confronted. Tormented by a fear that the moment he stepped out of the precentor's house, Toms would be on his trail, looking for an opportunity to do the job properly this time.

Hang on a moment! Why didn't he share his knowledge about Toms with Adam and let him pass it on?

Fool! Adam said to himself. That was easy. Because there was no way Sanford could know about the link between Adam and Wicken. He thought Adam was just a doctor called in by the Hanwells. Adam was certain he had never mentioned Wicken in Sanford's presence, and no one else in the house could have told him.

Sanford's work was most secret, as was the true nature of Wicken's role. So, Adam now suspected, was the knowledge Sanford had about Toms. The knowledge which had persuaded him to denounce Toms as a traitor. The poor fellow couldn't speak out to anyone here without violating whatever oaths he had sworn to keep silent about the nature and content of his work.

What Adam had to do to persuade Sanford to speak was to show him one of Wicken's letters. That would be proof that he was part of the secret and could be trusted to get word to Wicken at once.

THE FIRST BLOW fell when Adam had just completed his break-fast. Looking at his mother's clock, he decided it was now permissible for him to go to Dr Hanwell's house in The Close to talk to Sanford again. He would have liked to go the minute he had left his bed, but that would have been contrary to all politeness. He might be in a great hurry, but he had not forgotten his manners.

He was just rising from the breakfast table, intending to put on an outdoor coat and hat, when Ellen came in. With her was a young man Adam recognised as one of the Precentor's footmen.

"Begging your pardon, Doctor," the footman said, "but my master asks if you could come to his house on the instant. He said to tell you the matter is important and he is sure you will agree you should be informed at once."

Dr Hanwell met Adam in the parlour. Adam had been greatly alarmed by his message. Now the look on the Rev Dr Hanwell's face was ample confirmation that something of the highest seriousness had taken place. Nor did he waste any words.

"Your patient has taken his own life, Dr Bascom. My gardener found his body this morning. He must have crept out into the garden at some time during the night and concealed himself in the large shrubbery beyond the main area of grass. There he cut his throat with his own razor. My wife, as you can imagine, is extremely upset. She blames herself in some way. I have been unable yet to convince her that she bears no guilt for what has happened."

"She certainly does not," Adam replied. "I can bear witness that she nursed Sanford with the care and devotion of a mother. What-ever has caused this is not of her doing. If anyone must shoulder blame, it should be me for not recognising an event of this nature might occur."

"Let us not talk of blame, Doctor. To take one's own life is a most serious sin in the eyes of the church. We both know that the balance of Mr Sanford's mind was much disturbed. I would incline to the charitable view that he did this in a fit of insanity. However, he left a package and a letter, addressed to you, in his room. Here they are.

Perhaps you will be able to enlighten us further when you have read them."

He handed Adam two items. One was a leather pouch, neatly sealed. By the feel of it, it contained no more than two or three sheets of paper, or maybe four at most. The other was a letter addressed to Dr Adam Bascom. That too was sealed. Adam set down the pouch for the moment.

"With your permission, sir," he said "I will read this letter at once. It is possible that it contains some explanation of Mr Sanford's action. Then, again with your permission, I would like to examine the man's body."

The Precentor gravely nodded acceptance.

Sanford's letter was a single sheet, written in a firm hand. It was undated, so he might have composed it at any time. If he had written it immediately before going outside to kill himself, it proved he was experiencing no fear or nervousness at what lay ahead.

My Dear Dr Bascom,

I must crave your forgiveness for my action, after all your care and attention to restore me to health. I am not ungrateful, but I am sure this is the only way for me to save myself and my family from yet more suffering. Please will you also assure Mrs Hanwell that no blame rests with her. No one could have been a more devoted and careful nurse. I only wish I did not have to bring her suffering of any kind. At least my chosen place to end my life will avoid spoiling her bed linen or carpet.

With this letter I have left a leather pouch. It contains important documents which must be sent at once to the person noted below. I would have done it myself, but other matters intervened. Please Doctor, I beg of you, do not seek to break the seal. To send it on, unopened, will be the last and most important service you can do for me. I believe I may trust you in this, for you have dealt with me fairly at every stage. Do not let me down now.

I do not end my life lightly. It is, for me, the only possible action, now that I realise I am cursed with the same disease that killed my beloved Sally. At least I can be with her and at rest.

I am, sir, your most humble and grateful servant,

Charles Sanford

The name and address written at the end of the letter were exactly as Adam expected: Mr P Wicken, Home Department, Whitehall, London. Adam turned to the precentor.

"I will not read out all that is here, Sir. Some of it makes no sense to me at present. But listen to this short passage, which I believe may free your wife from any sense of blame for what has happened."

When he had finished, Dr Hanwell thanked him and led him out into the garden. All was exactly as he had described. Sanford's body was almost entirely concealed. He had presumably not wanted to alarm any one in the house, assuming the letter would be found before his corpse. The cut he had made to his throat had been done in a single, quick stroke, with no signs of hesitation or nervousness that Adam could see. It was the act of a man firmly determined on his course of action.

When the two men returned to the parlour, Adam took up Sanford's letter again.

"One thing is this letter does puzzle me, Reverend Sir," he said. "Mr Sanford refers to a disease that he has recognised in himself. I saw no signs of disease when I examined him. Only the dreadful blow to his head. Can you suggest anything that might account for his words?"

The precentor looked puzzled. "But of course, Doctor. He must mean the fits he suffered of late."

"Fits?" Adam said sharply. "What fits were these?"

"But he discussed them with you," Dr Hanwell said. "At least, that is what he told my wife. She said he had talked with you about them at length. You examined him and pronounced them distressing, but of no great seriousness. You told him people recovering from a bad concussion often reacted in that way. In time, they would pass and he would recover fully."

"He said nothing to me I assure you," Adam said. "Nothing whatsoever."

"But why would he lie to us?"

"That I cannot say. But you imply that your wife knew all about them."

"Indeed. Twice or three times, she told me, she had found Mr Sanford fallen on the floor, with foam at his lips and his body in a kind of spasm. Shall I ask her if she feels well enough to join us? Then she may tell you herself."

When Mrs Hanwell came in, the signs of crying were plain on her face, but otherwise she had herself firmly in hand. Her husband put his arm about her and would have begun right away with the request to relate what she knew of Sanford's fits. Adam stopped him, so that he might read her Sanford's own words. As he hoped, they caused her to brighten a little.

"I could not think what else I could have done, Doctor, but now those words reassure me a good deal," she said. "I will grieve for a life cut off and for a young man I had come to consider almost a member of our own family. But I will no longer blame myself."

"That is as it should be, madam," Adam said. "Now, if you feel well enough, it would greatly assist me if you could tell me all you can recall of the fits Mr Sanford suffered of late."

"But he told you of them," the lady protested.

"No, my dear," her husband said quietly. "He did not, whatever he said to you. The good doctor assures me he had heard nothing until I happened to mention them a few moments ago."

"That is so," Adam added. "He could not conceal the problem from you, since I gather you had found him in the midst of at least one fit. Since I was never present when one occurred, he could keep me in ignorance, whatever the reason. By assuring you he had discussed them with me, and even reporting what I had said, he could prevent you asking me about them yourself."

"I had decided to do just that, Doctor," Mrs Hanwell replied. "They seemed to be coming more often, which worried me. So did the casual way you dismissed their importance – at least as he represented your response."

"Can you describe what you saw?" Adam said. "Fits come in many guises, so I need to understand what happened to Sanford as precisely as I can, before I can form an opinion about the cause."

"Twitching, foaming at the mouth, a kind of bodily rigidity," Mrs Hanwell said. "His eyes would be rolled back and I would swear he had no consciousness of what was happening."

"Epilepsy," Adam said at once. "That would be my guess."

"Could it have resulted from the blow to his head?" the Precentor asked.

"It could. Yet what he writes in this letter suggests a belief in another cause. He says he is 'cursed with the disease which killed my beloved Sally.' That must mean that he has seen epilepsy before."

"Sally again," Mrs Hanwell said. "Who can she be?"

"Can you catch it from another?" the precentor asked.

"No. I have never heard of such a thing," Adam said. "It may be caused by a trauma, such as a blow to the head. It may have some other cause we do not yet understand. Without those words, one of those would have been my assumption in this case. Yet it would have provided no explanation for why Mr Sanford should seek to conceal his fits from me. No, I suspect this Sally is related to him in some way. Epilepsy is often suspected of running in certain families. If he had a relative who suffered epileptic fits, he might assume that his concussion had hastened what must have happened anyway."

"Can it be fatal?"

"Sometimes. Rarely of itself, I think. Some choke during a fit by swallowing their tongues. Some harm themselves in falling. As you suspected, Mrs Hanwell, a bad fit causes unconsciousness, together with a loss of voluntary action. If the sufferer fell into the fire in the grate, for example, he or she might be severely burned before being able to get themselves clear."

For some moments, they stood together in silence, each wrapped in imaginings of the fears that must assail anyone suffering a severe period of epilepsy. Then Dr Hanwell recalled them to practical matters.

"And so it ends, Doctor," he said. "I will summon one of the cathedral's own constables and have the body taken to a suitable place.

Will you need to examine it further to be sure of the cause of death?"
Adam shook his head. "Then I will contact the coroner, who will
arrange the inquest. I imagine it will be held tomorrow and he will
need your presence."

Adam had planned to return to Aylsham the next day, but there
was no chance of that now. His visit to Sir Daniel must be postponed
another day at the least.

"Fortunately," Dr Hanwell continued, "the cathedral exercises its
own jurisdiction over persons and events in The Close. Several of the
canons and prebendaries, including myself, are justices of the peace.
All that is necessary can be done with the greatest despatch. What
about informing the poor man's family? Have you any idea where
they live, doctor?"

"None," Adam said, "but I know someone who will. With your
permission, I will leave you now and hurry back to my mother's
house, so that I may send off a letter by the next post available. We
may hope to receive a speedy answer."

As luck would have it, Adam had just reached his mother's
house when he saw a man on a fine, black horse come to a stop
outside. From his appearance, this must be a King's Messenger
come from Wicken in response to his last letter. Hurrying forward,
Adam called out to the man at once. He took the letter Wicken had
sent him and knocked on the door. When Ellen came, he asked her
to bring the messenger some refreshment while he waited for the
letter Adam would give him to take back to London. The man would
not accept an invitation to sit a while in the kitchen, saying that he
must stay with his horse to guard against it being interfered with.
Indeed, such a fine beast was already drawing a good deal of
attention.

Thus it was that Adam dashed off the briefest of letters to Wicken,
informing him of Sanford's suicide and asking for details of his
kinfolk. At the last moment, aware of how his own curiosity would
react to such a bald statement of calamity, he added two sentences. In
the first, he assured Wicken that he was almost at the final point of
solving the mystery that surrounded Sanford. In the second, he

promised to come to London as soon as he could to explain all in person.

That done, he handed the King's Messenger his own letter and the packet Sanford had entrusted to him. The man stowed both in his saddlebag, then rode off along the street, already headed for London.

ALL ADAM WANTED WAS rest from what had proved so far a day of high tension and drama. It was not to be. Now he received a second blow, much worse than the first. Just as he was about to go to his room to change for dinner, Ellen announced that William the groom had arrived from Aylsham with a message for him.

Adam found William in the yard. The lad must have come in some haste, since the horse that had drawn Adam's curricle was flecked with sweat. This must be the new beast that Giles had bought for him. Betty would not have broken out in a sweat unless the hounds of hell themselves were chasing her – and maybe not even then.

Before his master could speak, William began to show off his new charge. "Her name's Fancy," he said, "and she be a strong and willing worker. Not as sweet-tempered as Betty though."

Only William could possibly describe Betty as sweet-tempered. He and that old horse loved each other more than most men ever love a woman. Adam had always found Betty lazy, cantankerous and bad-tempered – especially if made to work harder than she wanted. This new horse, he hoped, would be more amenable.

Eventually, Adam managed to interrupt William's explanations of Fancy's finer points to ask him for the message he had brought. William dug into his pocket and handed it over.

"A servant from Lady Fouchard brought it this morning, master," William said. "He did say it be most important that you should get it as soon as possible. So I gets the curricle out at once and comes to Norwich, in case you needs me to take you home straightaway."

It was as Adam most feared. Lady Alice wrote in haste. Her

husband had died peacefully during the night. His long agony was over. She added that she had sent word to her husband's great-nephew at once. He was now the baronet and would inherit the estate. She imagined he would be arriving as quickly as he could cover the twenty-eight miles or so from where he lived. It was going to take all her strength to deal with him.

Adam knew her husband's will would allow his young wife to remain at Mossterton for the remaining span of her life, or at least until she married again. That was usual. During that time, she would also have full use of all the estate's income. Neither provision would be of pleasure to the new baronet. He was known by all to be heavily in debt.

Lady Alice's letter ended with thanks for Adam's kindness to her husband in his dying days. She hoped he would also be a good friend to her as she learned to live on her own again. It was almost too much for Adam. His eyes filled with tears and he bent his head low so that William should not see such unmanly grief.

Adam's dearest wish was to set out for Mossterton Hall at once to bring Lady Alice what comfort he could, but that could not be. There was the inquest to be held on Sanford first. He could not leave before that was completed.

After a few moments, Adam managed to recover himself. "There's no haste to return to Aylsham," he said, his voice heavy with grief. "I'm sure my mother's housekeeper will find you somewhere to spend the night. We will go back home after I have completed various business here tomorrow."

Dinner proved a somber meal. Adam had nothing to say and ate little. The two deaths that day had left him dazed and confused. In Sanford's case, so many questions crowded into Adam's mind he was unable to imagine how he might ever sort them out. But it was the death of Sir Daniel that affected him most. Not since his own father's death had he experienced such a torment of grief and loss – and that for a man he had known for barely two weeks. However he tried to still his emotions, they assailed him with such misery that he knew not how to proceed.

Sensing Adam's mental turmoil, his mother and Miss LaSalle sat silent, as if in a house of mourning. It was the more surprising, therefore, when Ellen came in to bring the news that the doctor had yet another visitor. This one had declined to come inside, she said, and was waiting for Adam at the front door.

It was Peg, come to explain he and Dobbin had missed the carter, who had already left for one of his regular trips to Fakenham and Holt.

"'E won't be back till day after next, I reckon," Peg said. "But don't 'e fear. Us'll catch up with him then. Reckon we'll tell 'im to come back through Aylsham next time, so as 'e can call on you – that's if 'e got anything worth botherin' you with."

"Thank you," Adam said. Then his mind began to work more clearly and he added, "It's likely I'll have to go to London before then. I would not wish the man to have a wasted journey. Look, I'll come back through Norwich on my way home, so it might be more convenient to meet the carter here, if he's around. If that fails, I can at least leave word that I'm heading for Aylsham again."

"Ah, right enough, sir," Peg said. "You knows 'ow to find me and I knows 'ow to find the carter. If you be goin' to take the stage to an' from The Maid's Head, you can always leave word there."

18

RETURN TO ALYSHAM

Adam's journey back to Aylsham after the inquest on
Sanford was uneventful. It was also surprisingly quick.
Adam was struck by the difference the new horse made.
Where Betty had dawdled and crawled, Fancy stepped out in fine
style, seeming eager to show her new master what she could do. Even
William found nothing he might use to provoke an unfavourable
comparison.

It was high time he returned to his proper life, Adam thought, as
his curricle rumbled into Aylsham. He had neglected his practice
shamefully. Only his old friend Peter Lassimer had prevented its
complete collapse. He must shake off this interest in mysteries and
tell Wicken that he must find someone else to pursue his interests in
Norfolk. After all, he had only become involved with Wicken and his
secrets by chance. Since he had not sought to assist the authorities in
that way, he might with a good conscience lay down a burden which
was becoming too onerous.

Thus fortified with virtuous thoughts of resuming what he imagined as the quiet and blameless existence of a country doctor, Adam
reached his house in a more peaceful state of mind, if not a happier
one. The death of Sir Daniel Fouchard still weighed upon him.

Before he left Norwich, he had written a lengthy and careful letter of condolence to Lady Alice. It was one entirely appropriate to their respective circumstances: she as widow and he as her newly-appointed guardian. That was necessary, yet totally insufficient in his mind. What he wanted above all else was to be able to meet with her and share his deep grief at the loss of a man he had begun to see as far more than a patient. Yet to obtrude on the lady's grief without an invitation would be grossly improper. For the moment, at least, he must keep his sorrow to himself.

No, he would take up his old life, beginning with a visit to Peter to thank him once again for all his help over the past few weeks.

It was not be be. Less than ten minutes after Adam had arrived at his house, yet another King's Messenger arrived bearing a letter from Mr Wicken. Sighing, torn between curiosity and fear of yet more demands, Adam sat down in his parlour and broke the seal. What else could that powerful and devious man be asking of him?

Adam was right about the demands. With little more than the most perfunctory of preambles, Wicken launched into a series of requests. Could Adam find out as much as possible about who or what Toms was seeking in Holt? How long had he stayed there? Had he stopped anywhere along the way? Wicken declared the strongest possible interest in Toms' activities. Let that be Adam's chief preoccupation. If Sanford had labelled the man a traitor, he must have had a reason.

That was how the letter began. Next came a part, written untidily and in a great hurry, which must have been added after Wicken got the package from Sanford. He wrote that it held much of great interest, but such as he might not discuss by letter. He needed to see Adam face to face. Then, as if realising at last what he was asking Adam to undertake, to the ruin of his medical practice, Wicken's tone changed. In place of a series of near orders came something closer to a plea for help. Could Adam please come to London as quickly as possible? He promised most solemnly to make all up to him afterwards. This was now a matter of such great importance to the government and the country he must ask for his presence with the greatest speed.

There was still another postscript. Wicken wrote that Amos Tugwell had once been a King's Messenger and would have known Toms as a result. However, Tugwell should not be seen as of any great importance. Some two years ago, he was suspected of passing secret information to a French spy. However, he had got wind of what was happening and escaped before he might be questioned. It was interesting that he had turned up again in Norwich, but nothing more. The only information against the man had been from an anonymous letter. After careful enquiries, it became clear the whole affair was little more than an unpleasant attempt to blacken his character. They would have told him so, had he not fled beforehand.

Adam sat back and tried to take it all in. So ... Tugwell too had been a King's Messenger. That must be how he knew Toms. He was probably afraid to greet him because he did not know he was no longer under suspicion. So much made sense. What did not become any clearer was why he should have followed Toms about Norwich and tracked him to Gressington. Nor why he should kill the man, as they assumed he had.

Toms too remained an enigma. Sanford had called the man a traitor. So much Adam knew before. What had he written in the package sent to Wicken? Had he explained the grounds for his suspicion? Had he convinced Wicken that the man was indeed betraying his country?

Sanford, Adam had realised, did not know Toms was dead. That would explain any plea on his part that the man should be seized as soon as possible. But Wicken did. It was too late to investigate Toms' actions and find evidence of betrayal. So why was Wicken so interested in what the man had been doing in Norwich? Did he hope to find other traitors in the city and the area round about?

Adam's mind seethed with possibilities and ideas. Yet that was all they were: ideas and theories. Without more evidence, he could see no way to sort them out. Wicken's letter implied he had fresh clues, based on what Sanford had written, but could not share them save at a personal meeting. What might they be?

Finally, Adam settled on three points. Wicken seemed to be ignoring Sanford's suicide and the death of the miller at Gressington.

He had even dismissed Tugwell as unimportant. Yet all pointed to him as the murderer of Silas Toms. None of this made sense to Adam. He decided to review what he thought Wicken was missing.

If Sanford had simply wanted a message to go to Wicken, he could have sent it before through either Adam or the Hanwells. None would have so far breached common decency as to open and read another person's letter. Why kill himself?

Secondly, the death of the miller. Toms had visited the man, despite not knowing beforehand exactly where Gressington was – save, presumably, that it was near to Holt. Soon after that visit – the next day – the miller was dead. Had Tugwell killed him? No! Adam sat up with a start. Tugwell, they thought, had borrowed a horse from the inn to follow Toms. Surely Peg had told him the horse was found back in its stable the next morning? If so – and Tugwell had brought it back – he could not have murdered the miller. When the man died, Tugwell was already back in Norwich.

Somehow, Amos Tugwell was at the heart of the whole mystery. Of that, Adam was now sure. Find out what he was doing and why and the rest must become clear. To rush down to London, as Wicken asked, would be foolish. The answers lay right here ... or nowhere.

Sitting back in his chair, Adam thought about what to do next. Miss LaSalle had urged him to go to Gressington as soon as he might. Was she right? It seemed she was, as she had been in so much else. When she had appointed herself as his assistant, he had treated the idea as a jest. Now he wanted more than anything to be able to discuss his thoughts with her. On his own, he felt like a man trying to fight with one hand tied behind his back.

Well ... she was not here, so he must do as best he could. First, he would go to Gressington tomorrow. If he avoided Trundon, he would not need to tell his brother what he was doing. He would not risk being told to mind his own business. If what he found looked to demand his brother's involvement, he would confess and apologise. Only after doing his best to understand what Tugwell had found would he consider going to London. If Wicken thought that remiss, he would remind the man that he was not under orders and could decide on his own priorities.

That brought Adam back with a jolt to the matter of his medical practice. It seemed he must abandon it again. Nor could he trust himself to visit patients while his thoughts were so engaged elsewhere. Perhaps Peter would consent to continue his deputising a little while longer? It was time to find out.

He found Peter Lassimer in his shop, serving an elderly lady who lived at the other end of the street. When she saw the doctor enter, nothing would content her but to rehearse all her symptoms again. But if she thought Adam might suggest some different remedy from the one Peter was mixing, she was proved wrong. Adam turned to his friend and, with a wink he hoped the old lady would not see, asked what he was making up.

"Exactly what I would have prescribed," Adam said, after Peter had told him. "You see, madam? You have here both medical men in this town and they are as one on the solution to your problem."

That caused the woman to beam with pleasure and declare she felt better already. Then, taking the small bottle Peter had given her and handing over two shillings in payment, she left the shop in great good humour.

After the door had shut behind her, Peter darted out from behind the counter to pull down the blinds and close the shop for the day. "Mrs Kent is a sad case," he said to Adam. "There is nothing whatsoever wrong with her. Indeed, she is as strong as a horse and likely to outlive us both, despite being nigh on seventy years old. She comes, as you will have guessed, for a different medicine: the pleasure of human company. Her husband died some years ago, her children are dead also, and even her few relatives in these parts are too infirm to travel to see her. Once in a while, she visits one or more of them. For the rest, she visits the shopkeepers in the town and comes to bring me yet another imaginary ailment."

"Yet you charge her for what you prescribe?" Adam said.

"Of course. If I did not, she would be mortally offended. It would show her that I acted only out of pity and she would never forgive me.

No, my friend. I invent a name for what I give her – as I did when you asked me now – and charge her a shilling or so. When she brings back the empty bottle, as she always does, I give her back half of what she gave me."

"It is sad to become old," Adam said, his thoughts turning once more to the death of Sir Daniel Fouchard. "Yet none may avoid it."

Peter looked at Adam for a few moments, then said, "I heard Sir Daniel has died. I am sorry for your sake, for, by what I hear, you and he had grown close."

"It's true," Adam said in reply. "I mourn his death almost as much as I mourned the death of my own father. Yet I had known the man for scarce two weeks."

"Affection does not measure itself by the time passed," Peter said. "How does the widow?"

"I do not know. It is too soon for me to pay a visit of condolence, I reckon. Besides, I will scarce sleep in my own bed two nights before I must go again. To London, this time. That is why I am here. To ask if you would look after my patients a little longer. It is a great imposition, I know, but I have some hope that matters are drawing to a close at last."

"You had no need to ask," Peter said. "Of course I will. I had, however, hoped you had come to tell me your news ..."

Adam hastened to reassure his friend. "Of course," he said. "That is another reason to be here."

"Come into the compounding room," Peter said at once. "Will you take some refreshment? Some coffee, perhaps? Susan makes passable coffee, but I warn you she needs a good time yet to be able to make tea a civilised person can drink."

"Susan?" Adam said.

"One of my new maids. It is a long story, but it must wait until I have heard all that you can tell me of you doings in Norwich. Susan! Susan!"

The young girl who entered reminded Adam all too much of young Molly Hawkins. The same stick-thin arms and emaciated body. The same sense that the clothes she was wearing – in this case a good, homespun dress and clean apron – had been made for a person twice her size.

"Susan," Peter said as she entered. "This is my good friend, Dr Bascom. Take note of him and tell Jane what I tell you now. Dr Bascom is to be admitted at any time and treated as an honoured guest. Now, make us some coffee. What is Jane doing?"

"'Elping cook prepare some vegetables, Master," the girl said, her local accent so thick that even Adam had some difficulty in making out the words. "Tatties."

"Very good," Peter said. "Thank you, Susan. You may go and prepare the coffee now." The girl scuttled away.

"Two maids?" Adam said.

"Aye, and together they barely manage to do the work of one. I have hopes of them, or I would not have taken them on, but they need much training in their work."

"Could you not hire an experienced maidservant to replace Annie?"

Peter sighed. "No, Bascom. I tried, I assure you. I never expected such a problem in finding a maidservant. It seems people in Aylsham have got the idea that I am ... how shall I put it? ... of a somewhat lecherous disposition. Since I wanted a maid who would live in, many mothers flatly refused to allow their daughters to work for me. In the end, I had to go to the House of Industry – the workhouse – and take someone from there. All that concerned the overseer was that he would have fewer mouths to feed from the pittance the parish allows him."

"And you chose two?"

"Blame that on too tender a heart. The overseer first brought out Susan. It seems her mother was a whore found wandering along the road and dragging her children behind her. She asked the parish for money for bread, but was turned down. Despite her lies, it was determined that she had no residency here. She was taken to the parish boundary and thrust over for the next parish to worry about."

"And the girl?"

"Susan is but fifteen, Bascom, so far as she knows. Her sister, Jane, is probably a year or two younger. They ended up in the House of Industry because our good Rector saw what was happening and asked their mother where she was going. As he must have suspected, the mother was headed for Norwich to take up her old trade. Once there, she could sell the daughters for a good price to one of the bawds on watch for country virgins to tempt jaded city palates. Thanks to the Rector, the mother was sent on her way as incorrigible. The daughters stayed to save them from a life of vice."

"In the workhouse."

"Where else? The Rector felt he had discharged his Christian duty by blocking their passage to Norwich. He was not going to feed them as well."

"So you have taken both."

"What else could I do? When I said Susan should come with me, she cried piteously, not wanting to leave her sister behind. In the end, I agreed to both."

"You could do no other," Adam said. "But can you afford an extra servant?"

"Neither seems to eat enough to keep a sparrow alive" Peter said. "But I will plump them up, I assure you. When my apprentice gets here ..."

"Your apprentice?" Adam interrupted.

"See how much you have missed while you were away," Peter said. "You see before you a Master Apothecary, newly admitted to the Freedom of the Guild and thus able to take on an apprentice. All the additional work I have been doing ..." He grinned at Adam, then went on, "... has made me rich enough to hire some help to run the shop. Joseph arrives next week, so I will have three young people on my hands. Fortunately, my housekeeper has finally agreed to move in and assist me in looking after them."

"I thought she was adamant she would live at home," Adam said.

"She changed her mind. One day she went back early and found her husband in bed with her youngest sister. She came back here and asked me if she might have use of one of the bedrooms. I agreed. I also treated the sister for two black eyes and bad scratches to her face.

The husband I treated for severe bruising to his private parts, a black eye and the loss of several teeth. I gather my housekeeper has not been home since and the sister has moved in with the husband."

Adam was amazed. All the time he had lived in Aylsham, he had thought it such a quiet and dull place. Now it seemed as bad as Norwich.

"Now," Peter was saying, "enough of my news. Sit here, drink the coffee I hope Susan will bring us soon, and tell me all. Leave nothing out! Life here is so dull that I crave all the excitement from the big city."

ADAM SCARCELY SEEMED to notice Hannah when he got home from talking to Peter. He handed her his hat and coat in silence. Then, with the manner of someone in a trance, he turned, went directly to his study and shut himself in. And there he stayed, seeking neither food no drink, until it was well after the middle of the afternoon.

Such odd behaviour by the master provoked a good deal of lively conversation in the kitchen. Each of the servants tried to persuade one of the others to go to Adam's study and find out what was going on. It was, of course, Hannah who finally accepted the task. Not only was she the most curious of them all, but, as housemaid, she risked least in disturbing her master. She could not pretend someone had come to the door, or that a letter had been delivered. She therefore equipped herself with a tray on which lay a coffee cup, milk jug and a cone of sugar. Mrs Brigstone boiled water ready and it was agreed that, if the doctor was tempted by the thought of coffee, Hannah would return at once to the kitchen. The coffee itself could be made in a matter of moments.

Hannah was soon back, bursting with eagerness to report what had happened.

"Well ..." she said, "When I gets to the door, I waits a few moments and listens real hard. 'Tis quiet as the grave in there. No sound of movement, no noise of a pen scratching on paper, not even the rustling of the master turning the pages of a book. Right eerie it was. Anyhow, I screws up me courage and taps lightly on the door. Nothing. So I taps a bit harder. Guess what happened then."

"Get a move on, girl," Mrs Brigstone said. "This ain't one of your silly novels. What did happen?"

"The master calls out, 'e does."

"And what does 'e call?" Mrs Brigstone asked. "William and I've both got work to do, even if you 'aven't. Out with it!"

"Go away!"

"What?"

"That's what 'e says. 'Go away.' Just that. What d'you think it means?"

"I think it means he wanted you to go away, girl," Mrs Brigstone said. "He's busy in there and 'e doesn't want to be disturbed."

"But what's 'e busy with?" Hannah said. "I think he's pining for someone. He ain't been right since he came back from 'is mother's house. He's in there, all alone, weeping over some token from that Miss LaSalle. Probably a handkercher."

"I thought you said you couldn't hear nothing" Mrs Brigstone said. "If 'e was weeping, you'd 'ave 'eard 'im."

"Not if he was weeping silently," Hannah retorted.

Mrs Brigstone was disgusted. "Go on!" she said. "Your 'ead be full of romantic nonsense, Hannah Neston. No wonder you got no room in there for brains. I expect 'e's tired and having a little sleep. Either that, or 'e's thinking about some difficult medical case. He's not the sort of person to go soft in the head over a woman. Not like that friend of his, Mr Lassimer, the apothecary."

William spoke now for the first time. "I did hear that Mr Lassimer's taken two sisters from the workhouse to be maids. Annie left, she did. I liked Annie."

"That Annie were nothin' but trouble," Mrs Brixton said. "You liked 'er? Pah! Far too many men liked 'er, if you asked me, not least 'er master. And she liked any passable man she laid eyes on. Same with these two. They'll be trouble as well, I expect. That sort always are. Still, it was a charitable act. The workhouse is a terrible place to be. No, what's much more to the point is that 'is housekeeper is moved in with 'im. That's never right, I tell you."

"But you lives here in the master's house," Hannah said.

"That ain't nothing like the same. The master's a proper gentleman. That Mr Lassimer's a … well, never you mind what he is."

William laughed. "She'd got to go somewhere," he said, "I 'eard she went home and found 'er husband rogering 'er younger sister. She laid into 'em both, so folks say. Left 'er 'usband rolling on the floor clutchin' 'is bollocks and 'er sister's face a right mess. Then she stalks back to the apothecary and 'e takes her in. What's wrong with that? I calls it a kindness. Cor, that sister of hers be a right trollop!"

"You watch your tongue!" Mrs Brigstone said. "I'll have no talk of trollops in my kitchen."

"But she is, Ma," William said. "You've said so yerself. I've 'eard you afore now. When she lost 'er position with the baker over bein' caught out by 'is wife lettin' the baker mess with 'er dumplings. Last night, their neighbours played the rough music for 'em and run 'em out of town. House be empty now."

Mrs Brigstone's eyes lit up. "So that's where you were last night, William. Gettin' mixed up in what don't concern you."

"They deserved it," William said.

"Maybe they did," his mother replied. "But that poor woman's got no home to go back to now, 'as she?"

"Now you say apothecary's housekeeper's a poor woman," her son objected. "A minute ago, you was suggestin' she and Mr Lassimer livin' in the same 'ouse weren't right. As if you believed they was goin' to be up to no good right away. Make your mind up!"

"Never you mind what I believe. Back to work the both of you! It ain't never any good to try to understand what the gentry do or why. They ain't like us. When the master's ready, he'll be ringing that bell for something to eat, mark my words. Besides, it'll be time for his dinner soon, and I've never known him miss that. Off you go! If his meal ain't on the table when he wants it, I'll be getting the blame."

All that Adam was doing in his study was sitting with his eyes shut, thinking furiously. On his walk back from Peter's shop, an idea had occurred to him. It was so outrageous – so far away from his previous theories – that he was tempted to throw it aside. Then, as he had been handing Hannah his hat and coat, the idea had returned with such force that he had no option but to take it seriously.

Thus it was that he had gone into his study and shut himself away from all distractions to think it through. The more he did so, the more attractive it appeared. If he accepted it, much that had been a puzzle to him until now could be cleared up. He would have solved the mystery of the miller's death, including why he had first been strangled, then shot. He might even be able to say who had done it. It seemed too simple, but, try as he might, he could find no clear objection to it save one. None of it could be proved unless the person involved was willing to confess all they had done.

There was the crux of his problem. There was the sudden headlong leap into the unknown. It would be all or nothing. Even worse, his chance of success depended on the character of a person he had never met and about whom he knew next to nothing.

For nearly three hours, Adam went round the problem again and again, looking at it from every angle. Nothing helped. He was always forced back to the original conclusion. He must either make the attempt, rash as it seemed, or give up the idea altogether.

Finally, forced from his circling thoughts by the combination of an empty stomach and a full bladder, Adam reached a decision. He would try it. He would risk all on a single throw.

Thus it was that, at nearly four in the afternoon, he threw open the door of his study and hurried outside to the Necessary House, calling for William as he passed through the yard. The instructions he gave the lad were precise. Horse and chaise were to be ready by half past eight the next morning and he would drive himself. He would be gone most of the day, so a nosebag for the horse was needed. William should take Betty and go to Adam's mother's house in Norwich with the note Adam would give him later. When he returned to Aylsham, he must be ready to groom, feed and rest Fancy in anticipation of taking his master to Norwich very early the next day, for they must arrive in time for Adam to catch the first available mail coach for London.

Next, Adam returned within and rang for Hannah. More instructions followed. He told her he would breakfast early and leave immediately afterwards. Mrs Brigstone should provide him with food enough to take to last until he returned, probably in time for dinner. He would then be at home one more night, before leaving for London soon after dawn the following morning. How long he would be away he did not know. On his eventual return to Norwich, he would stay with his mother for a day or two. He would try to send word of when he would come home again.

Hannah relayed all this to Mrs Brigstone in the tones of someone announcing the imminent end of the world. "What can it mean?" she said at the end.

Mrs Brigstone's reply was typical. The woman had no imagination. "No idea," she said. "I expect he's up to something, but it's not my business to worry what it is. Now, if you've nothing useful to do, Hannah Neston, I can find you plenty of work to keep you busy."

Hannah fled.

19

THE FINAL PIECE

The weather the next morning was truly wretched. A dank, wet mist had blown in off the sea overnight. Even worse, a thin drizzle was now falling; the kind that seems nothing, yet wets you to the skin in a few minutes. Every twig, every blade of grass, every person or animal forced to be about that morning was drenched in cold water. And all buffeted by a wind that blew, it seemed, direct from the Arctic.

Betty would have objected most violently to being taken from her stable on a day like this. Fortunately the new horse, Fancy, seem to enjoy the outing and stepped out with a will. Meanwhile Adam sat hunched in the curricle, wrapped in almost as many clothes as he would have worn in the depths of winter. Beside him on the seat, his medical bag was prominently displayed. Few highway robbers would bother with a local doctor on his rounds. None were likely to be carrying anything worth stealing. Besides, even the most hardened criminals were reluctant to waylay a doctor bringing help to the sick. What none could know was that today Adam's bag contained not medical materials but a brace of fine pistols, fully loaded. Adam did not expect trouble. Given the dreadful weather, he felt sure any sensible robber would be wrapped up warm at home, not lurking on the side of the road getting wet and cold. Still, it was well to be prepared.

There was a time when Adam would not even have considered the possibility of robbers on such a short journey as this. Now, the troubled times, the lack of food for poor people and the general sense of animosity towards the gentry had produced a rash of robberies in the county. He could have asked William to drive him and provide an extra person to deter any attack, but today he wanted none to know where he was going. It was too risky.

The most direct route to his destination would be north through Saxthorpe and Holt, but that must take him along the road towards his brother's home at Trundon Hall. Too many people knew him in that area and might report to his brother that he had been seen. Instead he left Aylsham by the main road towards Cromer. It would make a considerable addition to the length of his journey, but he hoped that the better road would enable him to move quickly. Then he would skirt the great estate of Felbrigg Hall, turn back towards Holt, and drop down to the coast at Salthouse. Thus he might approach Gressington in such a way as to reach the mill before approaching the village itself. If luck was with him, he could arrive and leave by the same route.

The journey proved to be uneventful. Few were about who did not have to be and all so wrapped against the cold and wet as to be unrecognisable. By the time Adam clattered into the yard of the mill and drew up on the side nearest the house, his teeth were chattering and the skin on his face felt numb from the cold and the rain.

The effects of the attack on the mill were still plain to see. Despite the passage of time, there were holes in several of the walls and scorch marks up the walls that faced towards the road. Had the miller's death brought all repair work to a stop? So far as he could see in the wet gloom, the mill itself was still operating. He could hear the splashing of the mill-race and the low rumble of machinery. Voices inside too. Enough must have been repaired to keep the business going. That is, if the damage had ever been bad enough to threaten the work. If Peg had been right, the rioters would have taken care to avoid harming anything of real importance. The mobs who clamoured for lower grain prices rarely did much damage. No point in demanding cheap flour if you wreck its source.

The house was quite untouched. He had not noted this on his last visit. Then he and his brother had been too eager to go where the body of the miller had been placed. Adam turned away from the mill and went towards the house. That was where the miller's wife was most likely to be found.

Now he looked at the building, he could see it was quite a substantial residence, more suited to a prosperous yeoman farmer than a back-country miller. Its walls were built of brick, as were most of the newer houses in this part of the county. These bricks, however, seemed but a few years old. All their edges were sharp and the mortar between them still pale and unblemished. It all struck Adam as suspicious. This house spoke of prosperity in an area known generally for being poor. The miller's profits must have been large to afford such a home.

The maid who answered the door to his knocking was plainly amazed to see anyone about on such a day. Adam announced himself, stressing the name Bascom, and asked to see the mistress of the house at once. In this village, the Bascom name carried great weight. He had no doubt that the miller's wife would see him, whatever she was doing.

The maid returned in haste and ushered Adam into the best parlour, saying that her mistress would be with him in but a few moments. Then, as she had been instructed, she asked him whether he would partake of any refreshment. Adam refused. He did not wish to prolong his visit in any way. The quicker he could get away, the less likely he was to be seen.

The miller's wife came in in a fluster. She must have tidied herself as best she could to welcome such an important visitor. Adam suspected it was not enough. She would have liked time to put on her best clothes. Now, since this was a working day, she was not dressed in formal mourning. Instead, she wore a dark woollen day-dress that was – as Adam imagined most items were in this house – covered with the lightest dusting of flour. To this she had added a clean cap and apron. For the rest, Adam would have to take her as he found her.

How had this woman come to marry a man so much disliked as the miller? Had she known of his misdeeds? Had she wondered where he went on certain nights when the tides were right and contraband to be brought ashore? Had she noted the items hidden inside or under the bags of flour when their carts left on deliveries? Surely she must have known something. Yet even if she had, very likely she would have been unable to speak out, either for fear of her husband or to avoid losing what they had.

"I am sorry to come upon you unexpectedly," Adam said, "but I will not stay long. You will recall that I was involved in the inquest into the murder of your husband." The woman nodded her head. "I told the court then that when I examined the ... corpse ... I found certain signs upon the neck that indicated he might not have been killed by the use of the gun."

"I do, sir," the woman said. "You thought he had been seized by the neck and strangled."

"No, madam," Adam said. "Not strangled."

This was the moment of truth.

"Hanged."

At that word, all colour left the woman's face. Indeed, she would have fallen had Adam not darted forward and pushed her into a nearby chair. This was what he had been dreading, but to pull back now was impossible. However cruel it felt, he must press ahead while she was off-guard.

"Where did your husband hang himself?" Adam said. "Where the body was found? There were marks on a beam above, for I saw them. I imagine you found him during the night, cut the body down, then shot him with his own gun. Why did you do that?"

Adam knew his questions were brutal, but he had no choice. The only way to get at the truth was to shock her into an immediate confession. The look of anguish on the woman's face, her rapid, shallow breathing and her eyes held wide and fixed on his showed him he had succeeded – perhaps almost too well.

"Oh God! Dear God!" she said. "You know all and I will be ruined. Mercy, I beg of you! That dreadful night still haunts my every moment. I swear I did not do it for myself. It was to protect my children. They are innocent in all of this. Now they will lose a mother as well as a father."

Adam sat down himself then and spoke as gently as he could. "Do not distress yourself, madam, I beg you. Tell me all and I will leave. None knows I am here. Another matter has arisen which demands that I know exactly what took place. Yet nothing compels me to pass my knowledge on to my brother, as magistrate, or any other person in this locality. If what you say convinces me that I am right, and your actions were indeed selfless, I promise that I will tell no one save the one or two I must. They are far away from here and will, I am sure, prefer to say nothing and allow the verdict of the inquest to remain unchallenged."

The woman was weeping, but the first shock was over and she seemed more in control of herself. Indeed, Adam had little doubt that she would feel a mighty relief at telling someone what she had done. He had not come to judge her. His instincts told him already that she had suffered far too much at the miller's hands during their life together. It was not for him to add to her woes.

Slowly but steadily she told him her story. How she had pleaded with her husband to change his wicked ways, but to no avail. How fearful she became when she knew there was contraband hidden under the flour in their carts. How he had beaten her and threatened her with still worse beatings if she breathed so much as a word of what went on at the mill.

"It was his love of money that drew him into the clutches of the smugglers, Doctor," she said. "Once he got involved, there was no way of escape. So long as he took an active part in their crimes, they knew he would not betray them. If he had drawn back, they would have killed him to protect themselves. In time he gained a measure of power over some of them, but never enough to be safe from harm."

The riot and attack on the mill had terrified her, but her husband had even then dismissed her fears. She almost came to believe he had brought about the riot himself. Several other mills in the area had suffered mob violence from people complaining about the high price of flour and bread. It would have been suspicious if his mill alone was spared. The rioters knew not to go too far, he had told her. If they damaged his business too much, they not only destroyed their main means of getting any flour at all. They risked incurring the anger of the smuggling gang. No one would risk that for a loaf of bread.

"It was the day he died that things went so wrong," the woman told him. "Those two men came here. They were at the root of it, I am sure."

"Two?" Adam said.

"Aye, two, Doctor, but not together. The first came openly in a chaise, as you did. He arrived just before noon. He and my husband seemed at ease with each other, for he called for good ale and they talked for a little time. When the first man left, my husband came into the kitchen with a big smile on his face. Yet all he would tell me was that there was good money to be made. Then he bade me forget I had ever seen such a person in our house and gave me a good clout about my head to help me to do so. He threatened the older children too. He was a cruel man."

"And the second man?" Adam asked.

"He came later. Perhaps around four or five. None saw him come either, so I cannot tell you if he had horse or carriage. Indeed, I did not know he was here until I went into the mill to tell my husband his dinner would be ready in an hour. There were no smiles this time. As soon as he caught sight of me, my husband ordered me back into the house. Nor did he ask for drinks to be brought. Nothing."

"How long did this man stay?" Adam asked. "Did you get a good look at him?"

"Not long, Doctor. And no, I barely saw him for a few seconds. Nor do I know what he wanted or what he said. All I can tell you was that my husband seemed to have aged twenty years and more during his visit. After the man left, my husband came into the house walking like a man in a dream. He refused food and waved me away when I tried to discover what was ailing him. Then he went to the cupboard you see behind you and brought out that terrible gun. He checked that it was loaded and went out at once, back to the mill. That was the last time I saw him alive."

The rest of her story was more or less as Adam had expected. When her husband failed to return from the mill, she took a lantern and went to find him.

"I saw a light in the room where the flour is collected into the sacks," she told Adam. "That was the room where you saw my husband's body. When I went in, I saw his body at once, hanging from the beam you mentioned. He had placed a lantern on a bench nearby, for it was getting dark when he went inside. He must have found a length of rope and fashioned a noose in one end, thrown it over the beam and tied the other end to an upright. He stood on a stool and stepped off."

"What did you do?" Adam asked.

"For while, I looked at him," she said. "I knew he was dead. I hated my husband, sir. He was cruel and uncaring. Now he had taken the coward's way out and left me and my children to suffer the mess he had made. I imagined the scandal and the pointed fingers. My sons branded for ever as the sons of a suicide. My daughter unable to find a husband willing to take on such a man's child. Then it came to me that I knew what I must do."

"Tell me," Adam said. "You will feel better."

"I stood on the stool and I cut him down, Doctor. That was no easy task, for he was much heavier than I am. That's why I had to leave him on the floor below where he had been hanging. I could not carry him and I knew dragging him must leave traces. Then I looked around for his gun. I knew he had taken it with him. I found it where he had set it on the lid of a bin. Fortunately, there was a good wind that night and there had not yet been time to repair all the damage the rioters had done. There were many loud noises, bangs and thumps from loose planks and damaged machinery. This is a lonely place at night, Doctor. Few use this road and we are a good way from the village. When the wind blows from the sea, as it did that day, no noise from here could be heard so far away."

She paused to collect her thoughts, then hurried on.

"I hid the rope as best I could and put the stool back where it had been. I could not untie the noose, so I cut that part into pieces. I carried them into the house later and burned them in the fire. The mark around my husband's neck was terrible. That I had to hide, or none would ever believe he had been murdered. No stranglers hands could make such a mark. So I took the gun, cocked it and ..."

"No," Adam said then. "Do not go on. I have heard enough. Now, I have a small flask of good brandy in my pocket. Here, drink some down. Drink! You have had a dreadful shock and I have forced you to relive something I am sure you would far rather forget. I will not leave here knowing that I have not done all I can to ease your mind and repair your health."

The woman drank from the flask itself, as Adam directed her. First cautiously, then more deeply as the spirit warmed her. When she handed it back, it felt empty.

"Now," Adam said. "I am going to leave. As I said at the start, none knows I am here nor why I came. Let it remain so. I will keep my promise, madam. You may set your mind at rest. I will tell none but those few who must know. They, I am sure, will agree to tell no one else. My brother will arraign none for this murder, for there are none to be found. The truth, should it be known, will set none at liberty. Instead, it will put you and your family into the very worst kind of bondage. I will not have such an act on my conscience. What will you do now?"

"My intention was to sell the mill as soon as the probate is granted on my husband's will. Then I will to leave this place and take my children to grow up where none will every have heard of the mill at Gressington."

"Yes," Adam said. "I believe that is the best course of action. I wish you better fortune in the future, madam. You have suffered enough for this life. May you now find happiness and peace."

The miller's wife would have thanked him and poured praise

upon him, but Adam waved all aside, saying he must leave as soon as he might. Every minute increased the chance that someone would recognise him and let slip a careless word that would reach his brother. As he was leaving, he had one last instruction to give.

"Your maid knows who I am, madam. Perhaps she has already told others. If you are asked, say that I was passing and called to see how you were faring, since I knew about your husband's death. If that is not enough, point out that I am a doctor and always on the look-out for business in the area. That would be true enough of most, even if it does not apply to me."

With those words, Adam walked back to his curricle, climbed aboard and set Fancy's path back towards the main road. Mrs Brigstone had given him victuals for the journey. Still, in such weather he determined rather to stop at the first inn he might find that could offer him hot food, good ale and a groom to feed Fancy and shelter her a while from the wet and cold.

20

LONDON

By the time Adam took his seat in the Norwich mail coach for London the next morning, he had already been up for more than three hours. This was not how he liked to start his day. His habit was to ease into things gently, rising at a respectable hour and eating a hearty breakfast at about nine o'clock. Only then would he venture upon the day's business. That morning, William and he had left for Norwich just before seven. The breakfast rolls he had been forced to gobble down when they arrived at the White Lion Inn in the Market Place were far from enough for a whole day. The coffee had been only just short of awful.

Adam surveyed the other passengers. Travel by the mail coach was more expensive than using the normal stage, so those who chose it tended to be from the better classes. That definitely seemed to be the case that morning. The mail had the distinct advantage that they would reach their destination in London after scarcely twelve hours of travel. Even so, a good many people preferred to go more slowly and enjoy proper stops for meals along the way. On this coach, the rapid delivery of the mail had priority over all else, including the comfort of the passengers.

Today the coach was carrying only four passengers. There was a middle-aged couple who looked like a merchant and his wife, or perhaps an attorney. Next a pretty young woman, travelling alone, which was unusual. Then Adam himself. The couple sat opposite one another. That meant the young woman sat across from Adam. No one spoke after some initial nods of greeting. Perhaps they too were suffering from the effects of such an early start. Indeed, the husband soon fell asleep, despite the bumping and lurching of their progress.

Adam knew this journey was necessary, for Mr Wicken had demanded it. Yet he did not relish the extra time away from his practice or the discomforts of yet another long journey. He determined he would tell his story, then make it clear to Wicken this was to be the last time he involved Adam in his activities. Neither his finances nor his reputation in north Norfolk could stand it. A physician who is never there when you need him is no physician at all.

The coach moved at a good pace. From time to time, loud fanfares of the coachman's horn warned the turnpike keepers to open their gates for the Royal Mail to pass unhindered. Within, all was silent, save for the creaking of leather and the rumbling of the wheels along the road. None spoke, not even the man and his wife.

Adam was glad of the quiet. Conversation amongst travellers was rarely more than an idle passing of the time. Besides, he had much to turn over in his mind before he presented Wicken with his solutions to the various parts of the mystery. Some still eluded him and he hoped Wicken himself might be in a position to fill those gaps. Indeed, his case throughout was no more than supposition and deduction.

There were only three unassailable facts.

Charles Sanford had been attacked and left for dead, then revived. Later he killed himself. Sanford's suicide – at least, the cause of it – was still almost as obscure to Adam as it had ever been. Silas Toms had been murdered. The miller at Gressington died by his own hand on the same day that Toms met his end.

No one would stand trial for any of these crimes. There was not a shred of firm evidence on which to base a case; nor, Adam believed, would such evidence ever come to light. Of those who could tell with certainty all that had happened – and there were but three – two were already dead. Those were Silas Toms and the miller. The third, Amos Tugwell, would doubtless also take his secrets to the grave.

Adam could, of course, have left matters alone and claimed he could not discover the truth. That was not his way. He did not like loose ends and uncertain outcomes. Besides, he had a shrewd idea that Wicken would continue to waste time, energy and resources on the problem for a good while yet. The reputation of his operation was at stake. An important member of his secret team had committed suicide and a King's Messenger had been murdered. He could hardly shrug his shoulders, confess to being baffled and move on. The king and his ministers would not view the death of an official messenger and the theft of the papers he was carrying as something to be ignored. No, it was incumbent on Adam to help Wicken lay the matter to rest. Let all be as satisfied as they could be with what had turned out to be a most complex investigation.

At Bishop's Stortford, the coach made its only real stop, beyond changing horses, which the skilled postillions could do in less than two minutes. All the passengers now climbed down to stretch their weary limbs. In the few minutes allowed, they must snatch what refreshment they could and attend to any more intimate needs. Then it was back on board.

But now there were only two passengers. The middle-aged couple, it seemed, had reached their destination. Only Adam and the pretty young lady were to continue to London. Once again Adam wondered at her making such a journey alone and unchaperoned. By the strict standards of propriety, the two of them ought not to share the carriage without anyone else being present. Still, needs must. Adam had to get to London as quickly as he could. The lady seemed quite unconcerned at travelling with only a man – and a young man at that – as her companion.

As they set off again, Adam took several surreptitious glances at her. She was dressed in fashionable clothes and her hair – a most fetching colour of auburn-red – was adorned by a neat bonnet in what he assumed was the latest colour and style. Yet there was something about her that suggested she was not a member of *the ton*: the highest and most fashionable levels of society. It was not just her willingness to travel alone. There was something in the relaxed way she did it. The ease with which she occupied her place. Both implied far more spirit and self-assurance than most daughters of the aristocracy would have. Was she perhaps the pampered mistress of some great man? If so, why was she travelling thus and not in one of his private carriages?

Adam was certain the lady was well aware of his careful and lengthy scrutiny, yet she gave no sign. Mostly she looked at the passing countryside or read in a small volume she carried in her lap. Sometimes she closed her eyes and appeared to be either asleep or deep in thought.

Adam's puzzling over the nature of this delightful person was interrupted by the coach making the most tremendous lurch. Perhaps a wheel had caught in a deeper rut or hole in the road. Perhaps one of the horses had stumbled or thrown a shoe. Whatever had happened, the young lady opposite him was thrown towards Adam with considerable force. Only his swift reflexes prevented her suffering some injury. As it was, she ended up wrapped in his arms and more or less seated in his lap.

For several moments, both of them seemed too stunned to respond. Then, as the coach continued on its way with no slackening of speed, Adam realised the position. The sensation of this female body held so close to his own might be delightful, but his grip upon her person was a complete breach of etiquette.

The lady must have come to a similar conclusion, for she said softly, "You may release me now, sir. I am quite unhurt, thanks to your prompt action in catching me. To prolong our unintended embrace seems more than a little improper. It is generally accepted that a lady should at least be introduced to a gentleman before she throws herself into his arms."

Adam was so embarrassed that he almost pushed her away from him and back onto the seat opposite.

"You need not be quite so vigorous in ridding yourself of the burden of my presence in your lap, sir," she said. "Nor blush so deeply at what happened. Neither of us intended it. We could not have avoided the occurrence. Now, pray tell me by what name I may address my kind rescuer."

"Dr B ... B ... Bascom," Adam stammered. "Dr Adam Bascom."

"Are you a physician, Dr Bascom, or a surgeon?"

"A physician, madam."

"So, Dr Adam Bascom, a physician of Norwich."

"Of Aylsham."

"Pardon me. A physician of Aylsham. And I am Miss Phoebe Farnsworth. Perhaps you have heard of me?"

Adam wracked his brains. Farnsworth. Farnsworth. He knew of no family of that name in Norfolk.

"I regret I have not, Miss Farnsworth."

"That is indeed regrettable, Doctor. But tell me. Are you a follower of the dramatic art, a devotee of the muses of tragedy or comedy?"

"I beg your pardon?"

"Do you attend the theatre, sir!"

"Oh ... no, not often. Indeed, hardly ever."

"Then you are forgiven for your ignorance of my name, but not for this unaccountable gap in your education. I find it hard to credit that such a learned person, as I am sure you must be, could have reached maturity without tasting the rare delights to be found in the better class of theatres. Especially when you have a fine, new theatre in Norwich upon whose stage some of the greatest actors and actresses of our day have performed."

"You are connected with the theatre?" Adam asked.

"I am an actress universally acclaimed to be approaching the pinnacle of her art, Dr Bascom. I am a member of the company of London's Drury Lane Theatre and take many of the most weighty supporting roles. That I have not yet acted in the lead is due to the presence in the company of one or two more established and older ..." she stressed that word "... actresses. However, I have just been offered the leading role in 'Romeo and Juliet'. It is to be presented at your city's theatre during the month of June."

"My congratulations," Adam said. "You are a tragic actress then?"

"I am a most versatile performer, Doctor. While I can say without boasting that I excel in tragic parts, my true forte lies in playing young ingenues and in comic parts. I am also a rare dancer, with, so I am informed, legs fit for a king to feast his eyes upon."

This sudden mention of such intimate appendages caused Adam to blush again.

"For a physician, sir," Miss Farnsworth said, "you are easily abashed by the mention of mere limbs. I hope you do not have to deliver many babies."

"Not so often," Adam admitted. "Yet I have done so. The situation is not similar to now."

"So I should hope," Miss Farnsworth said, laughing. "I have been compromised enough for one day. Now, Doctor, let me move and sit beside you, if you will permit it. That way, should any fresh jolts throw either of us from our places, we will fall most properly upon the floor or the seat opposite, rather than into one another's arms."

For Adam, the rest of the journey passed in a blur. Miss Farnsworth proved the most delightful of travelling companions, in manner and speech as well as looks. She told him of her life on the stage. She expounded the merits of various playwrights and managers. And she so rarely described the joys to be experienced in the theatre that Adam came to believe his life had been much impoverished by their absence.

At one point, she even explained why she was travelling alone.

"I was accompanied to Norwich by Mr G ... no, I will not give you his name. I will simply say he is a fellow-actor and member of our company. Our purpose was to make certain final arrangements with the manager of the Norwich theatre for the roles we will play there. To travel with him is quite proper, even if no one else is present. It is well known he does not enjoy ... well, shall I say that his tastes do not run to any intimate relations with women. As a doctor, I'm sure you understand what I mean. That also lay behind him insisting on staying behind in Norwich when we were to leave. I had to return, since I am due to take an important role in tomorrow night's production. He has no acting engagement until next week. He met a young man at the theatre during our stay for whom he conceived a considerable ... regard. It seems his feelings were reciprocated. So he is determined to pursue this ... friendship ... for as many more days as he can. All this he told me just as we were due to leave, Doctor. I had no chance either to dissuade him nor find any other person to travel with me."

"A most difficult situation, Miss Farnsworth, as I can see. Well, you may set your mind at rest as regards myself. I am not of your colleague's ... persuasion ... no, not at all. Yet I believe that I am enough of a gentleman not to take advantage of any person in distress, let alone a woman."

"I never doubted it, Doctor. Now, we are almost at our destination, I think. We stop at The Bull and Mouth in St Martin's le Grand."

"But how will you proceed to your home?" Adam said. "A lady cannot be abroad in London at this late hour on her own. Never mind propriety. It would not be safe. Please allow me to escort you to your dwelling. I could not rest knowing you to be upon the street without proper escort."

"You are indeed a gentleman, Doctor, but there is no need. Both my colleague and I had no intention of travelling further immediately. The landlord of the inn is a great aficionado of the theatre. Before we left, we arranged for rooms to be held ready upon our return. But where are you going, Doctor?"

"To be frank, I have no idea. I suppose I hope to be able to find a room at a suitable inn nearby."

"By no means," Miss Farnsworth cried. "There was no time to acquaint the landlord that my companion would not be with me, so he will have held two rooms as we agreed. I'm sure he will be delighted to let the spare room to you, for otherwise he will be at a loss for the night's payment."

Yes, Adam thought. You are quite right, though I don't doubt he will complain mightily to the missing actor when he does appear. Aye, and do his best to gain recompense for his 'loss' from the man.

"That would be helpful," Adam said. "I thank you."

"Don't thank me, Doctor. Thank G ... my colleague and his roving eye. Now, I see we are almost there. It has been a most pleasant journey, Dr Bascom, thanks to you. I pray you, when you return to Norwich commence your education in the theatre as soon as you may. Come and see me tomorrow night too. I can promise you a fine entertainment. I will look out for you and be most disappointed if you are not there."

What could Adam do but promise to attend, provided a ticket was available.

"Do not worry about that," Miss Farnsworth said at once. She felt in her reticule and handed him a small round piece of metal, like a sovereign. On it was cast the name of the theatre within a decorated border, the year and the words, "First Gallery".

"Some of us have such things," she told him. "It will give you immediate access to some of the best seats in the house. Pray return it to me after the performance. It is not unusual for patrons to come backstage then, so you may deliver it to me in person and tell me how you enjoyed the evening."

Since the coach arrived and came to a stop as she spoke, there was no chance to talk further. Only, as he helped her down, she made as if to stumble a little and planted a single, soft kiss on the tip of his nose. Then, with a most unladylike giggle, she left him and hurried to greet the waiting landlord.

ADAM SLEPT well that night and arose the next day feeling refreshed. He had hoped to encounter Miss Farnsworth at breakfast, but it was not to be. The landlord explained that she would still be abed at such an hour. Those involved with the theatre rarely rose early. Many nights they would not be able to return to their rooms before midnight or the early hours. The performances might not end much before eleven and there were always admirers wishing to be seen afterwards.

If that was disappointing, Adam's breakfast turned out to be satisfactory in both quality and quantity. He ate with a will, for he had fasted for much of the day before, and consumed several cups of excellent coffee. He was now wondering how he might best find his way to Wicken's office. Then the landlord announced a carriage had arrived for him. How Wicken could have known where he spent the night, when he had not known himself until shortly before he arrived, Adam could not guess. Perhaps it was better that way. To enquire too far into the man's sources of information might prove disquieting.

"Well, my friend," Wicken said, when Adam had taken some refreshment. "You have once again proved of inestimable help to this department."

They were seated in the grandeur of Wicken's office and Adam had finished yet another cup of excellent coffee. Now it appeared his host had decided it was time to attend to business.

"Thanks to your discoveries, Doctor, we now know how information was taken from this building and conveyed to our enemies abroad. We have blocked up that passageway at once. If we cannot take satisfaction in seeing all the traitors punished, we can at least be certain their future actions will be a good deal harder to undertake."

"So it was Toms," Adam said.

"In part at least. Who his contact was we still do not know."

"He had none in this country, I believe," Adam said. "I was warned by a friend that it was easy to make complications where none existed. Indeed, he quoted Occam's Razor to me. I was too slow at the time to apply his advice correctly. Later I saw how it applied to this case. We were both adding elements to the puzzle that did not exist. Toms was the only spy in your midst. I imagine he did it for money and passed his information straight to persons overseas. There was no one else. No one was needed."

Wicken stared.

"You wrote to me that the man Tugwell had been under suspicion at one time. Later you realised the charges against him – made only via an anonymous letter – were false. That is correct?"

Wicken nodded in agreement. He seemed too shocked to speak.

"My belief is that Toms was the source of that letter. Tugwell must have come to suspect him. Perhaps he saw some suspicious behaviour or noted Toms being where he should not have been. He was probably going to communicate his suspicions to the proper person, but Toms got wind of it first. The attempt to fix the blame on Tugwell was to prevent him from placing it where it was well deserved."

"We were already suspicious," Wicken said. "Until recently, we kept no special record of which messenger carried which package. Each was given to the next man available. Then it became clear that our enemies were receiving information which could only have come from this building. In our attempt to discover the traitor, we at once set a clerk to record a number against each package in a ledger. It indicates the messenger to whom that package has been entrusted. But how did you work all this out? I was about to tell you what I have discovered, but you have stolen the wind from my sails."

"I could guess only the outline, Wicken, and will be glad to have my guesses confirmed by the detail."

The story Wicken now unfolded was lengthy and complex. It began with sources of information abroad. They showed messages were reaching the French with details of British plans and policy discussions. Some of this could be traced back to Whitehall and to the building where they now sat. By a process of elimination, those seeking the traitor began to focus on the King's Messengers. It seemed quite possible that one or more of them might be involved. By using a thin, hot blade to lift the seal on the documents they carried, they might read the contents and replace the seal intact. Only a most careful examination of the seal would reveal the tampering.

That was when two things happened. First, the system of recording which messengers carried each document was introduced. That was when they received the anonymous denunciation of Amos Tugwell and went to arrest him. He had flown, which seemed proof enough of his guilt. But when it was noted that the theft of information proceeded at the same rate as before, they began to suspect he had been innocent all along.

Now, thanks to Adam's earlier messages, the clerk who recorded each messenger's packages had been questioned closely. In the end, he confessed the truth. Toms sometimes came to his desk and gave him half a guinea to buy grog in the nearest tavern, saying he would see all safe in his absence.

"We examined the entries then with great care, Doctor. Many had been altered. The book no longer gave a true account, which was why it revealed nothing of what was taking place."

"But what of Toms and Sanford?" Adam asked. "I can see what might have caused enmity between Tugwell and our traitor, but not how Sanford came into it?"

"The message from Sanford that you sent on to me explained all," Wicken said. "Sanford often worked into the early hours of the morning. At such a time, the building was deserted, save for the messengers who were on call. He admits he sometimes fell asleep. That, he believes, was how Toms discovered him one night and used the chance to steal his notes on a document he was decoding. Of course, he did not know it was Toms at the time. That the notes were gone was certain. Who took them was not."

"But why did he not tell someone?" Adam asked.

"The silly fool knew he would be reprimanded for his carelessness and for sleeping at his desk. In his mind, only by going to his superior with definite proof of the thief's identity could he erase the stain on his reputation."

"Did it happen again?"

"It did. Only this time it was after Toms had come to his desk, shaken him awake and given him a drink of what he said was brandy 'to liven him up'. Of course, it had been drugged so he fell asleep even more heavily. That time no papers were missing, but he was certain some had been read – perhaps copied. It seems he was a most methodical worker and noticed that those were not quite in the same place when he awoke as they had been earlier."

"But still he said nothing."

"Indeed, Doctor. He thought he would be dismissed from his post. Instead he became desperate to find the culprit first and use him as an offering to placate us."

"Did he not suspect Toms?"

"Of course. The idiot thought he would set a trap. He had been given several documents from our supposed French spy. All were written in code. One night, he left them where they might easily be seen – on the top of the pile – then rested his head on the desk and pretended to sleep. He imagined Toms would not be able to resist stealing them and could be apprehended in the act. Nothing happened. He tried again. Still nothing. Of course, by the third night, the effort of staying awake to catch the thief had taken its toll. He fell asleep in earnest. When he awoke, the papers had gone."

"Yet even then he stayed silent?"

"Of course, Doctor. He had left secret papers in plain view, fallen asleep and let them be stolen. Without proof of the thief, the only punishment would be his."

"Thus came his melancholy, I imagine," Adam said. "He knew himself to be a fool and a traitor – at least by omission – and he feared he must soon be discovered. All it would take would be for Toms to report finding him asleep one night. His reputation would be ruined, along with his career."

Wicken agreed. It was at that point, he explained, he had sent Sanford to Norwich, hoping to cure him of his nervous debility. Perhaps the man imagined he could set all behind him. After all, nothing had been said about his lapses. Neither Toms nor anyone else had denounced him.

"Then Toms brought him the last package," Adam said.

"Yes. According to Sanford's letter – which is riddled with outbursts of self-loathing – Toms was open with him. He said he knew all about Sanford's mistakes. Now he would make sure he was punished as he deserved, unless he did as he was told. This time, Sanford was to make a copy of one of the coded documents in particular, together with his decryption. He must give these to Toms as quickly as possible. Toms was not interested in the other documents. He could send them back or burn them as he wished. Only he must do as he was told or be exposed and – so Toms said – hanged."

"Toms wanted proof," Adam said. "He wanted to show his French paymasters their documents were being intercepted and deciphered. I wonder how much that was going to cost them?"

"You were correct that Sanford had recovered most of his memory, Doctor. Only the actual night of the assault was still unclear. He knew time had passed, yet Toms had not returned. In Sanford's tormented mind, he imagined the man had returned to London and already denounced him. Your attempts to keep him indoors he interpreted as a concealed imprisonment. Thus he might be taken up and born away for trial and execution. Now he carried out the action he had planned before he was struck down. He wrote down all that he could, then took his own life rather than face up to what he had done."

Adam shook his head. So much promise destroyed by a simple unwillingness to admit to working too hard and falling asleep at his desk. Well, maybe there was more to it than that. The man must have been suffering from some kind of mental instability to view the world as he had viewed it. He must have some ingrained fear of admitting he was less than perfect. They would never know.

"That is as far as I can go, Doctor," Wicken said. "For the rest, I am in your hands. Tell me what else you have discovered."

Adam began, not with the attack on Sanford, but with Toms' time in Norwich before then. He explained how Tugwell had caught sight of him, then tracked him around the city. How Toms had had himself conveyed to the mill at Gressington to meet with the miller.

"Why?" Wicken asked.

"To arrange passage out of the country, I expect," Adam said. "If, as I believe, Toms alone was the spy, he may well have realised that you were closing in. His attempt to make Sanford provide proof of your ability to read French codes was to be his final means to wealth and security. With that in his hands, he would be certain of a most cordial welcome in France and ample reward. Unfortunately, Tugwell had followed him to the mill as well. After he left, Tugwell confronted the miller. What he said, I do not know, but it was enough to frighten the miller out of his wits and cause him to hang himself."

"Hang himself?" Wicken protested. "You told me he had been shot."

"So he was," Adam replied, "but only after he was dead. His wife was never a willing party to his misdeeds. He beat her to keep her silent. Yet once he was dead, she refused to allow his manner of dying to stain his children's lives. She shot him to try to hide what he had done. As with Sanford, even the meekest person will turn against their tormentor when there seems no other way."

"You know this for certain, Doctor?"

"Yes. Maybe I should not have done, but I gave my word that I would tell only such as must know and they would then keep silent in their turn. The poor woman has suffered enough."

"Hmmm," Wicken said. "Well, I will not see you forsworn. Since her husband cannot now be punished, I see no reason for her to bear the blame. Go on, Bascom."

"Tugwell killed Toms, as I told you by letter. He also carried Sanford back to the precentor's house where he might be tended. Then he disappeared. I imagine he is already far away from Norwich."

"I will not seek him out," Wicken said. "Though he has committed murder, the man he killed would have died anyway at the hangman's hands, if we could have caught him. I have no pity for Toms. Indeed, Tugwell has done us a great service. Toms was unable to inform the French of our ability to read some of their secret messages. Had he been able to do so, that would have been a bitter blow to this country. Toms, the traitor, and Sanford, the fool, can do no more harm. Nor can that treacherous miller. I will make sure none of this is made known, Doctor. Thus our enemies will stay ignorant and our own reputation will be unsullied by foolish comments in the press."

"Now, Wicken," Adam said, "About my practice ..."

Wicken held up his hand and stopped Adam going further.

"Hush, Bascom," he said. "Do not reproach me. You cannot know how much I have reproached myself on that score over the past few weeks. But I have found the solution, I believe." He opened a drawer in his desk and pulled out a letter.

"Take this letter," he continued. "It is from the Comptroller of the Privy Purse. His Majesty has seen fit to repay your loyalty and efforts for this country himself. The London Gazette will announce tomorrow that you have been granted a pension of £500 per year by royal command. That will, I believe, more than make up for what you may have lost."

"I do not deserve this," Adam protested. He was stunned by such a turn of events.

"You do. There is no doubt of that. Firstly because of the great service you have done in clearing up this muddle. Secondly because your talents are wasted as a country doctor. And thirdly because I may need your help again and I will not have your ruin on my conscience. Tush, man! Be grateful. You can hardly refuse the King's personal token of thanks, can you?"

Of course, he could not. To do so would be the most terrible insult to the crown. He took the letter, opened it and read its contents. An annual pension of £500! That was a gentleman's income in itself. Add what he might earn by treating certain selected patients and he would be a man of means. Best of all, he would be his own master, freed from the need to accept unpleasant tasks just to pay his bills.

21

A NEW START

For the rest of the day, Adam was too unsettled by Wicken's narrative and the granting of a pension from the king himself to spend his time sensibly. Tomorrow, Wicken had arranged a government post-chaise to take him back to Norwich. That still left a good part of the afternoon and all the evening free. All he could do was sit in a coffeehouse and try to work out the implications of the royal bounty. Which patients would he seek to keep? Should he try to sell his practice in Aylsham or ask Peter to take over all the local work he had been doing? Should he even stay in Aylsham? Norwich would be a more sensible place to live. It would give him access to a good number of professional colleagues, as well as libraries, regular lectures and ... well, the theatre.

There was no doubt in Adam's mind that he would keep his promise to Miss Farnsworth. He must attend her performances that evening, however tired he felt. He also had to return the special ticket she had loaned him. To do so other than in person would be discourteous or worse. No, he decided, he would go to the performance and make of it what he could – which he suspected might be little. Then he would go backstage, return the ticket and bid her a pleasant evening. That done, he could return to his room at the inn with a clear conscience and try to sleep before tomorrow's journey.

That small metal token, he found, was a magic key to entry at Drury Lane. Merely by showing it, he was allowed in. Then he was conducted past the other theatre-goers, shoving and elbowing each other to get better seats. Finally, he was shown to a seat from which the whole of the stage was within his view. Once seated, he glanced around and was amazed at what he saw. The whole front row was occupied by grave-looking men. He even recognised one of them: Mr William Windham, MP for Norwich. He was once a close associate of the great Charles James Fox. Now he had moved from his orbit through his firm opposition to any accommodation with the revolutionaries in France.

"Are you wondering who they all are?"

The sudden voice from the seat beside him made Adam jump. His neighbour had been seated when he arrived. Adam had been so bewildered by all he saw about him that he had done no more than nod a greeting to the man.

"I recognise Mr Windham," Adam said. "I come from Norfolk and he is one of our members of parliament. The rest I do not know."

The other man counted them off on his fingers. "Mr Joshua Reynolds, The Duke of Portland, Mr Canning, Mr Gibbon, Lord Grenville, Mr Sheridan, Mr Windham and ... yes, Viscount Townshend. There must be no parliamentary business tonight."

"Such great men patronise the theatre?" Adam said.

"Naturally," his neighbour replied. "They're cultured people who appreciate the arts. Besides, the theatre is the best school for oratory you can find, other than sermonising. Which politician hasn't stolen tricks from both preachers and thespians?"

Adam hadn't though of that, but any further conversation was prevented by an actor coming to the front of the stage to deliver the prologue.

Afterwards, Adam couldn't even recall the name of the principal play, let alone the burlesque comedy which followed. All that stuck in his mind was the compelling delivery of the principal actors. How emotions welled up in him at the tragic fate of the character played by Miss Farnsworth and the roars of applause which greeted the end of each act.

When the burlesque came on stage, he saw Phoebe Farnsworth at her best. She was strikingly pretty, deliciously flirtatious and not a little naughty in the way she twirled and kicked up her feet. The audience had many glimpses of what were, as she had told him, most attractive legs. In the tragic play, she had provided solid support to older and more experienced members of the cast. Here she was undoubtedly the star. She knew it, revelled in the shouts from the pit and blew kisses to those who stood up to throw flowers onto the stage in her honour.

Twice at least, she spotted Adam. The first time, she waved and smiled. That made several young bucks turn around to see which of their rivals might be the recipient of such a personal greeting. The second time, perhaps noting the rapt expression on Adam's face, she stopped for a moment in her progress across the stage, put both hands to her mouth and blew him an elaborate kiss. His embarrassment and confusion amused her, for she stopped and did it again. Now her many admirers were all staring at him. Several were muttering to their neighbours; all wore expressions of anger.

"Know her, do you?" his neighbour said. "What did you do to deserve that? There's hundreds of men in London who'd give a good deal for a greeting like that from our darling Phoebe."

"I first met her on the coach yesterday," Adam muttered. "She gave me the ticket for this seat."

"Ye gods! You're a fast worker and no mistake. Just met her yesterday and she's blowing you kisses? I wish I knew your secret. You don't look like that Signor Casanova, but you act like him."

By now, Adam wanted the floor to open up and swallow him. Yet he could not quell a small burst of pride at the same time. What would his mother think if she could see what Miss Farnsworth had done? She wouldn't be so certain then that he had no skills with the Fair Sex. That thought brought on another, far less welcome one. What would Miss LaSalle make of this; or Miss Jempson; or even –

Heaven forbid! – Lady Alice Fouchard? The theatre was a dangerous place.

The evening ended to more rapturous applause and loud shouts of "Encore!" Adam left his seat and looked for someone to tell him how to make his way behind the stage. Eventually, he was directed to a small doorway and found himself in a strange world of dust and ropes and piles of bits and pieces. The front of the theatre might be ornate, but back here no money had been wasted on anything but the essentials. A man dressed like a carpenter showed him the way to the dressing rooms. Yet it still took him several minutes to find the right one. In the end, the sound of Miss Farnsworth's merry laughter convinced him to knock on one of the doors.

"Come in! Come in!" Adam heard Miss Farnsworth call out. When he did, he found the room quite packed with young men, all jostling and pushing one another in their attempts to get close to their idol. Quite unsure what to do next, he stood by the door. Miss Farnsworth saw who it was and came to his rescue.

"Out! Out! Out, all of you!" she cried. "Enough of your flattery. Go! Here is a good friend with whom I wish to speak in private. Go, I say, my lord! Your father may have many acres, but I know you to be in debt to your eyeballs and beyond. Out, sirs! I will speak with you no more tonight, whatever you promise."

All the time she was speaking, Miss Farnsworth and another, much older woman – presumably her maid or duenna – were pushing men out through the doorway. Only when all had gone did she turn to greet Adam.

"I am so glad you came, Doctor," she said. "I hoped you would, but men promise many things that they fail to perform. Did you enjoy the evening? Did you like my performance?"

"I enjoyed myself immensely," Adam said and meant it. "You were … I cannot find the words … exquisite, amazing. In that death scene, I wept as if you were my own flesh and blood upon your bed of pain. In the burlesque, you were quite the most striking and accomplished person on the stage."

Miss Farnsworth gave him a grin that caused his heart to move in strange ways within him.

"If you sing songs like that," she declared, "you may come and sing them every night! Did you hear him, Meg? He said I was exquisite and amazing."

"I did hear him, Miss. Quite a gentleman of taste, I should say."

"Oh, Doctor! You have made my evening with your words. Sadly, you have come rather late to deliver them. Ah, thank you for that ..." Adam had just remembered the ticket she had given him and now returned it with a low bow. "It was well given indeed. Now, it is late and I have still not removed my costume. I must ask you to leave me. Look for me in Norwich, sir, for I shall look for you."

With these words, she darted forward, put her hands up to Adam's face and pulled his head down so that she might place a warm kiss full upon his lips. He was so bewildered and flustered by this that he could not even manage to wish her goodnight as she pushed him out through the door. Only when it had shut behind him did he manage to take a breath and realise what she had done. In a haze of happiness, he stumbled back the way he had come and left the theatre to find a chair to take him back to the inn. There would be little sleep for him that night.

"How vexing!" Sophia said. "You were ahead of me there, Doctor. I had not even considered suicide."

Adam, Miss Sophia Lasalle and his mother sat in the drawing room on the evening of the day after Adam's return to Norwich. Thanks to the government post-chaise, his journey back had been uncommonly quick. Yet it had still been late when he reached his mother's house. The long journey, the early start and, above all, his sleepless night before had all taken their toll on Adam, young and fit as he might be. He had lain in bed until eleven, then rose, wolfed down an enormous late breakfast, and retired again. Only now, after dinner, was there an occasion to tell the two ladies what he had discovered about the deaths of Sanford, Toms and the miller.

'I must say I find it hard to follow," his mother said. "This Toms was a spy, you said?"

"Not so much a spy by conviction as an opportunist," Adam replied. "He wanted money and saw a way to gain it by selling material to the enemy. That must be a temptation to all who handle sensitive information."

"You do not defend him, surely," his mother said in disgust. "The man was nought but a common traitor. He would have been a murderer, if he had not been murdered himself first."

"Quite so," Adam said. "It was chance that brought him to Norwich – and chance that placed Amos Tugwell here to see him. Tugwell, as I told you, was the man he had tried to send to the gallows in his place."

"You may see chance, Adam, for I know you to be a sceptic in these matters. I see the hand of Providence. The mills of God grind slow, as the Bible puts it, but they grind exceeding small. Toms deserved his fate."

"What confuses me," Sophia put in at this point, "is why Mr Sanford killed himself. So far as I can see, he had done nothing so terrible that it would lead to more than a severe reprimand."

"Ah," Adam said. "You forget that he never knew Toms was dead. He had branded Toms a traitor and almost been killed for that. Yet he had still not been able to communicate his knowledge to anyone in authority. He was trapped in Norwich all the time he had been unable to recall past events. Even when he had remembered, he must deny it. Thus I still kept him here. Toms had been free to arrange ways to discredit what he might say – even to brand him as the traitor and have him executed. I also think he was much ashamed of his weakness in failing to confront Toms as soon as his suspicions arose."

"But he could have confided in you, Doctor. You would have seen that Mr Wicken was told at once."

"He knew nothing of my connection with Wicken. I did not tell him and I am sure neither Dr Hanwell nor his wife would have done so. So far as Mr Sanford knew, I was nothing but a local doctor."

"Sally!" Mrs Bascom called out. Everyone else jumped. "I knew you had missed something out. Did you find out who Sally was?"

"In the end," Adam said. "Mr Wicken quite forgot to tell me until I was about to leave. Sally was Sanford's youngest sister. It seems the poor girl suffered from epilepsy and often fell into fits. Sanford had received a communication from his home but a day or so before all the other events. It told him that she had died. It seems she suffered a severe seizure and fell upon the fire in the hearth, and before anyone could pull her off, her clothes burst into flames. By the time the fire was doused, she was badly burned. The local doctor did all he could, but she died two days later from her injuries. She was but twelve years old and Sanford had doted upon her. I think I mentioned Mrs Hanwell told me how Sanford himself had begun to suffer epileptic seizures. They were probably due as much to his concussion and his fretting about what Toms might be doing as anything else. However, there was a family history of epilepsy, as you see. I suspect that further stiffened his resolve to end his life."

"Poor man," Sophia said. "I pity him. Both Toms and the miller received what they deserved. Mr Sanford might have recovered, given time enough."

Mrs Bascom had had enough of such gloomy thoughts. "All this is in the past," she said. "What we should be looking to is the future. I can scarce credit that His Majesty has accorded you such a signal honour, Adam. Indeed, I am near bursting with pride. When I tell Lady Grandison and her grand friends of this, I wager none of them will look down upon our family any longer."

Adam sighed. "Do not broadcast it to all the world," he said. "I do not wish to become notorious again amongst the ladies of Norwich. It was bad enough last year."

"I thought you enjoyed it," Mrs Bascom said. "The Honourable Miss Jane Labelior is always asking about you. The thought of royal favour will much increase her curiosity. Perhaps I should invite them all to tea again, so you can renew your acquaintance."

The look of horror on Adam's face caused her to break into laughter.

"What will you do, Doctor?" Sophia asked. "You are becoming a great man and a wealthy one too. Soon you will have no more time for your old acquaintances." Her voice sounded almost sad.

"Never!" Adam declared. "You cannot think me so base as to throw aside those who have helped and supported me until now. I may have been lucky enough to catch His Majesty's fleeting attention, but I am the same man as before. To be honest, Miss LaSalle, I have not had time to consider my future. Nor will there be time, at least for a while. I must return to Aylsham tomorrow. There, I assure you, my friend Lassimer will be as eager to hear all my news as you and my mother have been. Then I wish to see if Lady Fouchard will receive me. Her husband's death is a matter of great sorrow to both of us. I have not had chance to give her my heartfelt condolences on her loss ..."

"Oh my!" Mrs Bascom cried. "I forgot in all the excitement. Your groom, William, came here yesterday with a message. That Miss Jempson you know sent her maidservant to your house in Aylsham to ask you if you could take tea with her and Lady Fouchard on Thursday next. Your housekeeper told her that she did not know when you would be returning, but she would ensure the message reached you as soon as it could. She reasoned you must stop here on your way, so sent William to ask me to tell you."

"I will write a reply at once, mother," Adam said. "No. If I take the chaise from The Black Boys Inn back home tomorrow, I will be there as quickly as the post. Then I can send Hannah around with my reply immediately. This is good news. I long to see Lady Alice ..."

"Why, sir?" Sophia said, with surprising coolness.

"Why? I told you. To convey my condolences. I knew her husband for such a short time, yet he came to mean a great deal to me. She will be deeply upset by his death, however expected, and I wish to bring her what comfort I may. I am now her guardian too."

"Is that all?" Miss LaSalle.

"What else could there be?" Adam said, quite bewildered by her sudden change of mood. "She has suffered a grievous loss, as I have. Perhaps we may share our grief a little and thus lessen it."

Sophia made a noise in her throat that sounded uncommonly like a growl. Then she said, "And Miss Jempson?"

Poor Adam was too excited to spot the trap now before him and he plunged onwards.

"As for Miss Jempson, I am always glad to see her, even in such melancholy circumstances as these. She is the epitome of those qualities most associated with the Fair Sex: grace, beauty, gentleness ..."

Sophia stood up. "Please excuse me, Madam," she said to Mrs Bascom. "I think I will retire to my room early tonight. I find I have a headache coming on. Goodnight to you both." With that, she walked quickly to the door and left.

Startled, Adam turned to his mother, but the expression on her face stopped his words. She was laughing at him again!

"Oh, Adam, Adam" she said. "What a booby you are! When will you learn to watch your speech? I cannot see how any young lady could manage to be in your presence for long and not feel herself insulted. Now, put all this out of your mind. Sophia will recover her poise – and her patience – I have no doubt. What else did you do and see in our capital city?"

"Nothing really," Adam said, in as offhand a manner as he could. "I had little time and was tired. I drank some coffee in a coffeehouse and ... er ... that was it."

"It serves me right for asking," his mother said. "Mothers, like sons, should know when to keep quiet and leave sleeping dogs to lie. Would you like another dish of tea?"

AFTERWORD

Did you enjoy this book?

If you did, I would be so grateful if you could leave an honest review, either on Amazon.co.uk, Amazon.com or your local Amazon website. Getting reviews is really important for any Indie author. Without them, it's hard to interest other readers and attract more sales. Thank you.

This is Book 3 in the series "The Mysteries of Georgian Norfolk".

What links these books together is their setting in Norfolk, England, in the period between The Seven Years' War in the 1750s and 1760s and the French Revolutionary and Napoleonic wars from 1791 onwards.

Most writers covering the same period set their books in London. But London isn't really representative of life in Britain today and wasn't then either. I choose Norfolk both because I live there and because it was one of the most diverse counties of England, encompassing shipping, manufacturing, England's third-largest city for part of the time (Norwich) and, of course, some of the richest agricultural land on this island. It also had a reputation for being turbulent, independent and often radical in its politics.

Book 1: "An Unlamented Death", set in 1791.

"An Unlamented Death" starts the series. When, Dr. Adam Bascom trips over a body in Gressington churchyard, he never imagines it will change the whole direction of his life. Adam should be devoting all his energy to his business, but it soon becomes clear the authorities are intent on making sure the death is accepted as an accident without further investigation. Adam's curiosity and sense of justice cannot accept this. He has no standing to would allow him to become involved formally, so he uses friends, old and new, unexpected contacts and even his own mother to help him get to the truth.

Book 2: "The Fabric of Murder", set in around 1760.

"The Fabric of Murder" introduces Mr. Ashmole Foxe, something of an enigma in Norwich. He claims to be a bookseller, yet his shop, which stands next to his fine city house, is rarely open for business. He dresses in the most fashionable clothes, is clearly a gentleman, seems well-educated and at ease in the company of peers and rich merchants, and his household is such as befits a wealthy bachelor. Yet where his money comes from nobody knows.

So why, when a leading cloth merchant in the city is found murdered and disaster threatens Norwich's most important trade, do the mayor and aldermen turn at once to Mr. Foxe to solve the crime?

Set against a background of a city where a glittering cosmopolitan life rubs up against filth and degradation, the race is on to find a cunning killer. At stake is the city's most important and profitable trade, plus the livelihoods of many thousands of those who live there.

More books are planned.

You can keep track of progress at my website, "Pen and Pension", where you'll also find regular blog posts about Britain and Norfolk in Georgian and Regency times.

ABOUT THE AUTHOR

William Savage is an independent scholar and speaker, as well as author of mysteries. His books are set in Georgian and Regency Norfolk during the period of the French Revolutionary and Napoleonic wars. They are not, however, about the fighting or the major political and military figures involved. What interests him more is recreating the experience of the bulk of the population, trying to get on with daily life in such turbulent times.

William's books are designed to be first-and-foremost 'good yarns' about interesting people in tough situations. While he strives for authenticity in setting and culture, these are stories, not historical essays.

He is retired now and lives not far from the beautiful North Norfolk coast in eastern England.

For more information
www.penandpension.com

Printed in Great Britain
by Amazon

32930986R00144